DEMONS AND DEADLINES

ELLA STONE

PAPER CAT PUBLISHING

ALSO BY ELLA STONE

BY ELLA STONE & HEATHER G HARRIS

The Witchlight Magical Mysteries

Text copyright © 2025 Ella Stone

Paper Cat Publishing

ISBN: 978-1-915346-63-6

Edited by Dayna Hart
Cover by Christian Bentulan

CHAPTER
ONE

When you have your entire life turned upside down, completely derailed and smashed to a million unrecognisable parts, so that you have to rebuild almost your entire identity from nothing, it gives you a sense of strength. It makes you think that you're prepared, and if something truly unthinkable were ever to happen again, you would be able to handle it.

Or at least, I did.

I mean, I'd been murdered and turned into a vampire at the same time as discovering vampires existed. My only support came from my best friend, who I thought I knew, only to find out she was a damn powerful witch and had taken her position of editor-in-chief at my old paper to help keep a lid on the paranormal world.

My fiancé, who I'd assumed would be by my side forever, ran out of the relationship faster than a gargoyle in a stonemason's. I'd packed up my life in London, moved to an island on the west coast of the States and taken up residence in the small town of Ravens Hollow. There, I took a position at *The Oracle* – the local paper – where, rather than working with normal humans (typicals, as we paranormal folk refer to them), my boss was a cyclops, and my colleagues varied from werewolves to fairies, and a copy editor I was pretty sure was concealing something behind the enormous skirts she wore every day.

But finding out that my mother – who'd walked out on me and my dad during a family holiday to the Seychelles – had been living here in Ravens Hollow for close to twenty years, spelled to masquerade as an elf with pointed ears and everything, when she was in fact, a vampire... Well, that was a step too far.

Thankfully, I wasn't alone when the discovery had happened.

'Elodie, what do you need from me right now?' The voice came from Alex. Local law enforcement officer, obscenely attractive lion shifter, and friend. Pongo, my Leonberger pup, sat by my feet, staring up at me expectantly.

'I... I need to think...' I replied. My voice trembled as I pressed my fingers into my forehead, trying to make sense of what I had just found out. My mother, who I had thought I would never see again, was there, standing in front of me.

The next voice that spoke was hers.

'I can see we have a lot to talk about,' she said.

I couldn't help but laugh. And not like a quick, bitter chuckle, but a full-bellied, have-I-lost-my-mind laugh. *A lot to talk about?* That had to be the understatement of the year.

It was hard to comprehend that this person talking in front of me, whom up to this point I had known as Amira, was actually *my* mother Maria. If it hadn't been for the beaded bracelet around her wrist, that I now recognised as one I'd made her when I'd been six or seven, and the picture of us framed on her bookcase I may have doubted it. But then again, maybe that was wishful thinking. There was something about the way she spoke. And how her nostrils flattened with every inhale and the way she chewed down on her lips. Even if she didn't look like the woman I remembered from all those years ago, I didn't doubt it was her.

'You don't have a sire registered.' Addressing what she felt was easier than addressing how she'd walked out on us all those years ago. 'Did you pay? Did you pay somebody to turn you into a vampire?'

I had been turned into a vampire because I'd stumbled onto a trafficking ring called The Guardians. This group of unscrupulous vampires took money from typicals before changing them.

It went against all the rules.

Sires were supposed to be approved and registered so that every vampire knew every part of their lineage.

But my mother was sireless.

'I didn't pay anybody, Elodie. It was a gift,' she replied.

'A gift?' I didn't try to hide my disgust, and I met her glazed eyes with a steely glare.

'I was sick, Elodie,' she said. 'It was serious. I was trying to get the doctors to help me, but they wouldn't listen. I went back and forth, getting worse and worse every week. You must remember it? You must remember how tired I was back in those days. How I struggled.'

This time it's a bitter laugh.

'We took a plane all the way to the bloomin' Seychelles, Mum. You can't have been struggling that much.'

Her chin dipped in the slightest nod as her gaze dropped to the floor.

'Maybe it didn't look that way to you. Maybe I did a good job of hiding it. But I promise you, darling, I was unwell. I'd been unwell for years, and I was tired of being ill. Tired of being tired. I wasn't being the mother that you deserved. That was all I wanted.' She drew a breath in, but before she could speak, I felt a hand slip into mine. I looked up to finding Alex staring at me, his face lined with worry.

'You don't have to listen to this now, Elodie,' he said. 'Take some time. We can come back when you're ready.'

Ready? How was this something you were ever ready for? And as for taking time, I knew from experience that it wouldn't change anything. Besides, Alex and I went there for a reason and no matter how much I despised the situation I'd found myself in, she might finally give me some insight into the vampires who had turned me.

'No, I don't want to leave,' I said, looking back at Alex as I spoke. 'I wanted answers. I want to know it all. Who changed her. Where they did it. How she's been hiding like this. I want answers, and I'm not leaving until we've got them.'

Maria – Amira – whatever I was supposed to call my mother, nodded her chin.

'Then perhaps you should sit down then love, it's not a quick story.'

W hat is it about being with your parents – even one that you haven't seen in years – that can turn you from a mature adult to a petulant little kid? Or maybe that was just me and my mother. Though a little petulance felt like the least she deserved. I didn't want to sit down. I didn't want to get comfortable in this flat which she had made her home while my father and I had been struggling to rebuild ours. But at the same time, my legs were abnormally weak, especially considering I was a vampire and should have been able to leg-press a small truck. Not that I'd ever tried.

And so I perched on the arm of her sofa and watched as her lips pursed slightly, as if she was going to tell me to sit properly, but instead she pulled out a dining chair and took a seat opposite.

Still on the floor, Pongo looked up at me and tilted his head. Even without the use of his buttons, I knew what he was asking me, although it was a question he tended not to ask at home, or at work. No, there he would jump on whatever chair or sofa he could, and normally had to be dragged off it. But here, he seemed to have developed manners. Not that I cared if he did or not. He could have slobbered all over Amira's cushions, and I wouldn't have batted an eyelid. Actually, I'd have quite liked that. But at a slight wiggle of my fingers, he jumped up onto the sofa next to me.

Alex was the only one who remained standing and, just like with Pongo, I knew why. He was waiting to see what I wanted. He would stay with me if I wanted. Or he could go and give me privacy. The choice was mine. With a slight dip of my chin, I nodded to the seat, and he wordlessly took a place next to Pongo.

Finally, all settled, I was the first to speak.

'Well, we're all ears,' I said, only to find my comment ridiculously amusing. The persona that my mother had adopted, Amira the fae, had unfeasibly large ears. It was by far her most dominant feature, and I struggled to stifle a giggle. There was nothing to laugh about, was there? I mean, apart from the fact that my mother had chosen to parade herself like an extra from a low budget fantasy film rather than stay with us. That was pretty amusing, if you had a seriously dark sense of humour.

'You have to know, I didn't think I'd ever get the chance to tell you all this,' her voice warbled. 'Not until you showed up on the island. But it's difficult to know where to start.'

'Why don't you start at when you planned on abandoning your family?' I suggested dryly.

Her nostrils flattened as she sucked in a breath.

'It wasn't like that, Elodie. It wasn't. I didn't plan on leaving you, but...' she paused. 'But if I'm honest, I think I always thought you'd be better off without me. Without my moods, my tiredness, my lack of patience. I could never be the type of parent your father was. It all came so easy to him.'

'No, it didn't,' I cut her off, already bored with her pity party. 'Dad listened. That was all it was. He got to know me. Spent time with me. I might not remember much about you being around, but I remember being at the bottom of your list of priorities.'

Her cheeks drew into a pout. 'I'm so sorry if that's what you remember, Elodie. I promise you, that was never the case. You were my whole world. You are —'

'The vampires.' I cut her off again. We came there for a reason and I was not letting her pull me into a well of emotion that caused me to forget my job. Pushing my shoulders back, I took on the role of Elodie Evergreen, investigative journalist. That's all this was, another investigation. And I was going to treat it like that. 'When did you first meet them? Did you deliberately hunt them out, knowing what they could do for you?'

'No,' she shook her head, her forehead crinkling as if she was surprised by my sudden change in tone. 'It wasn't like that. Well... not at first.' She paused again and drew in yet another lung full of air. Patience with my sources had always been one of my greatest skills as a journalist. Listening to people. Knowing when to press them for more, and when to give them time to collect their thoughts, so that they didn't clam up. It was like second nature to me, normally. But now, I could see that Amira needed time. She needed space, mentally, to regather herself. Yet I had no desire to give it to her.

'Was it in the Seychelles? Is that where you met them? Or was it back in London?'

'It was on holiday,' she nodded. 'On our third day there.'

I did the maths in my head. She had disappeared the

day before we were due to leave, and they'd booked a fort-
night's holiday. That meant for ten days, she'd been
walking around with her tip family, aware that the para
world existed and not said anything.

'You and your dad were playing cards. I don't know
what the game was—'

'Shit head,' I said, before cursing myself for once again
crossing that line between daughter and journalist. 'He
taught me shit head that holiday.'

'Right.' She pursed her lips. 'I'm sure you're right. Well,
you were playing cards, and I went for a walk. Wanted to
find somewhere for a drink and ended up walking into the
staff area and finding this little cabana.'

In my head, I was transported to that scene from Dirty
Dancing, where Baby goes up the steps towards the party.
Is she going to tell me that, as well as being a vampire, she
also moonlighted in clubs and crawled along a dance studio
floor with a young Patrick Swayze? Right now, nothing
could shock me.

'Are you saying that the hotel staff were vampires?'
Alex's voice reminded me he was still there. And that I was
meant to be asking questions.

Amira shook her head. 'Not all of them. I don't think.
There were four of them there, though. In the cabana. Three
had drinks; I thought they were cocktails. Bloody Marys.
Then I saw the fourth one drinking more directly. Straight
from the source, so to speak.'

I looked to Alex. 'Vampires drinking from tips in the tip
world. Guessing that goes against the rules?'

'Yeah, I mean you can get special dispensation and
stuff. Apply for permits if you have a willing donor, but out
where people could see you? Definite no.'

I took a moment to contemplate what I'd learned so far.

Was seeing a vampire feeding while chilling with their vampire friends more or less traumatic than my first encounter, I wondered? It was a tough call. I guess they both ended the same way.

'So they turned you,' I said, guessing the rest of the story. 'They turned you for seeing what they were doing.'

'No!' Amira appeared genuinely shocked by the question. 'No, I don't think it ever crossed their mind. The one who was being fed from, she was a witch. She wiped my memory. Or at least, she tried. But the next evening, when I was sitting at dinner with you and your father, it all came back.'

'Okay...' Alex said slowly. I could feel his eyes boring into me, and I knew he was thinking the same as I am. Did the memory spell not work because the witch didn't know what she was doing, or because my mother had more in her heritage than the average Jo? Maybe it's the same reason my blood healed Ines. It was definitely a conversation I wanted to have with him. Though not at that precise moment.

'So what did you do once you knew?' I asked. 'Once the memories came back.'

'I thought,' she replied.

'You thought?' Of all the answers I'd expected her to give, that wasn't one of them. Personally, if I'd been on holiday with my husband and child and discovered there were vampires on the island, I would have been on a plane out of there faster than a piglet at a hog roast.

'Care to tell us what you'd thought about?' There was definite sarcasm in my voice, but I didn't care. It felt like she was drawing this out, deliberately.

'I thought about how that could be a way to help me. To help with the sickness that doctors had refused to acknowledge. I thought about how much better you would be without me. Wondered if I could actually do it. And when I realised I could, I went to them and asked them to change me.'

'And they agreed?'

'No. They tried to wipe my memory again, but it lasted even less time. By the time I'd woken up, they were back. The third time they tried, it didn't work at all. One of them suggested killing me, but thankfully, the others feared that would draw unwanted attention to them. Besides, I think they were a little intrigued by me, if I'm honest.'

'Wow.' I wasn't sure what else I could say. What I remembered from my mother, she was a distracted woman, busy with work. But she'd also been kind of plain. Someone who would melt into the background. Certainly not someone who would approach vampires multiple times in order to get what she wanted.

'I couldn't go back to being what I was, Elodie. Not when I knew there was a possibility of being more, of being better... of being well.' There was pleading in her voice, as she looked away. You didn't need to be a vampire to read her expression. The shame was written all over her face. 'While you and your father got on your plane, I watched. I stood there in the airport, hidden at a distance, and watched as you held your head against his shoulder and sobbed into his arms before boarding that plane and disappearing out of my life. I promise you, Elodie, so much of me wanted to run after you. So much of me wanted to get onto that plane and forget the stupid idea, but I couldn't. I couldn't forget what I'd learned. Forget there was a chance for me.'

It's only when a sharp pain pierced my palms, I realised my hands were clenched into such tight fists that the nails were digging into the skin. If it was any other person then perhaps I would feel a fragment of sympathy for them, but I just couldn't.

'You didn't even *know* that you were that unwell. We could've gone to the hospital together. We could've demanded the doctors do something. Find the cause.'

'I didn't want your childhood to be spent like that,' she said. 'No kind of mother wants their child to grow up like that.'

She was playing the hurt mother, the doting parent who did what was best for her child, but I still didn't believe it.

'So what? You just spent the next few months lazing in the Seychelles until they finally did what you asked of them? Until they finally changed you?'

'It wasn't quite lazing about,' she said. 'I tended to their every need. I was their acolyte, if you will. Hoping that they would change me. Hoping they would make it official. But they wouldn't.'

She paused, and my mind filled in the gaps. Anything they needed. Did they feed from her? It's a question I wanted to ask. A question I would have asked someone else if I was interviewing them. But I couldn't do it with her.

'Other vampires came and went, and one of their visitors was a younger woman. I don't know how old she was in vampire years, but we grew close. She felt sorry for me. I could see that. She'd had a family of her own, and things were complicated.' She drew in a breath. 'Then one night...I thought she was going to feed from me, but instead...she did it.'

'She turned you?' I felt my eyes widen, and not only because I'd just got the answer about feedings. The only way I get my haemoglobin fix is by taking my shots in a cappuccino from Weirdoughs.

'I thought it was an impulsive decision,' Amira continued. 'Something she decided, spur of the moment. But then she handed me a new passport, with a new name, along with some money and a plane ticket to LA and instructions on how to reach the island.'

So her transformation hadn't been anything like mine at all. She'd chosen it all, and had someone there to guide her. Even if that guidance was basically limited to sat nav capabilities.

'Was she the one that told you to turn into an elf as well? Did she tell you how to do it?'

'It's a glamour,' she said. 'And no, that wasn't her idea. When I arrived, I met this young witch, Nyrah. She's lovely. You've seen her a few times, I think.'

'Nyrah's been doing this to you?' I wouldn't't've thought it wasn't possible to feel any more pain, but I considered Nyrah a friend. To know she'd been doing this – helping keep my mother hidden – made the bile sting at the back of my throat.

'Nyrah doesn't know who I am,' Amira said, reading my expression. 'She doesn't know where I came from. Nothing like that. She just knew I needed to stay hidden.'

'Why? why did you need to stay hidden?'

'Because that was what the vampire told me to do, and I owed her. The last thing I wanted was to give her a reason to regret her choice. I may have not known her well, but she was powerful. I knew that much.'

As we fell into silence, I considered everything I'd learned. My mother had been changed willingly into a vampire. She'd left us to become immortal. That should have been all I could focus on, but instead, there was something else, niggling at the back of my mind. My mother had become a vampire around nineteen years ago. An unregistered vampire who had made it on her own in a paranormal community without documentation. She had done what her sire had said, and stayed hidden, and in doing so... in doing so had made vampires see it was possible to skip the red tape and turn as many humans as they wanted. And maybe turn a profit too.

The words choke in my throat. 'The Guardians exist because of you.'

THREE

Well, I came here wanting information about The Guardians, and it looks like I'd found it. If what she'd said was true, mum – Amira – may well have been instrumental in them starting out. If not, it was a ridiculous coincidence, and I'd long since stopped believing in them. I had a lead. My stomach clenched. A decent scoop would be the perfect thing to distract me from the chaos of my life, and I was pretty sure I had one.

'Are you in contact?' I said, trying to keep my excitement under wraps as I slipped my journalist head back on. 'Do you have a way to contact your sire? A name? A telephone number? Any way to get in touch?'

Amira shook her head.

'The others would call her Em. But I didn't know if that was Em as in a name, like Emily, or just the first letter. And I never heard from her again. She made it clear that if I did see her again, it wouldn't be a good thing.'

Threats to keep quiet. This Em may not have taken

money, but she wasn't sounding like the most altruistic person either.

'And you've never seen her here in Ravens Hollow?' Alex asked what was going to be one of my next questions, though I'd already guessed what her answer was going to be.

'No, I'd have recognised her. I'm sure of it. She was a striking young woman.'

It wasn't a lot to go on at all. A striking female vampire. I needed more than that.

'What about any of the others who were there with you? The other vampires. The witch who tried to wipe your memory.'

Her lips pursed.

'I wish I could help you, Elodie...really I do. But I can't.'

'Can't or won't?' I replied. Once again, I'd let my professionalism slip. Pongo nudged his nose into my thigh, clearly hearing the strain in my voice, and I gave him a quick smile as I rubbed the back of his neck, trying to at least pretend I was okay, even if he knew I wasn't.

'It's not personal, Elodie,' Amira said. 'It's about safety. All our safety.'

Had any other source said the same to me, I would have been disappointed, but I would have backed off. Accepted it, at least until I'd found a way to ease their concerns. But this was different. This was personal. She had chosen vampirism over her human family, and now she was choosing to protect these scum bags, rather than help me.

'You okay, Evergreen?' Alex said, brushing the back of my arm. I wasn't sure whether he was asking about the story or my mother, but either way, I didn't think I could offer him a decent answer. And so, for the first time since I stepped foot in her flat, I shifted the attention away from my mother and onto me.

'Do you know what I am?' I was looking at Amira, ignoring Alex, but I knew he'd understand.

'What you are?' Amira echoed tilted her head to the side. 'You're a vampire, right? That's what I read about you. That's what I learned.'

'What about with the blood? Do you know why that happened?'

'Blood. What about blood? You don't drink it?'

She shook her head, confused, and for a split second, I was tempted to tell her what had happened the day before.

I'd been following a story, trying to work out why several people in the town, including two of my colleagues, had been hexed. Despite Whip telling me not to confront the person I believed to be behind it all alone, I'm not very good at listening. Not when there's a story involved.

Anyway, the short version was that I found myself under attack by a load of werewolves, despite it not being a full moon. And although I came out pretty much unscathed, apart from a nasty bite on my arm that bled like hell, the Beta of the Amber Pack, Ines Ortega, was less lucky. Her sister, in wolf form, attacked her while she was still human, leaving her for dead.

There had been a brief moment, when I'd actually considered feeding from her, but thankfully Pongo had brought me back to my senses. My own blood dripped onto her wounds and sealed them. It wasn't, as far as any of us were aware, a general vampire trait. And it was something I was trying to keep to myself for now, because the fewer people who knew about it, the better.

And by the look of pure confusion on my mother's face,

she didn't know what I was talking about. So it was better to keep it that way.

Amira leaned forward and clenched her hands on her lap.

'Elodie, I promise I was going to talk to you at some point.'

'Now that I was on the island, you mean,' I clarified. 'What if I hadn't come here? What if I hadn't been turned?'

Her chin dipped and wavered. 'I've been thinking about that too, I promise. I was following everything you did.'

She moved over to a bookshelf. From the bottom, she pulled out what appeared to be a photo album.

'I've been following you every step of the way,' she said as she opened it up. It was full of clippings. Newspaper articles, and though I didn't look too closely, I was pretty sure they were all by me.

'You were doing so well,' Amira continued. 'I was waiting for a time when me reappearing in your life didn't confuse matters.'

Alex let out a scoff at how ridiculous that remark was.

'I think that's what you call wishful thinking, Mother,' I said, unable to stop the bitterness from spilling out.

Once again, Pongo was alert to the change in my tone, though this time, he rested his paw on my hand.

'It's okay, boy. I'm okay,' I said, before pushing myself up to standing and stretching my hand out towards Amira.

'Thank you for everything you told us around your changing,' I said, my voice the most formal it had been since I'd arrived. 'If you remember anything else, or feel comfortable telling us any more, you know where to reach us.'

'Elodie, please.' Her voice quivered as she reached out towards me. 'Can we not—'

'No,' I replied, not even sure what it was she was going to ask me. 'This is going to take some time. A lot of time. I guess it's lucky for you we're both immortal. Come on, boy,' I called Pongo over to me, 'we've been here long enough.'

CHAPTER
FOUR

Being out of her apartment might have given me the physical space I needed from this elf-vampire mother I'd assumed was dead, but it hardly helped with the mental issues at all. My mind was an absolute wreck.

'Is there someone you can talk to?' Alex asked as we stepped out onto the street. Ahead of us, white sand merged with crystal blue seas. 'I mean, you can talk to me if that helps. I ain't going to tell nobody.'

'Thank you,' I said. 'But I don't know. I don't know what the right thing is to do right now.'

'You want to get a drink? Don't have to talk. Just sit, if that's what you need.'

I twisted around to look at him.

'You're a good friend, Alex. You know that, right?'

A smile flickered on his lips, but I couldn't help but see sadness in his eyes. Then again, it had been less than an hour ago when he'd told me he thought I was rushing things with Whip. That I should slow down, maybe date a little and see if there was someone I was better suited to.

And I knew he'd meant him, even though he'd denied it. My relationship with Whip now felt like one of the most uncomplicated aspects of my life, and there was no way I wanted to do anything to change that. Even if I did feel a safety and comfort around Alex that I'd rarely experienced around someone before. Especially not so quickly.

'Let's just walk,' I said, turning away from the beach, and towards the road that led us back to the station and paper.

It was a sign of how distracted I was that I didn't even put Pongo on his leash. I wasn't actually sure where it was, and had a horrible feeling that I'd left it at Amira's, but it didn't matter. They had more at the station from when they'd had police dogs. I could just pick one up from there. And Pongo was perfectly good at keeping to heel.

As we walked, my mind was a fuzzy mess. One of my first instincts was to call my best friend, Donna, who was also my former editor back in the UK, but given that it was only midday here, it was some crazy hour of the morning there, and there was no way I could disturb her. I already did that way too often. Besides, I wasn't even sure what I'd say.

And so we walked in silence.

Only when we reached the paper did Alex pause. 'You heading there, or you coming with me to the station?'

Whip was in the station. I wasn't sure what I was ready to tell him, but I really didn't want to deal with whatever questions were waiting for me at the paper either.

'I want to pick up Pongo a leash,' I said. 'I'll come with you.'

At the mention of the word station, Pongo's tail began beating against my leg. The station was home to his best friend and there was a one hundred percent chance she would to be there, given that she couldn't actually leave the building.

'Pongo! There's my good boy!' The station ghost whizzed through the reception desk to crouch down on the floor next to my dog, before standing up and looking at me. 'Elodie, I'm glad you're here too,' she said, in what very much sounded like an afterthought. 'I've located a box of dog treats. I knew I'd put them somewhere a while back. Could you open them for me? You've just got to move that cupboard over there, the one next to the filing cabinet, so you can pull out the second drawer. I would ask one of the others, but you know, they have proper jobs, and given that you spend as much time here as you do at the paper, I assumed you'd be able to spend a few minutes helping me?'

Wow, I was barely even listening, but I still caught enough to know that I, or at least my profession, had been insulted.

Thankfully, Alex replied. 'I'll do it, Josephine. Just show me where,' he said, as he instinctively knew I needed him to step in and come to my aid. 'And whilst we're at it, can you tell me where we might find another leash?'

As Alex moved to shift the furniture and get Pongo some snacks that were probably decades old, I walked through into the main station office.

Raven's Hollow Police station was an impressively large building and, if what Josephine said was true, one of the oldest in the town. As well as the reception and the office area, which included an open plan section where Raquel and Alex normally worked, and a separate office for Whip, there were also questioning rooms and cells, none of which I had ever seen. And all of that was on the ground floor; the first floor, as far as I was aware, was all Whip's apartment, but I'd not yet been up there to see. Though if our relationship continued to progress the way it had been doing, I was sure I would at some point. After all, he'd stayed at my place a couple of times now, even if the first time had been on the sofa so he could keep an eye on Pongo in case he'd been hexed.

'Hey Elodie, how did it go?'

Raquel was sitting at a computer in the open plan office. Her father Bobby was my boss at *The Oracle*, and they were good people. The whole family had made me feel at home here in Ravens Hollow, although her question unexpectedly threw me.

'It?'

'You were going to see if you could track down a sireless vampire, weren't you? Isn't that where you and Alex have been?'

It had been naïve of me to think that I'd only get questioned about my morning if I'd gone to the paper. But as Raquel stared up at her desk, looking at me expectantly, I found myself at a loss for words. Apparently, I couldn't even think up a decent lie on the spot any more. Not that minute, anyway.

'Is he in?' I said, instead, gesturing to Whip's office.

'Yeah,' Raquel nodded, frowning slightly. 'He's got a lot to deal with, you know. After Welcoming Woods.'

Welcoming Woods, indeed. That was where Ines's pack had taken a potion to transform into werewolves and attacked me. I'd seen jellyfish-infested waters more welcoming than that place.

'Thanks,' I said, before moving over to Whip's office, knocking once on the door, and opening it up.

'Is it important?' he said, without even looking up from the desk.

'Kind of, yeah.'

His head snapped up the moment he heard my voice.

'Elodie?' He pushed his chair back and hurried around the desk as I closed the door behind me. 'How did it go? Did you speak to the vampire? Does it look like it could be a lead to The Guardians?'

He was the most beautiful man. Dark, brooding and chiselled. And normally, knowing that I got to kiss him was enough to cause an unprecedented grin to cross my face, but even as he placed his hands on my hips, I struggled to muster even the smallest smile.

'Elodie, what is it?' His face dropped. 'What's happened? Are you okay?'

It didn't matter how much I didn't want to cry in front of him. The burning behind my eyes was starting again, and unlike at Amira's house, I knew I couldn't keep it in.

'Just out of interest,' I said. 'How do you feel about dealing with large amounts of emotional trauma from someone you're not officially dating yet?'

CHAPTER
FIVE

Before now, I had only told Whip bits and pieces of my childhood. We weren't at that stage in a relationship where we knew the ins and outs of everything each other had been through. I wasn't even at the stage where I knew what his actual age was, but that was something I preferred not to dwell on too much. If he turned around and told me he'd been present when the Acropolis was built, I wasn't exactly sure how I'd take it.

However, he did know that my mother had left, and that it had been just my father and me for almost as long as I could remember. He knew that I had given up ever thinking I would see her again, or even wanting to. So, I gave him the stripped-back version of how our meeting had gone.

'She got a vampire to change her, all those years ago. I just can't believe it.'

I saw the shock registering on his face.

'Are you sure it's her?' The first question out of his mouth was a sensible one. 'She could be lying about the glamour. Couldn't it just be some kind of trick?'

'I'm not sure what anyone would gain by pretending to be my mother,' I replied truthfully. 'It's not as if they could expect a positive relationship between us. And it's not like I'm some old widow they might hope to inherit millions from.' I'd never really thought about the whole work-life thing as a vampire, but pensions definitely felt off the cards now that I was going to be twenty-nine for all eternity. Did I want to work forever? Thankfully, I adored my job, and no two days were ever the same, meaning I was unlikely to get bored with it. I could almost imagine how good I would get at the investigative side of things if I had centuries to tune my instincts. I shook the thoughts away and considered what Whip had said to me.

'Besides, it's her,' I continued with a sigh. 'I know it is. She had clippings from my first newspaper articles. A bracelet I made. It was her. God, I thought life on this island couldn't get any more chaotic.' I was pretty sure I would rather face another half-dozen werewolves than have a repeat of that morning.

'You've only been here a couple of months,' Whip said, though I'm not sure if that comment was meant to comfort me or not.

Silence began to form between us, but before it settled, there was a sharp knock at the door.

'No, it's not a great time,' Whip called out, but rather than whoever it was, taking the hint and coming back, the door opened. Alex stood behind it.

'Sorry, it's me. I just wanted to check if you were okay.' He was looking at me as he spoke, and didn't shift his gaze as he stepped in and closed the door behind him.

'You were with Elodie when she met Amira?'

Alex nodded, before finally acknowledging Whip's presence. 'She told you about her?'

Whip's face was unusually hard. 'She did. She told me everything, and this isn't to go out of this room. Not unless Elodie is okay with it, you understand? There will be consequences if you tell people. I promise that.'

I'd never heard Whip speak so sharply to him. But I was already aware that my siren sort-of-boyfriend had a definite jealous streak. He'd shown that the first time Alex stripped off in front of me. Not that it was a gratuitous strip. It was to shift to his lion form. But still.

'It's fine Whip, I trust him. He knows I trust him.'

I did. Truly. And he deserved that trust.

Now didn't seem like the right time to tell Whip about what my blood had done to Ines. So far, she, Alex and I were the only people that knew it had healed her, but whether that had been a one-off thing, or to do with her being a werewolf, or maybe linked to how sunlight wards didn't work half as long on me as other people, we had no idea. Alex had suggested I should mention it to Whip, though, just to see if he could shed some light on the matter. But I was going to save that for another time. One when he hadn't already threatened one of his best friends out of worry for me.

'Was there anything else you needed?' Whip said, still focused on the lion shifter.

'No, it's all good, boss.' Alex glanced at me, and offered a smile. 'You know where to find me if you need anything,' he said, before disappearing out of the office and closing the door.

A second silence started to swell, and I knew I should probably go. Raquel hadn't been lying when she'd said that Whip had a crazy amount of work to do. But before I could even stand up, the siren spoke again.

'Why don't you spend the weekend with me?' he said,

both his voice and the question catching me by surprise. 'I've got a couple of hours more work I need to do here before I can leave. You could head home, grab Pongo's food and then we can go to my place when I'm done.'

'Your place? As in the flat above the station?' I asked.

It wasn't that I didn't want to spend the weekend with Whip, I absolutely did, but I suspected Josephine wasn't confined to the downstairs part of the station, and the last thing I wanted was her sweeping in on our conversations. Not to mention other things. I felt like I needed a little more space.

'The flat's where I stay when I'm working a lot,' he said. 'I've actually got another place. In Peppers Bay.'

Peppers Bay was the exclusive part of the island. Over on the west coast, next to the Forlorning Forest, the area of land was a cause for much debate for island inhabitants, as paras and werewolves were banned from hunting there, which was stretching the rest of the island's ecosystems to its limits. That had been why Ines's sister, Sophia, had started hexing people. To raise awareness and spur the council into action. But Peppers Bay was also where all the wealthy people had their cliff-side mansions with views out to the ocean, private docks, and goodness knows what else. I'd been there a couple of times. Most recently, to talk to Prue Parsons, the so-called journalist who ran a vlog and was basically a glorified gossip columnist.

I couldn't imagine Whip living somewhere like that.

'It's nice to have somewhere to escape to,' he said. 'To get out of town. Being in my job and everything, you can't really have a day off and wander about Ravens Hollow without someone accosting you about one thing or another. So I bought a place a couple of years ago.'

'Right.... In...Peppers Bay,' I repeated.

I still couldn't picture it, but the idea of being away from the town – and therefore my mother – even if it was only by a couple of miles, was too good of an opportunity to pass up. The last thing I could deal with was bumping into her while I was walking Pongo. Or worse still, have her turning up on my doorstep. It wouldn't be the first time.

'Okay. I'll get my things and meet you back here in two or three hours. I probably need to drop by the paper and check if there's anything Bobby needs me to write up before I go.'

'Sure thing.'

He walked around to where I was now standing, then he took my hands and pressed his lips against mine. Every kiss I'd shared with Whip had been unique; full of sparks, and tension and promise of what would come. But this one? It was pure tenderness. And when he pulled away, his eyes were gazing deep into mine.

'What you said when you came in, about dealing with emotional trauma, we'll find a way around it. And that relationship part too. If you're happy with that, then so am I. To make it official.'

A relationship with Whip. That was... insane. Never in my life had I imagined I would end up with a man like him. Who cooked for me and cared for me and made me feel like I was the most precious thing in the entire world. But before I replied, a thought entered my head. I shifted back from him slightly.

'If I'm actually going to be in a relationship with you, I'd really like to know what your actual name is. I mean... it's not really "Whip", is it?'

His eyebrows rose.

'You want to do this now?' he said.

'I really do.'

With a low groan, he dropped my hands, moved behind his desk, and pulled open a drawer. He rifled through it for a second before tossing something over to me.

It took me a moment to realise it was a passport.

With normal vampire reflexes, I caught it and opened it to the photo page.

My eyes went first to the image of Whip. I didn't know it was possible for someone to take such a good passport photo. He looked like a freaking model. Yet as my gaze shifted to the name, my eyes widened, and I let out a giggle.

'Really?' I said, grinning.

'Elodie...' His face didn't show a hint of the amusement I was feeling. 'You tell anybody, and I *will* know where to bury the bodies.'

'You have my word.' Rather than tossing the passport back, I walked over to him, kissed him on the lips, and dropped it back into the drawer. 'Your secret is safe with me.'

CHAPTER
SIX

Back at the paper, the entire crew was in working. Bobby, the editor-in-chief, was in his office, while everyone else was squirreling away at their desks. As Pongo hopped onto my seat and curled up – clearly exhausted from his long morning walks and escapades with Josephina, I took a moment, simply to stand there, and feel a deep sense of gratitude.

Diego and Theodora were back at work, but less than forty-eight hours ago, they had still been under the effects of the hex planted on them by Sophia. Bobby had told them they could take as long as they needed to recover, but all six of us at The Oracle were workaholics. Well, except perhaps Diego. I was fairly sure he only came to work for the snacks and to get away from his own pack politics. But still, I wouldn't change it for the world. And seeing them all working caused a strange sense of normality to run through me after everything I had already experienced that day.

'You're back!' Chloe said with excitement, as if I'd been gone for days, not just a couple of hours. But then, she was the one most often out of the office, reporting on the island's various sporting events. It probably felt strange to be one of the people left in the office while others were out.

'Everything alright?' Diego asked, looking up from his desk 'You smell... emotional.'

'Emotional has a smell?' I replied.

He sat back in his seat, probably happy for an excuse to stop work. 'Hormones excreted when you're emotional smell,' he told me. 'And you reek, so you got a lotta of emotions coming off you right now.'

I lifted my armpit and took a whiff. Was it the most ladylike thing to do in my workplace? No, was Diego right in saying that I smelt of emotions? I hardly thought his choice of word, 'reeked,' was fair, but there was definitely an aroma there, that wasn't the average sweat pits stench.

'Maybe you could give me a hand identifying some different smells sometime,' I said, diverting conversation away from me. 'I'm guessing if you can smell them, then I should be able to too?'

'Sure. I'll let you have a whiff of me next time I'm bored. Happens pretty often.'

I couldn't help but crinkle my nose. 'Thanks. I think.'

'No worries.'

'You okay?' Chloe asked. 'What happened? Did you not find the vampire? Or did you find the vampire, and they were horrible? Did Alex go with you? Has he already gone back to the station? Did you and Alex have an argument? Did you and Whip have an argument?'

As a fire-fae, Chloe had so many amazing talents. But asking succinct questions was not one of them.

'No, I didn't have any arguments with anyone,' I clarified. 'I just had a pretty big bit of unexpected news.'

'About the sireless vampire?' she asked. 'What did they do? Did they do something?' While I was grateful that she was clearly worried about me, it wasn't something I could go into and once again I was glad I'd gone to the station first. I wasn't sure how I would have dealt with the bombardment of questions if I hadn't spoken with Whip and got it all off my chest.

'I'm fine. It just took a turn I didn't expect.'

'Really? Why? Did they—

'Clo?' Dylan called out from across the office. 'How 'bout you give Elodie a bit o' space, yeah?'

'He means stop pestering her,' Diego joined in.

As much as I loved Chloe, and she was my closest friend on the island, I was grateful to the guys for interjecting. She wasn't great at knowing when to let things go. Still, I felt a flush of guilt as her cheeks turned almost as pink as her ombre hair. Though within a heartbeat, she was back to the questions again.

'Do you want a drink?' she said. 'We thought we might go out for a celebration, now that everyone's out and everything. We were going to do it next week, but I'm sure nobody would mind bringing it forward, if that's what you need? I can ring Mick too, see if he can make it.'

I moved to my desk, which was opposite hers, and lifted Pongo off the chair, placing him on the dog bed only two feet away.

'Celebratory drinks sound great,' I told her as I sat down. 'But next week would be better for me. I've actually got plans this weekend. I'm spending it at Whip's.'

'You are?' her jaw hung lost. 'You mean you're spending the weekend there as in... as in the way a girlfriend would spend the weekend at her boyfriend's?'

'I guess you'd say that, yes,' I tried, but failing to hold in my grin.

'Oh, my god. Eek!' she squealed, jumping up and down.

'We are going to have to double date. Oh my god, that would be amazing. The whole weekend. Tell me you've shaved? Do you need to book in a wax? I can ring Elise. See if she can book you in."

'Stop. Stop now.' Diego growled from behind his desk. 'I'd rather be hexed than listen to this.'

Chloe's eyes met mine, and she struggled to stifle another giggle. As much as I was normally one for a professional working environment, I was incredibly grateful for the way the conversation was distracting me from everything I'd learned about my mother earlier that morning.

'I'm serious about the double date though,' she continued, lowering the volume of her voice by a fraction. 'We have to. It'll be so much fun.'

'Absolutely,' I replied, trying to sound as genuine as possible.

Despite all Chloe's efforts to introduce me to Mick, the only time I'd actually met him was when I was hunting down a lead for a story. And my impression of him hadn't been all that favourable. Not with the way he had looked me up and down, seemingly forgetting he had a loving fiancée I happened to be good friends with. They were a strange pairing, that was for sure. I didn't know how long they'd been together, but from what Chloe'd said, they'd been engaged now for three years, with no sign of a wedding date set, even though she was clearly keen to get married.

It was stranger still when you threw Dylan, the advertising guy, into the equation. Chloe frequently described Dylan as her best friend, and his unrequited love was apparent to everyone except Chloe. The poor man hung on her every word and the more I saw them together, the more I couldn't help but think how perfectly suited to one another they were. But maybe that was just because I hadn't seen Mick and her together. And the last thing I wanted was to push my own ideas of what a relationship should be onto somebody else. After all, it wasn't like my ex-fiancé was the pinnacle of supportive partners.

'I just came to see if there's anything I need to write up over the weekend,' I said. 'Before I head off.'

'Well, Bobby's in his office. He and Diego have been fielding phone calls for hours now. It's weird. I always heard about what it was like when a new beta or alpha was found – how chaotic things could get when a wolf pack's hierarchy was disrupted – but I'd never seen it in person.'

'One of the packs is changing leadership?' I asked.

There were five wolf packs on the island, all identifiable by the colours of their eyes. The Onyx wolves had black eyes, Peridot had green, and the Lapiz wolves, which was the pack Diego was part of, had blue eyes. But the only ones I'd ever had anything to do with were the Amber wolves, of which Ines Ortega was the beta.

'Which pack?' I said, not that I expected to know any of the people involved.

Chloe looked at me, her head cocking to the side, as if I'd made a joke. 'What do you mean? It's the Ambers. Everyone's vying for the beta position now that Ines has been stripped.'

'What?' I said.

'You didn't know?' she asked.

I shook my head, feeling a lump form in my throat. Was this because Sophia had injured her? Ines had told me that she had to be the one to fight Sophia. To defeat her. Otherwise, she was effectively conceding her position in the pack. But she *had* fought her. She had brought her sister down in wolf form, even though she herself was only human at the time, and she had nearly died because of it.

She didn't deserve to be stripped of her position; she deserved to be Alpha. After all, she'd been doing that job in her father's absence for as long as I'd been on the island.

'You should talk to Bobby,' Chloe said. 'Or Diego. They know more about it than me,' she said.

I nodded, offering her a quick, quiet 'thanks', before looking at Diego. Like me, the wolf had acute hearing, and I'd no doubt he'd heard everything we'd just said.

His eyes met mine, and he let out a slight sigh. 'Come on. We'll talk to the boss together. No doubt he's got things to fill me in on, too.'

CHAPTER
SEVEN

I didn't hold back.

'She's no longer the beta? Because of what happened?' I wasn't aiming my question at Bobby or Diego individually. I wasn't even sure I was hoping for answers. I just had to get it out. 'Do they have any idea what she went through? She almost died... I mean, she could have died.' The last thing I wanted to do was out myself just cause I was angry. I hastily tried to backtrack. 'The fact that she was barely injured should be all the evidence the alpha needs to know she won that fight fair and square.'

Diego let out a long sigh. I hadn't noticed before, but he looked tired, and I didn't think it had anything to do with the hex he'd previously suffered. No wonder he didn't want to listen in on Chloe and my conversation about intimate waxes.

'It's even worse than that, unfortunately,' he said. 'They didn't just strip her of her position. They've cast her out of the pack.'

'What?' My anger reached another level. I could feel the

adrenaline roaring behind my ears. If Diego had thought I'd reeked before, I could only imagine what I smelt like now. 'Can they do that? How?'

'The alpha of the pack can do anything they want,' Bobby said. 'That's the way it works.'

'But Ines's father is the alpha, isn't he?' I'd never met Pedro Ortega before, but I had heard of him. He roared from afar, and everyone cowered at his every word, even from a distance. But Ines had been keeping the pack running on a day-to-day basis. It was Ines trying to do the best for her people.

'How many has he cast out?' I asked, thinking of all those wolves who had followed Sophia to overthrow Ines. Bobby and Diego exchanged a look.

'What? What is it you're not telling me?'

The two men exchanged a look, as if trying to persuade the other to speak. In the end, Diego took the plunge.

'She's the only one,' Diego said eventually.

'What?!' That was it. My fangs were out with such speed that both men jumped back. Although why Diego was afraid, I had no idea. I'd recently learnt that werewolf blood was poisonous to vampires, but I guess that wouldn't stop me from snapping his neck if I wanted to. Which I didn't.

No, I wanted to snap this damn Alpha's neck.

In as measured a manner as I could manage, I retracted my fangs, then took a deep breath in, before starting again. Slowly.

'I'm sorry. Are you telling me that they threw Ines out of the pack, but not Sophia? How is that right? Sophia nearly killed her. She took a potion and became a wolf when it wasn't even a full moon. Surely she should get cast out for that?'

'She'll get punished, for sure,' Diego said, 'but it won't be that bad. She challenged the beta. There's nothing to stop her from doing that.'

'And what about hexing people? The alpha's fine with that, is he?' I was getting dangerously close to fang territory again, but tried my best to rein it in. 'He's fine with the fact that she nearly killed you, another wolf? Another beta? Husband of an alpha?'

I got that politics were weird. I mean, you only needed to look at the tip world to see that, and I was sure being a para added a whole other heap of complications to the matters, but this...this was just cruel.

'Pedro thinks Ines should've known what was going on with Sophia and the others,' Diego said. 'And, speaking as another beta, he's right.'

'Seriously? You're on his side?' Anger flashed through me, and I noticed the way Bobby stiffened, as if he was worried I might genuinely lunge for Diego.

'It's more complicated than sides,' he said.

'Ines was trying to better the whole island. Protesting to the mayor about hunting rights that would help *all* wolves. Not just the Amber Pack.'

'I get that, but maybe it shouldn't have been her priority. If she'd been focused on the pack, she might've seen how obsessed Sophia was getting. Maybe she could've stopped things before they got that far. Maybe casting her out wasn't the right decision, but I think that stripping her position was. Until she earned it back. And I like her. A lot. But you can't let friendships get in the way of doing what's right.'

My fangs may not have come out again, but my jaw was so tightly clenched I could feel rattling through my skull.

'So what happens now?' I asked. 'What happens to someone cast out of the pack?'

Bobby looked at Diego, waiting for him to respond, but he didn't. It was like he couldn't let the words leave his lips and for the first time I smelt the slightest hint of aroma that was different from what I normally scented rising from my colleague. Was it terror?

'I don't think they have the easiest time,' Bobby said eventually. 'We've had a couple of stripped werewolves in town before. They still change, of course. They're still were-wolves. But wolves are pack animals. They hunt together. Live together. Solitary life don't suit them.'

'Can't we find a way to make her less solitary?' I said. 'There must be something she can do. A job maybe. Or somewhere she could volunteer. Just so she's still around people if that's what she needs.'

'It ain't just about bein' around people,' Diego said. 'It's about bein' around other wolves. But you know, sometimes cast-out wolves find each other. She'd have to leave the island, but there's packs of folk shunned from their original ones. She could maybe find a home with one.'

My heart was aching for Ines. I had never considered her a friend, but I'd always thought we'd get that way, once I'd been on the island a little longer. She was someone who fought for what she believed in. She had a strong sense of what was right and wrong when it came to the island. And when it came to her people. To see her deserted like this; it was enough to break my heart.

'It's not okay,' I said, a feeling of hopelessness flooding me at the fact I could do nothing to help the situation. 'It's not okay at all!' With that, I turned around, walked out the office, and slammed the door behind me.

EIGHT

'You okay?' Chloe said when I reappeared at my desk. It was probably a sign of how furious I looked that she only asked the single question. And that Pongo jumped straight off my seat the instant he saw me coming.

With a noise remarkably like a grunt, I flopped down.

'I can't believe the pack would treat her that way after everything she's done for them,' I said. 'You'd have thought some of them would have stepped up for her.'

'Maybe they did,' she said. 'Or maybe they were too scared to.'

It was a definite possibility. If standing up for Ines meant risking being cast out themselves, I could see why they'd be reluctant. But surely one or two must have.

Given my mood, I knew I was unlikely to get any work done, and I was about to ready myself to leave when Chloe's phone chimed loudly. My muscles tensed. I knew exactly what the sound was, and it didn't me feel any better.

'Really, Chloe?' My voice was laced with as much judgement as a school-yard mum when one of the other parents forgets World Book day. I couldn't believe she was still getting notifications from that damn sea witch Prue Parsons and her Ravens Hollow gossip site.

'I know.' Chloe's face dropped in shame. 'I keep promising myself I'll delete it, but it's really addictive.' She shook her head, as if physically trying to shake Prue off her. 'No, that's wrong. I'll delete it now. Right now.' She opened up her phone and her fingers hovered over the screen, as if she was about to do exactly what she's said, but instead her hands lingered, as she frowned.

'Okay. That's weird.' Her voice was little more than a mutter, but perfectly clear. To me, anyway.

'What is it?' I asked, annoyed that my interest was piqued by the damn gossip hound.

'It's Prue,' Chloe replied.

'Obviously.' My words came out far more curt than I'd ever normally speak, but given the day I'd had so far, I wasn't going to hold it against me.

'I'm mean, the video is of Prue,' Chloe clarified. 'She's talking to the camera. Well, actually, no. She's crying. Look.'

She handed me the phone, turning up the volume before passing it over.

With her red hair unusually dishevelled and black mascara streaks running down her face, it was indeed Prue, though she looked even worse than when she'd been hexed.

'I just... it's just so difficult, being on your own like this,' she stuttered as she drew in gulping breaths of air. 'And everybody thinks I'm a horrible sea witch, but I'm not. Yes, I'm a sea witch, but I'm doing something for the community. I'm trying to make a difference. But people take it so personally. And that's hard. Really hard.'

I couldn't hear a heartbeat, given that it was a recording, but from what I knew of her, it was hard to believe she was genuine.

'Just another ploy to get more followers and subscribers,' I said, handing the phone back to Chloe. It will have got out that Sophia told her where to go to record Diego. She's probably got blowback from that. Deservedly so in my opinion. 'She'll be back to her vile pieces tomorrow. You mark my words.'

Was I being overly harsh to Prue? Maybe. Was it deserved? Absolutely. She was an embarrassment to the name of journalism, and I was hardly the only one on the island with a personal reason to dislike her. My arrival in Ravens Hollow had been announced by her posting several photos of me in a lion onesie, and yet she had actually had the guts to smile and say how pleased she was to meet me the first time we met. No, there were few people in the world I had as little time for as I did for Prue Parson.

Chloe, however, continued to stare at the video. 'Yeah... I just can't believe this. I've never seen her do anything like this. It just doesn't feel right.'

'Please put it away,' I said, yet before she even moved, that same chime rang out again. 'There you go,' I said, with more than a hint of smugness. 'I bet that's her laughing at all the people who thought she was being genuine.'

'I don't think it is,' Chloe replied, as she hit play on the second video. Once again, it was Prue. And once again, she seemed to be sobbing.

'I just wanted to apologise for the video I posted earlier in the week. It was wrong. So wrong. And all the ones I've ever posted that have hurt people. That's not who I am. That's not who I want to be. And from now, you will see a different side to Prue Parson. A kinder side. You have my word.'

It didn't matter how genuine she sounded; I wasn't falling for it.

'She has to be joking, right?' I said. 'She loves it when her videos get traction. About time she felt a bit of her own content came back to bite her.'

I was about to ask Chloe to put it away again, when Diego and Bobby appeared.

'Have you seen the videos Prue just posted?' Chloe said, holding up her phone. 'It's not like her at all. Elodie thinks they're fake, but I'm not sure. What do you think?'

'I think you should get that witch out of my face now, before you need to buy yourself a new phone,' Diego replied.

Apparently, his threats were more believable than mine, as Chloe immediately did what he said.

'Weekend started early for y'all has it?' Bobby said, his single eye shifting between Chloe and me.

A brief flicker of annoyance rose in me, only to fade almost instantly. He was probably right. Since I'd got back, all I'd done was talk to Chloe and rant at him and Diego. It wasn't the most productive use of my time.

'Actually, I was hoping to head off early. Just needed to check if there's any work I need to get on with over the weekend. I'm going to head to Whip's. Not sure how much reception I'll get over in Pepper Bay.'

'Pepper Bay?' Dylan let out a low whistle from the other side of the room, while Diego looked entirely non-plussed. Bobby's look was far more serious, and I had the distinct feeling that one of his fatherly lectures was on the horizon.

'Now, I ain't tryin' to sound like your pops,' he said, 'but you're takin' things slow, right? I like Whip, but I don't want you to deal with any heartbreak. You've been through a fair bit already.'

'You don't know the half of it,' I muttered to myself.

Diego frowned, and I cursed myself. Sometimes I forgot he had supernatural hearing too. I waved my comment off with a flick of my hand.

'It's fine, honestly. It's fine. And we're taking things slow. Just seeing a different bit of the island, that's all. In a nice manner. And it'll be good for Pongo to see a bit more, too.'

Bobby didn't look convinced. 'Alright, well, have a good time, and try to relax.'

'You know I could say the same to you,' I replied with a smirk, only for him to let out a long groan.

'Chances be a fine thing,' he muttered. He was right. Beautiful island or not, Ravens Hollow was not the place to come to for a quiet life. But then, I'd never been good with quiet.

CHAPTER
NINE

There was no point in staying at The Oracle, when I obviously wouldn't get any work done, and as much as I'd tried to ignore Chloe's comment about getting a wax before I spent the weekend with Whip's, it wouldn't hurt to have a quick shave. Then there was the whole overnight bag issue to think of. Did people swim at Peppers Bay? Would we? It made sense to pack a costume in case. In which case, I would want to take clean clothes to put on afterwards. And would Whip have extra towels for me to use?

But worse than all that was the nightwear conundrum. I had never been a lingerie person. It wasn't that I didn't like it. It was just that Andy's idea of a wild night involved watching two episodes of CSI in an evening, rather than one, and he insisted I only wore a hundred percent cotton to bed. Unlike most of Andy's foibles, this one was a sound and texture thing, rather than an allergy, though he never seemed to complain about such things when he wore golf gear or cycling shorts.

Play. Play. Pongo hit on his button.

'Sorry buddy,' I said, glancing down at him. 'I will. I've just got to work out what to take first.'

I had a couple of cute matching sets, but they were far skimpier than I'd normally wear and hardly comfortable, and the last thing I wanted was to be distracted by a butt-severing wedgy during a critical moment. Mostly, I slept in an oversized T-shirt, but I didn't want Whip to think I was going for the whole casual buddies sleepover thing. Unless that was what he wanted. Which I was ninety-nine percent sure he didn't. But that damn one percent had me in a spiral.

It was no good. The idea of spending a night at Whip's – at another man's house – just wasn't something I could get my head around. I couldn't make this decision on my own. While continuing to rummage through my drawers with one hand, I picked up my phone with the other, ready to call Donna when the doorbell rang out.

Chucking a dodgy pair of grey knickers – that looked more like a well-used dishcloth than anything remotely sexy – back into the drawer, I mulled over who it could be. Theoretically, I should have still been at work, and others were still at the paper. Whip was waiting for me to ring him so he'd know I was ready to leave. So who did that leave? My stomach lurched. Amira?

A mixture of nerves and anger rolled through me. I thought I'd made it perfectly clear to her I needed time before I'd be okay to talk, and I hadn't meant a couple of hours. Out in the hallway, Pongo began bounding up and down as he wagged his tail. It didn't seem like the type of response he should have to my mother, but if it was, then maybe that was a good sign.

With trepidation shifting me into full alert mode, I headed downstairs, only to catch a familiar scent wafting through the air. Not Amira then. That was good, though the nerves didn't fade entirely.

'Alex,' I said as I opened my door. 'What are you doing here?'

For a man normally so full of confidence, Alex looked decidedly nervous as he twirled a piece of his long hair around his finger. I was tempted to sniff him, just to help my scent training, like Diego had suggested, but before I could do something stupid, like stick my nose in his armpit, he spoke.

'Hey Evergreen. Just wanted to check how you were doing. After everything. You didn't exactly say much on the walk back.'

'Oh, well I'm fine, Alex, really,' I sounded convincing, to myself at least. Though if an aroma for lying existed, there was a good chance it was wafting from me in droves. 'I mean, it's a lot to get my head around, but I'll be fine.'

'You're right,' he nodded, his gaze dropping to his feet, which were shuffling ever so slightly. Yup, he was definitely nervous.

'What is it?' I said. 'Are you okay? Has something else happened? Something with The Guardians?'

'The Guardians?' he frowned. 'No, I mean, it's not that. It's just, I wanted to say sorry about earlier. For what I said about you and Whip. You know. Not rushing things.'

God. Him and Bobby combined. I got that they only cared, but really, it was like they didn't remember I was a grown woman capable of making my own decisions. Although Alex having the decency to come and apologise was something I respected. A guy that apologised off his own bat, would have been something I'd put high of my list of desirable characteristics before I came here. I still did.

'Alex, it's okay. I get that you were just trying to look out for me.'

'Yeah, thing is...' His feet shuffled again. 'Whip's a great guy. He is. But with you, he's different. Like... possessive. Look how he was today. He's never spoken to me like that before. Ever. And it's not the first time he's been like that with you.'

I knew exactly what incidents Alex was talking about. From the way Whip had deliberately tried to make me think Alex was all brawn and no brain to how he had been that afternoon. Yet, I felt the need to defend Whip. Especially now we were definitely an item. Besides, after years with Andy, who only ever worried about me falling ill or hurting myself if it interfered with me paying my half of the rent, I was okay with having a man who was a little protective. And in Whip's defence, it wasn't like I hadn't got into a fair heap of trouble since my move here.

'He's going through a lot,' I said. 'He's got a lot going on at the minute.'

'You're right, he does,' he nodded as if in agreement. 'But he always has a lot going on.' Alex bit down on his bottom lip as he dropped his strand of hair and cracked his knuckle instead. 'I'm just saying. Be careful, alright? I feel like something about him is different around you, and I don't know what it is. It worries me. And if you've got any sense, it'll worry you too. I know you're planning on spending the weekend at his, but I don't know if that's a good idea.'

'What?' It took less than a split second for the shock to transform into anger. I felt the way my spine lengthened as my back stiffened. 'Let me get this right? You turned up here to apologise for sticking your nose into my private life, and also to stick your nose in again?'

Alex shook his head, his hair remarkably like the mane he possessed as a lion. 'No, that's not what I meant to do—'

'That's exactly what you meant to do.' The fury was radiating from me now. 'Alex, you're a friend. A friend who wants more—'

'Elodie that's not—'

'But that is not going to happen.' I didn't let him finish. I was way too mad for that. 'Whip and I are a thing. And I'm a grown woman, capable of making my own decisions. You're overstepping the mark. Seriously overstepping it.'

As a journalist, confrontation was not something I'd been able to avoid, but my personal life had always been an entirely different matter. I could count on one hand the number of times I'd had stand-up arguments with friends, and I'd probably still have all my fingers left. But Alex had pushed me too far.

'If you want to save anything that's left of this friendship of ours, which you say you value so much, then you need to leave, now.' My voice growled. So much so that Pongo slunk behind my legs. And yet Alex remained exactly where he was.

'I get it, I do. I can see why you'd fall for him. But you've only been here a couple of months. You've only known him a couple of months—'

'Exactly the same amount of time I've known you!' I shouted, any pretence of calmness gone. 'But I should pick you instead?'

'No, that's not what I'm saying!' He momentarily dropped his head before lifting it up again and raising his hands as if admitting defeat. 'Forget it,' he said, already turning to leave. 'I just wanted to make sure you're okay. Have a good weekend, Evergreen.'

TEN

Needless to say, the encounter with Alex left me more than a little pissed. It wasn't the first time I had been called out about dating the wrong guy – Donna had done it on an almost daily basis when Andy and I had first got together. And weekly during all the years that followed. But that had been a very different situation. Donna was my closest friend. And it wasn't like I didn't enjoy hanging with Alex, but platonic relationships with men weren't something I had navigated before, other than in a work environment. But if he thought that gave him cart-blanche to say what he wanted to me, then he was very much mistaken. If I wanted to be lectured like I was a child, I'd have rung my dad.

The thought of my father caused a thousand knots to contort in my stomach and a tight ache to squeeze around my chest. How could I look at him again, now that I knew Mum was alive? And *in* my life.

I've never lied to my dad. Not unless you included the reason that I'd moved to Ravens Hollow, but that had been complicated. I'd had to be sparse with the facts, not wanting to throw his entire world upside down by telling him his baby girl had been turned into a vampire. But I'd still told him as much truth as I could; Andy and I had broken up. I needed to find myself. It was going to be an entirely fresh start for me, and I had a job at a small paper. All of that was true.

But this, my mother being here, in the same town as me, and that we had spoken to each other multiple times – even if I hadn't known it was her first of all – that was a far bigger lie by omission than my lack of pulse. I hated it. I hated it, and I hadn't even done it yet.

But I couldn't tell him the truth. Not without opening a way bigger can of worms than I could stomach. Because while I knew Dad and Aggie's response to what I'd become would be nothing like Andy's had been – they would stick by me no matter what – the paranormal world was something they simply didn't need to know about.

A new wave of anger hit me as I picked up my phone and fired off a quick photo of Pongo to my dad. At least that way he'd have had some contact from me, and it would hopefully buy me a few more days before he wanted to talk, and by then I would have worked out how to deal with Amira. There was nothing to stop her from making contact with him after all. Perhaps I could make that part of my agreement of speaking to her.

Cuddle. Cuddle. Cuddle. The sound came from out in the living room, repeated over and over on the button.

'You want a cuddle, do you, Boy? That sounds good to me.'

Once again, the *no Pongo on the sofa rule* was broken, as he leapt up and dropped his head onto my lap.

'Who knew we'd have two men fighting over us, hey?' I said, though even as the words left my lips, I wasn't sure they were true. To start with, Whip hadn't needed to fight. I'd been his from day one. And Alex was insisting that jealousy wasn't the reason he was acting so possessive. But I wasn't convinced..

'Come on boy,' I said, ten minutes later, when Pongo started to fall asleep on my lap. 'We still need to pack, and that means getting all your things, too. We don't want to keep Whip waiting, do we?'

∼

WHEN WHIP TURNED up at mine an hour later, he was holding an extra-large Weirdoughs takeaway cup which, from a single whiff, I could tell was a mocha with double shot of O-negative.

'I didn't know how many you'd had today,' he said, only for a smirk to rise on his lips. 'But I figured the worst-case scenario was that you don't fancy sleeping much tonight.'

'That's the worst-case scenario, is it?' I said, arching an eyebrow.

'Hey, I'm just being a good boyfriend at the beginning of a relationship. You'll get no pressure from me. Unless that's what you're into, that is.'

I couldn't help but roll my eyes as my lips involuntarily found his again. So what if he got a bit jealous of Alex now and then? I wasn't sure how different I'd be, if there was some gorgeous girl hitting on him under my nose, the way Alex had done more than once in front of Whip. Not that we'd been together at the time.

'So you wanna put your bag in the truck, and we can get going?'

Whip's truck was a sizable pick up, with more than enough room for all my stuff, Pongo and his massive bag of dog food, and probably a family of bear shifters too. It was definitely the sensible option for driving over to Peppers Bay. But as I went to agree, Pongo locked up at me with those big eyes of his, that had finally shifted from blue to brown. I loved my Mini, Maureen, more than I ever thought it was feasible to love a vehicle. But if there was anyone who enjoyed riding in it even more, it would have been him.

I turned to Whip unable to stop the smile twitching on my lips.

'You're okay to squeeze in, right?'

CHAPTER
ELEVEN

Could I see over any of the cars in front of me? Absolutely not. Was there room for me, Pongo, another person and luggage at the same time? No, there was not. Was I worried about the rate at which my dog was growing, meaning that at some point he would not fit in the car at all? Absolutely. Which is why I was pleased I'd made the decision to drive Maureen to Peppers Bay. Besides, the lack of room meant it was perfectly reasonable for Whip to have his hand resting on my lap the entire time.

'I heard about Ines being stripped,' I said to Whip as we drove out of town. 'I really can't believe that. The pack was everything to her.'

'I know. Werewolves preach about putting family first, but some of their ways are archaic. In my opinion, anyway. But hey, I guess it's worked for them for thousands of years. Who are we to question it?'

'You're right, I guess,' I said. 'It's just... all of this is going to take a lot of getting used to.'

'It is.' He glanced across and looked at me. 'But this

weekend, you don't have anything to worry about. Are you hungry? I thought about doing some baking. And I got a couple of dehydrated O-negs from Omar that I can add for you too, if you want?'

'I'm sorry?' I glanced away from the road just long enough to look him in the eye. My surprise wasn't just at finding out you could get dehydrated blood for cooking with. 'You bake too?' I said.

He shrugged. 'Hardly patisserie standard, but I can whip up a loaf or lemon tart if you fancy it?'

'Fresh bread? You make fresh bread?'

'And I do a mean French toast too,' he grinned.

God damn it. Maybe I should have brought the stretchy grey pants after all.

'Is it safe to go into the sea over at Peppers Bay?' I asked, moving the conversation away from food, although I would have happily spent the entire weekend sitting on Whip's sofa being fed like some Ancient Egyptian Queen. 'I've not been in since I moved here.'

'You what?' It was Whip's turn to look surprised. 'You haven't been swimming since you got here?'

I opened my mouth for some excuse, but the fact was, I didn't really have one. I'd been on the beach plenty of times, watching Pongo, sitting and having drinks, but I'd never been that strong a swimmer as a human – and although I was pretty sure that would've changed now that I was a vampire, just like with running, it wasn't a risk I wanted to take. Not without someone to go with me. Other than Chloe, there wasn't really anyone I'd ask to go for a dip with and so much of the time she was with Mick. It just hadn't happened. And it wasn't like I was planning on going anywhere soon either, so I assumed I had plenty of time to get into the ocean after the next couple of centuries.

'Yeah, Peppers Bay's great for swimming,' he said. 'Though, if we want a tad more privacy, we'd be better off in my pool.'

'Of course you have a pool,' I said, letting out a sound that was somewhere between a groan and a moan.

'It's just a small infinity pool,' he said, the grin sparkling in his eyes.

'You really are full of surprises, aren't you?'

'You've no idea,' he said.

As the road thinned, I recognised it from the path I'd taken to Prue Parsons' house. Though rather than following the road on the left, Whip indicated I turn down what could only be described as a track, heading through the forest.

'I like my privacy,' he said, gesturing around us. It was just dense trees and wildlife.

'I can tell. I'm guessing you don't have guests very often.'

'Alex and Raquel have come over a couple of times, but that's it. And Nyrah, but she's normally helping me with ward stuff.'

'Three people. You've had three people visit your house. How long have you lived there?'

'I had it built about... oh, fourteen years ago now.'

My head shook as I let out a laugh. 'Whip, how the hell could you have not had more guests over in fourteen years?'

'If I want to see people, I stay in town. Have them up to my flat. This is my escape. When I want to get away from folk.' His words made sense, yet before I could say as much, he carried on. 'But maybe at some point, if you like it here, we could invite people round.'

Whip had pulled my attention from the road so many times already, but this had to be the longest I stared at him.

So much so, that it was only Pongo barking in the back that reminded me I had to focus.

'You mean host a dinner party?' I said, when my eyes were back on the road. 'Like *us*? As a couple?'

'That's exactly what I mean,' he said. 'If you fancy it?'

'That sounds perfect,' I said, unable to stop the grin from taking hold of me.

Was I rushing into things? Absolutely. Bobby's voice, reminding me to take things slow echoed around in my head. But it was hard not to rush into things when Whip was this damn perfect. There had to be skeletons in his closet; I knew there were. He'd pretty much told me as much. But right now, I was happy to close my eyes, open the door, and suck them up with a Hoover. They didn't need to be thought about. Not for now, anyway.

Finally, the trees broke, and in front of us was an extended log cabin, the entire thing raised about ten feet off the ground.

'You have a house on stilts?' I shook my head in belief as I drew the car to a stop in front of the architectural masterpiece of wood and glass.

'I like the view of the water,' Whip replied, opening his door only for Pongo to barrel out over him before he'd had a chance to get his belt off. 'Come on, let me show you around.'

'Looks like we both want the tour,' I laughed.

CHAPTER

TWELVE

The inside of the house was just as beautiful as the outside. The white walls of the entrance hall were decorated with four mammoth paintings – watercolours, acrylics, oil pastels – all depicting views of the water. Of course, I knew Whip was a siren. It had been one of the first things I'd learned about him. But I'd never really thought about how important the water, particularly the ocean, must be to him. Here, in his Pepper's Bay home, I finally saw how fundamental a part of him it was.

'Try not to get too much mud on the walls, boy.' I glanced down at Pongo. I'd already accepted that I would lose whatever deposit had been paid on my house. Pongo had already well and truly left his mark, from muddy paw prints by the door when he tried to let himself out, to the large tomato stain on the carpet when he'd pulled the pizza box off the coffee table (even though he could reach it perfectly well and knew he wasn't meant to eat it). He'd also chewed through two lamp cords, although one of those was at the office, and Chloe had helped get me a replacement before Bobby noticed. Yup, just because Pongo was house-trained didn't mean he didn't make a mess. Hopefully, this weekend would be different.

'Are you coming through, or do you want to spend all weekend in the hall?' Whip called from further in the house.

With one more knowing look at Pongo, I followed him. Although three steps later, I was glued to the spot, my heart clenching in my chest.

Whip hadn't been joking about the view. With the extra height, we could see all the way to the mainland, not that they could see us. The barrier guarding the island acted as a cloak, too. Even if you knew about it, you wouldn't be able to see it from over there. Though at that moment, my eyes were solely on the water.

Every shade of blue shimmered as it reflected the afternoon light, while just a short way from the shore, a pod of dolphins was playing in the waves.

'I think this is the most beautiful thing I've ever seen in my life.'

'I used to think so,' Whip replied quietly.

'Used to?' I turned to face him. His eyes were trained on me.

He stepped closer and brushed a strand of hair behind my ear, his thumb grazing my cheek as he did so.

'Raquel told me I'm moving way too fast by inviting you here this weekend,' he said.

'Is that right?' I laughed. 'Funny, because Bobby said exactly the same thing.'

'And Alex... he's less than happy about this connection.'

'You think?' I didn't want to bring up Alex coming to my house. Besides, Whip already knew how his colleague felt, reinforcing the point wasn't going to help anything.

'It's weird though, isn't it?' Whip continued, his hand

slowly cradling the back of my neck. 'I don't feel like things are moving fast. I just want to spend time with you. There's nobody else I want to spend my time with. Does that sound ridiculous?'

'No. That sounds exactly the same as I feel.'

I leaned forward to kiss him, but before our lips touched, he shifted back slightly.

'But if you do ever feel that it's going too fast, you'll tell me, won't you?'

'I'll tell you,' I said. 'Now... are we talking or are we kissing?'

I leaned in until my lips were pressed against his, his warmth flooding through me, spiking my adrenaline. Would it be wrong to spend an entire weekend kissing? It didn't feel like the most productive use of my time, but there was definitely nothing else I wanted to do more. Nothing else I could do out here. Yet as I felt my weight disappearing into Whip's hold, a sudden thought struck. I wanted to spend this weekend getting to know the new man in my life, but there was more than one way to do it.

'Elodie, you okay?' Whip frowned as I broke away from him.

'Yes, yes.' I placed my hands on his chest. 'Everything's perfect. Absolutely perfect. Only...' I bit down on my lip as I gazed up into his eyes. 'I had something different in mind for us to do. Something very physical, that'll get us both very sweaty. What do you say?'

A smirk twisted on his lips, as a hint of pink coloured his cheeks.

'I'd say I'm all ears.' He grinned.

～

'Okay, I'll be honest—when you said we were gonna get physical, this wasn't what I'd been expecting,' Whip said.

'Oh.' I tilted my head to the side, my expression a picture of pure innocence. 'What did you *think* I meant?' My lips twisted into a grin, desperate to hear his reply, even though I knew he was too much of a gentleman to say it. 'Just hear me out.' I said, back in focused mood. 'This is something I really need to do. I've been thinking about it since Macoy Belkin. I just need some basic defence moves. Maybe a couple of attack ones too.'

We were out on his wooden deck, and the afternoon sun had taken on all the deepest shades of pinks and orange. I'd already taken a few snaps, ready to send to Donna and Dad. But first I wanted to do this. I wanted Whip to teach me to fight. Properly. If my last encounter with the werewolves had taught me anything it was that vampire strength and no skill would only get me so far. And that wasn't something I was willing to accept.

Whip's lips pursed. 'There's no way you're going to take no for an answer on this, is there?'

'Nope.' I pronounced the p with an extra pop, just to reinforce my point. 'And don't go easy on me. I'm pretty strong, you know.'

'I'm well aware,' he said. 'But out here, there are people a heck of a lot stronger.'

I will admit, that was a sobering thought. The werewolves had been strong, yeah, but I hadn't considered them any stronger than I was. The issue then was that I'd been fighting four at once. And as for Macoy Belkin, well you'd expected the head of the Mermaid Mafia to be able to fight, wouldn't you?

A muscle twitched along Whip's jaw, and I didn't know

if it was because he was considering what to do or because he still wasn't keen on the idea of me fighting.

'Just because you're teaching me doesn't mean I'm gonna go out there looking for trouble,' I clarified, feeling the need to put his mind at ease. 'It just means I'll be better able to defend myself when it finds me.'

'Why do I hate the way you use the word *when* instead of *if*?'

His smile glittered, causing my heart to skitter. It was that smile that had first made me realise I was in serious trouble when it came to the local Chief Inspector, although now I couldn't help but feel a sense of smug satisfaction, too. It had taken even less time than I'd thought to wear him down; he was going to help me fight.

With a resigned sigh, Whip took a step away from me. 'Alright, well, the first thing we need to sort out is your stance.'

'My stance?'

'Yes. If you can't hold yourself properly, you'll be easily barrelled over from the side. That's the quickest way to end a fight, and not the way you want to end it.'

I clenched my jaw. The only reason I hadn't drunk from Ines Ortega when she'd been bleeding in her home was because Pongo had barrelled me over from the side and knocked some sense back into me. With that in mind, it was probably a good thing I hadn't done this training earlier. But now I knew werewolf blood was deliberately designed to lure vampires in and poison them, I wouldn't make that mistake again.

'Okay. Stance,' I said, accepting that he was right to start with the basics.

'You need to plant yourself. Shift your legs further apart.'

I'd taken the suggestion a little too far. I looked like a comic book drill sergeant, with my legs three feet apart. I shuffled them inwards slightly.

'Better. But you need to move your left one back a bit.' I did as he said. 'Right. Are you balanced?'

'I think so?' I said, a little confused by the question. Surely the fact that I wasn't flat on my face was a sign I was balanced, wasn't it?

'Let's see.' In two strides, Whip came up beside me. I tensed myself, ready for impact, only for him to do little more than tap me on the shoulder.

'Really?' I offered him my most withering look. 'You wouldn't be able to knock over a dandelion with that. If you're going to help me, it has to be a challenge.'

'Fine, you asked for it.' He shoved me a little harder, but not enough to make me wobble.

'Meh.'

Third time, he actually put some welly behind it. My feet wobbled, and I staggered slightly, but somehow, I managed to stay upright. A tingling sense of satisfaction filled me as I caught the look of approval on his face.

'You really are incredibly strong,' he said.

'Well, I can take zero credit for it,' I replied. 'But now we know I can stand, how about we do some of the other stuff? The kicking and punching.'

As if to demonstrate my point, I swung my leg high into the air, only for Whip to catch my ankle. Any pretence I had of balance vanished. I wobbled and fell straight into his arms. His look of impressed surprise was quickly replaced by a cynical frown.

'Let's not run before we can walk, okay? If you're going for a kick, go low. The shin. The back of the knee. You've got so much strength behind you, if you hit the right spot, you'll floor someone.'

'That's what I want to do,' I said. 'Right, show me where to hit.'

Whip's frown hadn't disappeared. Instead, it had taken on a new seriousness.

'Just remember this is a *practice*, right? I'll tell you if you hit the right place. You don't need to go too hard.'

'Are you scared, Chief Inspector?'

'Of you? Always. Right, go for the back of the knee, okay? And use the bottom of your foot or your shin. Don't use the top. That's when you're likely to injure yourself as well. Okay, let's give it a go...'

THIRTEEN

We had continued our training practice for close to an hour, after which he'd run me a bath in his freestanding tub. I had wondered if, half hoped, he was going to join me, but instead, he had a shower before he got started on dinner. In true Whip style, he hit the ball out of the park with a Thai curry, although it was hard to think about how delicious the food was when my mind was somewhere else. Were we rushing things? Yes. Did I want to? Yes… but also a tiny bit no. There was no way in the world I could consider Whip a rebound from Andy. You didn't rebound onto people like Whip. No, you fantasised about them. But I wasn't sure how to act in a relationship that didn't involve an entire lecture if I forget to separate his whites from his pale blue shirts. And I sure as heck didn't know how to bring that up in a conversation.

'You don't have any photos up,' I said, halfway through the meal as I tried to push the undeniable elephant out of the room. 'Do you not have any? You know, family and things. Your sister?'

Since becoming a para, I had learned the myth about

vampires not being visible in photos was a lie. And Whip was close to his vampire stepsister, so I'd assumed he'd have a couple of pictures of them together. But the only things on the bookshelves were books, and the only images on the wall were the expensive-looking paintings.

'I only have a couple and they're at the flat. You know. As I spend more time there.'

'Right? Does she ever come and visit. I'd love to meet her.'

'I wish,' he said in a tone that ended that topic faster than I'd expected. And in its place, a silence started to take hold. But as much as I tried to find a way to break it, my mind was coming up empty.

'You're worried about tonight.' Whip said. There was no question in his words.

'No...' I started, only to change my mind. 'Maybe a little.'

His smile lifted, but there was no hint of amusement in. Just something like looking remarkably close to adoration.

'Would it make you feel better if I told you I'm nervous too?'

I half choked on my wine. I had seen him with his top off, albeit far too briefly, when he was getting out of the shower. The only thing he needed to be worried about was being claimed by medical science for a study of the perfect body.

Not that my issues were body related. No, Pongo's daily walks had me more toned than I'd been in years. Another reason for loving my furry companion, although he was currently sulking, having been told by Whip that the white leather sofa was a definite no for him and his brown fur.

'Look, we've slept in the same bed before,' Whip continued. 'And from what I remember, we had a perfectly good time. Even though I kept my clothes on.'

It was true, we had. Kissing Whip was like being transformed into the leading lady of a romcom film. I could only imagine what it would be like when we took it to the next stage. But whether or not that was going to be this weekend was something I hadn't made my mind up on.

'It was pretty good, yes,' I said, coyly.

'Right. So if that's all we do, that's fine. I know you've got a past, Elodie. I'm not oblivious to that. And the last thing I want is for you to regret moving too fast. So when you're ready, you're ready. Put it this way, I'd sleep next to you in a full diving suit if it meant I got to hold your hand when I wake up in the morning.'

His eyes locked on mine.

'I'm not sure if that's romantic, or incredibly creepy,' I replied.

'I see that now, but it was meant to be romantic.' He leaned over the table. 'Definitely romantic.'

'I got that.'

'Good.'

As we kissed, all the worry that had been itching the back of my mind flooded from my body. Of course, he wouldn't expect anything from me. This was Whip we were talking about. And there was no way I was taking him up on the diving suit option. Not when I'd already seen those abs of his.

I've just had the most romantic weekend of my life.

I FIRED off the message to Donna from Whip's ensuite Monday morning.

When can I call you?

It was strange to think that a weekend which had started with me kicking, punching, and holding Whip in a headlock could end up being romantic. And no, it wasn't because I discovered I had a secret thing for that. Though who knew what the future would hold? I was in a committed relationship with a siren, who respected every part of me, as he had very much proven time and time again over the weekend. Yup, I needed to talk to Donna. ASAP.

After years of thinking what Andy and I had was mature and sensible in a way most relationships would never be, I was finally experiencing those things that everybody talked about.

A man who topped up my water while I read by his pool. Who rubbed lotion on my back, not because it was needed – my sunlight ward dealt with all of that – but because he wanted to touch me. Who kissed me the moment he woke up, not caring about morning breath. And the feelings of infatuation and adoration were very much reciprocal. My chest throbbed, close to bursting half the time. And it didn't matter what Whip was doing, whether he was baking breakfast muffins or loading the dishwasher or standing waist-deep in the pool, I couldn't take my eyes off him.

Okay, the pool was where it was most difficult. I mean, the man was ripped. Tall and toned, and everything you saw in films and magazines, but never really believed existed in actual reality. And he was *there*. Not only was he there, but I got to touch him, and hold him, and kiss him.

There was only one tiny downside to this relationship. Although it was one that was definitely going to get bigger over time. Physically, anyway.

'I don't think he liked having to sleep outside the bedroom,' I said to Whip on Monday morning.

Pongo had woken us multiple times during the night, hitting his buttons. Most of the time, he was just hammering on my name. Whip had tried to be patient, but no matter how much he said he was okay with Pongo coming into the room and sleeping on the floor, I knew that wasn't entirely true. Besides, the floor wasn't going to be acceptable to Pongo. He normally spooned me when I slept, and he was clearly having difficulty accepting this intruder into the equation. Whip's suggestion of taking the buttons away felt sensible.

Until I remembered the lamp cords.

The last thing I wanted was for Pongo to chew through Whip's place in protest. And so, I had spent the remainder of the night out on the sofa, creeping back into bed just before dawn, when Pongo was asleep.

'We're going to have to come up with an arrangement that works for all of us,' I said, as I packed up my things, ready to head to work. 'Maybe you and him need to spend some time together. I mean, he's used to having me to himself all the time, and he doesn't really know you.'

Bedtime had been the worst, but it certainly hadn't been the only time Pongo had tried to stop Whip and I getting too close. When Whip had moved his sun lounger next to mine, Pongo had jumped between us, and at dinner, he had dragged his food bowl over to the dining table so that it was directly under Whip's chair.

'What are you suggesting?' Whip said, tilting his head to the side as he looked at Pongo. 'You think I should take him to the station?'

I wasn't sure what I'd been thinking at all, but now he'd

said it, it felt like a surprisingly logical solution. Even if it meant being without Pongo for a bit.

'He'd have to be with you, in your office,' I clarified. 'It's not going to help if he's just with Josephina the whole time.'

'I could manage that. What do you think, boy?' Whip said, looking down at Pongo. 'Fancy coming to the station with me today?'

Pongo didn't hesitate. *No*, the buzzer rang out.

I crouched next to Pongo. 'What do you say, boy? Whip's got lots of good treats at the station. Meaty chews.' Pongo's head tilted to the side. 'Do you want to go to the station with Whip today? Stay with him and get lots of meaty chews?' I tried using my most cajoling, upbeat voice. His foot hovered above no, again. 'Big treats,' I stressed again.

Finally, his paw came down. *Yes*.

While it wasn't possible for the electronic buzzer voice to sound begrudging, I was pretty sure Pongo's action was. Still, I chose to ignore it as I stood back up and turned to Whip.

'There you go. Easy,' I said with a grin.

'Yeah, just one problem,' Whip replied, his brow thoroughly furrowed. 'He's going to be even more angry when he realises I don't have any meaty chews.'

'No worries,' I said, pecking Whip on the lips. 'We can pick some up on the way.'

CHAPTER
FOURTEEN

As we drove back into town, I couldn't control my smile. Even if I was simultaneously bracing myself for the countless questions I'd have to deal with at the paper. But that was fine. What we had and hadn't got up to was no one's business but our own. I was the happiest I could remember being in a relationship, *ever*. That was what counted, and that was what I would tell anyone who asked.

Of course, I was pretty sure most people were happy in a relationship when they were only a week or so in, and given our immortal statuses, long-term took on a whole different meaning. But for now, I was happy. With him. With however things were going.

'Are you okay?' I said, glancing over at Whip. We'd both had points over the weekend when we'd checked our phones and work emails – being a workaholic doesn't fade just because you're dead – but this was the first time I'd seen him with a frown on his face.

'Been a break-in in town,' he said. 'At old Flo's place. Poor woman.'

'Flo's place? I don't think I know it.'

Ravens Hollow was only a small town, but it was a town nonetheless, and I still hadn't yet explored every nook and cranny. Or even every bar, for that matter.

'It's a little beach shop, one road over from Nyrah's salon. Dunno how the place's still running. I've never seen anyone in there in the twenty years I've lived here. But she's always there, with a smile. Sweet old woman. Certainly not caused me any trouble.'

Break-ins were traumatic whenever they happened, but I knew from interviews I'd done at the paper in London that trauma could be even more pronounced if you were in the building when it happened.

'Is she okay?' I asked. 'Was she there for the break-in?'

'I don't think so,' Whip put down his phone as he turned his attention to me. 'Sounds like you think there's a story brewing.'

'Probably,' I admitted. 'If there's a thief targeting shops in town, then the people in Ravens Hollow need to know.'

'If there's a thief targeting shops, Flo's place is a strange choice to start with,' Whip replied.

This was the first time all weekend we'd mentioned the conflict of interest our jobs presented. I was an investigative reporter, meaning I needed to turn over stones and dig in places the police sometimes didn't want me digging. And by the police, I meant *him*.

So we'd come up with a set of rules. Number one: I wasn't allowed to listen in on any of his conversations with my supernatural hearing. Yes, I *had* done that once. Maybe twice. Was I proud of it? I was a vampire and a journalist who'd been using the skills I had at my disposal, so that was a tough one to answer. But it was wrong, – not just from a relationship point of view – and agreed not to do it again. The second rule was that I'd share anything I picked up, hearing, scent, or otherwise, with the police if it helped with a case. And the third was to remember it's our job. Not our lives. And while they meant a lot to us, other things, including our relationship, mattered, too.

'Are there many break-ins in Ravens Hollow?' I said, trying not to sound too much like a journalist, even though I could feel myself already slipping into work mode.

Whip shook his head. 'I can't remember the last time one of the shops was hit. There're occasionally house break-ins, normally due to too much mango hooch, but other than that, no. Not knowing what kind of wards people can have on their places acts as one heck of a deterrent.'

'What is it with this place and that hooch?' I said, as we drove past the auto shop where Mick, Chloe's fiancé, and his brother Larry made the liquor. 'I mean, it's not like you can't get other alcohol on the island.'

Whip looked at me, his gaze narrowing as if confused by what I was saying. 'Have you *tried* the mango hooch?' he asked.

'I keep meaning to.'

I had a large crate of it at home. Alex had brought it for me, on discovering that I'd never tried the local liquor. It had been waiting for me when I'd woken up after the mermaid venom. But so far, it remained untouched. If I was going to have a drink in the evening I was a vodka and Coke girl, or white wine with a meal. It felt like I needed a proper get-together to crack into the hooch. A get-together I'd not yet had. Besides, Sophia had used the drink as a conduit for her hexes, and that had made me a little less tempted to try it.

'It's like sunshine in a bottle,' Whip replied. 'Sunny day,

the waves lapping at your feet and a glass of mango hooch.'
He let out a long sigh. 'It's tough to beat.'

'Maybe that's why Chloe's still with Mick,' I said absentmindedly. 'For the hooch.'

Whip snorted beside me. 'They're a strange couple, for sure. But then, what would people think of a cursed siren and a vampire?'

A grin rose on his lips, and I couldn't help but reciprocate it.

'Well, that sounds like a disaster waiting to happen.' I joked.

'Doesn't it just.'

Whether it was fate or good fortune, we drew up to a stop signal. As I stopped Maureen, Whip leaned across the gearstick and kissed me on the lips. Softly at first, and then more firmly, to the point that I could have easily lost myself in the moment and forgotten about everything I had to do that day, had a car not beeped its horn behind us.

'See?' I grinned. 'Definitely a disaster.'

CHAPTER
FIFTEEN

'Where's Pongo? Is he okay? What happened? Did something happen to him? You should have told me!'

I shouldn't have been surprised that Chloe's first question – or rather questions – as I stepped into the office were about Pongo, rather than my weekend. I had to admit, I'd felt a little empty as I'd driven Maureen from the station to here, then even more so as I'd walked up the stairs to the office. Like I was missing a furry, slobbery, extra limb. This was the first time I'd been to work without him, and assuming he lasted the entire day with Whip, it would be the longest time we'd spent apart. Though, to be fair, being unconscious from mermaid venom probably counted in some ways too.

'He's with Whip,' I said, trying to sound casual as I slung my bag over my shoulder and pulled out my laptop. 'The two of them are having some bonding time.'

Chloe's eyes widened. 'Oh my gosh. Seriously. Whip's doing doggy day care? That is so cute. Oh my god, you two really are serious. This is serious!'

I rolled my eyes, trying to play it cool, despite the fact I was desperate to tell her all about the cute little things Whip had done for me over the weekend, including baking red velvet cookies to disguise the colour the dehydrated blood gave them. Next to Weirdoughs drinks, it may well be my favourite manner to ingest my daily dose of O-negative. And I'd got all the extras in my bag to snack on too.

'We're taking things very slowly,' I said, tactfully ignoring Chloe's question about Whip and I being serious. Diego had told me when I first arrived in Ravens Hollow that you just learned to tune out half the things Chloe asked you. At the time, I'd thought he'd been a little rude. Turned out he was just experienced.

'Not that slowly, if you spent the entire weekend. And you did, right? What's his place like? You still haven't explained why Pongo's at the station? Oh my god, is he going to train Pongo to be a police dog?! He would be the cutest.'

Cutest? Maybe? Most disastrous? Absolutely. Pongo's only way of apprehending a criminal would be to slobber all over them, and he'd need several hours nap after every sprint.

'They're just getting to know each other, that's all,' I replied. 'If Whip and I are going to keep spending time together, then he and Pongo need to get on.'

'You mean they didn't get on?' Chloe's smile evaporated entirely. Instead, her bottom lip was trembling; she looked like she was about to cry. 'What happened? I thought Pongo loved everyone. Did something happen?'

'No, nothing happened.' I didn't think that mentioning how I had to spend half the night on the sofa to stop Pongo from being jealous was a sensible thing to say. Especially not when it would almost certainly lead to questions about the other half of the night. 'We just thought it would be a good thing to do.'

'Gossiping again? What a surprise.' I swivelled around in my seat to find my oversized, one-eyed boss standing over me. It was a sign of how distracted I'd been that I hadn't heard him coming. 'And where's the fluffball?'

'He's with Whip!' Chloe got in there before I could reply. 'Elodie says they need bonding time, but she won't say why. It sounds to me like something happened. Don't you think that sounds like something happened?'

Considering he only had one visible eye, Bobby was the master of rolling it. He let out a groan before ignoring Chloe all together and continuing to talk to me.

'You and I have work to do,' he said. 'We've got a break-in to investigate.'

'I know,' I said, standing up. 'Flo's beach shop. Whip told me on the way here.'

'He did, did he?' I couldn't tell whether the grunt was a disapproving one or not. Either way, I chose to ignore it.

'Come on then,' I said, walking over to the door and throwing him a glance over my shoulder. 'Or do you want me to do this by myself?'

'Like heck I do.'

~

WHIP HAD ALREADY TOLD me that Flo's place was on the street next to Nyrah's, but I hadn't put two and two together to realise what that meant. It was only a five-minute walk from Amira's place too.

Whip had done an impressive job of keeping me distracted from the thought of my mother over the week-end. But now I was back in town, and like it or not, so was she. At some point, I was going to have to give myself time to process it all. Thankfully, the fact that I was on a story meant that this was not that time.

'Are you okay?' Bobby asked as I gripped the steering wheel so hard it caused a slight crunching sound.

'I'm fine. Just... just...'

I trusted Bobby. I really did. He had been like a father figure to me from the moment I'd arrived on the island and wasn't afraid to call me out when he didn't like the way I did things. Everybody I'd ever spoken to had nothing but respect for him, and I knew he would keep my secret about my mother. The same way I knew both Alex and Whip would. That wasn't the issue. The issue was that every time I spoke it out aloud, I had to admit it was true to myself all over again. Admit that my mother had left us to become a vampire. Admit that she was, in part, to blame for The Guardians, and therefore what *I* was.

And that just wasn't something I could face right now.

'Yes, yes, I'm absolutely fine... sort of,' I said, relieved to find a parking space so that I could get out of the car, which was growing stuffier and stuffier by the second.

'Flo's is a beach shop, right?' I said, as we began walking the last part of the journey. 'What does it sell?'

Bobby hummed slightly before he spoke. 'Well, it's gone through countless makeovers these last ten years. Flo's always been there. Truth be told, I dunno how she's kept it runnin' all that time. Never seems busy.'

'Whip said the same. And she's never thought of selling?'

'No need to sell it. She's got two nephews lined up, desperate to take o'er the place. But she's been there her whole life. My guess is, she don't wanna move on.'

Given that I wasn't exactly sure which shop we were

going to, I let Bobby lead, while wondering what we'd face. I'd covered plenty of break-ins in London before. Particularly ones that seemed to be part of gang networks or strategic theft rings. Those tended to be synonymous with efficiency: a smashed window above the door to let them in, then limited mess, as they swiftly took what they needed.

Other times, when the break-in hadn't been so well planned, it would be messier, with things tipped over, drawers rifled through and displays overturned. But generally speaking, the chaos stayed *inside*. Because once they were in, that was where they focused.

But as we approached the strip of shops, there was no need to ask Bobby which one was Flo's. A line of yellow police tape had already been put up, not just outside the building, but two feet onto the sidewalk too. My stomach knotted, and a gasp of surprise left my lungs.

'What the hell happened here?' I said.

SIXTEEN

The entire door had been hammered in. I couldn't tell by what, but the metal had massive dents in it, and the glass front had been shattered, along with a fair chunk of the brickwork. And it wasn't just a case of mortar having crumbled. Someone had battered the building with enough force to crack the bricks. It was a surprise the building was still upright. If I hadn't known better, I'd have thought a car had driven into it. Or rather, several cars.

Bobby and I walked together towards where Raquel was speaking with a petite woman dressed in a German-style dirndl. One of the things I loved about Ravens Hollow was the freedom people had to dress and express themselves however they wished. And this old lady's choice certainly spoke to that. I assumed she had European heritage, something I'd add into the story when I came to write it. Adding personal touches about the people involved always made the articles more engaging. Although her choice in accessories made the outfit even more unique: fur cuffed, elbow-length leather gloves. Given the weather here, I couldn't help but wonder if they were hiding something similar to whatever was beneath Theodora's skirts.

The police officer offered her father a quick nod, as she continued her conversation. 'I'll leave you for now, Flo, but don't worry, we'll find out who did this,' she told the woman before heading over to us.

'Well, that's one hell of a mess,' Bobby said his voice heavy.

'Crazy, right?'

'Any witnesses?' I asked.

Raquel shook her head. 'No. And I've never seen anything like this before. But I'm hoping a couple of shops down the road might have CCTV cameras pointing in this direction. I'm going to head there now and see what I can get.' She looked between us carefully before adding, 'She's pretty shaken up, okay? Just... don't pry any more than you need to.'

'As if,' Bobby said, and Raquel rolled her eyes.

Despite his concerns about Whip and me moving too fast, Bobby had been the one to convince me that a relationship between us could work, if we set boundaries the way he and his daughter had done. It was a piece of advice I hadn't yet thanked him for, but I would.

'Do you want me to do the talking here?' Bobby asked. 'She knows me, so it might be better.'

'Whatever works best,' I said.

He smirked. We both knew what that meant. Countless times, Bobby had told me to stay back and not ask questions. In fact, when I'd first arrived in Ravens Hollow, he'd insisted I wouldn't be doing any investigative journalism until I understood the paranormal world – and the town – better. And yet here we were, six weeks later, already on my third case, and we were both aware that there was very little chance I was going to stay quiet. Still, it was amusing that he tried.

Close up, it was easy to see the tears around the old woman's red-rimmed eyes, and her gloved hands gripped at her apron. Her gaze remained fixed on the shop, as if she couldn't quite comprehend how something like this could have happened.

'Flo?' My voice was soft as I approached her. 'My name's Elodie. I'm here with Bobby from *The Oracle*. We wondered if we could ask you just a couple of questions about what happened. I know you've already spoken to Raquel and the police, so we don't want to take up too much of your time. It's just, we'd like to tell people what happened here. If that's okay with you?'

She turned, looking genuinely surprised to see us there.

'I don't understand why somebody would be so violent. So cruel,' she said. 'Cruel.' The way she rolled her r's was an impressive trait and another hint towards a Germanic heritage.

'I understand,' I said., and I really did. I couldn't imagine that buckets, spades and inflatables were worth much money. Certainly not compared to some of the other shops down the road. There was a jeweller's, an independent art gallery and apothecaries, all of them seemed like more sensible targets. This looked personal.

'I don't know if you've had much of a chance to check,' I said quietly, 'but do you know if much has been taken?'

She sniffed and cleared her throat. 'If it's not been taken, it's broken. Useless. Inflatables. Pierced. Buckets. Smashed. Useless. If this is Henrik... if this is Henrik, then he will never get hands on this shop. Never.'

'Henrik? Who's Henrik?' I cast a glance at Bobby as I spoke. 'Did you tell the police you think he's behind it?'

Flo sniffed again, wiping her nose with the back of her hand in one long, almost absent motion.

'He's my nephew. The eldest. They've both been on at me for years to give up the shop. Want to run it themselves. Always telling me their big ideas.' She scoffed as she shook her head. 'I don't know why I go to theirs for supper. Always it ends in a row. Always it ends with them telling me what I should be doing. But for him to do this...? Yes we got cross... but this... Henrik's my nephew. They're my nephews....'

As her breaths shuddered, I placed my hand gently on her shoulder.

'I'm so sorry you're having to go through this, Flo. How long have you had the shop? A long time, right? Has it always been in your family?'

There was no point rehashing questions the police would've already asked. Besides, I wasn't after the same thing. They were after the criminal. I wanted to write a piece on this woman, on what she was going through and maybe get a few more details that would lead me closer to the why.

She sniffed again, a sad smile curling at the corners of her lips.

'Not in the family, no. I bought it. Always wanted to run a shop. My mother, she was a mermaid. My dad was a billy goat shifter. Odd combination, you'd think, yes? But they were happy as anything, they really were. People used to laugh when they'd see him in his goat form, splashing away in the waves with her. I used to love it.

'And this shop here, this was my favourite. This was where I spent all my allowance. Sweets, spades, anything. When it came up for sale, it just felt right, you know? I don't make much money. I know that. I'm sure people laugh. But it's not about money. It's about standing here, watching people, like I watched my mother and father. It's about the memories. You see?'

I did see. I could see she loved the shop far more than the bricks and mortar it was made of. And given how I'd got attached to the heap of yellow metal that was Maureen, my Mini, I was hardly going to judge her for it. Feeling the story form in my head, I was about to ask her what her plans were now and whether she intended to get the shop back up and running. Papers loved a revival story, and this certainly had that potential. But before I could, a figure came rushing towards us.

'Aunt Flo! Oh my goodness, this is terrible. Terrible!'

The man looked to be in his late forties and was shorter even than his great-aunt. With his long, narrow chin and small manicured beard I could definitely see the goat genes that were accentuated further as he skipped towards us.

'This is awful! Aunt Flo, you should've rung me. Why didn't you call me?'

'You know exactly why,' Flo bit back. 'Tell me you didn't. Tell me you didn't want the shop that much.'

His jaw dropped, lengthening his face even further. 'You can't be serious, Flo! I would never, I could never. Never!'

Noticing Bobby and I for the first time, he spun round to face us.

'Whatever it is you've got, this is *family* business and you're not welcome here right now.'

'This is *shop* business,' Flo replied sharply, 'meaning *you're* not welcome here either.'

A deeply exaggerated wounded expression crossed his face.

'Auntie Flo… you can't mean that. You *can't*.'

I was momentarily taken back to the conversation with

my mother before the weekend, the way she'd desperately wanted me to listen, and how I hadn't been ready. How I'd wanted Alex there, just so I didn't have to be on my own with her. Was that what Flo wanted? I got the feeling that, no, an audience was the last thing she needed. Whatever conversation was about to happen between Henrik and Flo, it was private.

'We'll leave you to it, Flo,' I said. 'And I'll send you anything I'm going to write before I print it, if you'd like to see it.'

'Do what you have to do,' she said. 'And his surname is Hoffman. Just in case you need it. Henrik Hoffman.'

Henrik stood fuming as Bobby and I turned and made our way back to the car. I'd already learned that it was good practice to put a fair distance between you and whatever para you were going to discuss, just in case they had supernatural hearing.

'So,' I said to Bobby as we I started the engine. 'Are you thinking it could be the nephew?'

'Not sure,' he replied. 'I guess it's time we do some digging.'

CHAPTER
SEVENTEEN

I couldn't believe how empty the office felt without Pongo. Sure, it was a lot easier to get work done without him constantly hammering his buttons, asking for food or snacks, or telling me that he was bored and wanted to go for a walk. But still, it was strange. Eerily quiet.

And I wasn't the only one who felt it.

'Is he gonna be gone all day?' Theodora asked from her computer, her voice carrying over the quiet clack of her keyboard. 'I wanted to see how he was doing with his buttons.'

The comment took me by surprise. I was well aware that Chloe adored Pongo – she even kept a jar of snacks especially for him – but Theodora wasn't the same. I'd never seen her take that much of an interest in him. Then again, Theodora really was a unique character... and not just because I didn't know what she was hiding beneath those enormous skirts of hers. She'd been at The Oracle longer than anyone but Bobby, but was the least sociable of us all, though she and Bobby were close. I knew from when she'd been hexed that she had no family on the island, but she never spoke of friends either. I got the impression that she was the type of person who liked to be on her own, rather than endure the company of someone she wasn't a hundred percent sold on. I just hadn't realised that Pongo was on the list of company she actually enjoyed.

'I haven't heard from Whip yet,' I said. I would have to message him at some point, though. We hadn't discussed plans, further than him having Pongo for the day, though given that he was back at work, I suspected he would be spending the evening at the flat above the station rather than going back to Peppers Bay. The question was whether we were going to spend any time together, too. Three nights in a row was probably more than enough for Pongo to cope with if I didn't want him to chew through something extraordinarily valuable at Whip's. And if I was being honest with myself, I was quite keen on heading home, too. Back to my little house with its photos and mess and lived-in warmth, even if that meant missing out on the infinity pool and Whip's California king. Staying at his place really had felt like living in a show home. Though I suspected it would be different at the flat above the station. After all, that was where he'd said he kept his photos and more personal items. 'I assume that if there's a problem, he'd ring me and tell me. So I guess he's alright having Pongo for now.'

'You don't think he'd *actually* ring you if there was a problem,' Dylan said from his desk, not even looking up from his computer.

'What? Of course he would.'

Diego scoffed. I wasn't surprised that the werewolf was listening into the conversation. Gossip and eating office snacks were two of Diego's most honed skills.

'No, he won't. You've just started dating, and that dog is the most important thing in your life. Pongo could eat Whip's most expensive shoes, pee all over his desk chair and god knows what else, and Whip would *still* tell you everything's absolutely fine.'

'That's not true,' I said, cutting my eyes around the rest of the office. Andy would've absolutely told me if something had upset him. Not that he would've looked after a dog... No, Andy was full of allergies. Having a dog was out of the question. Still, he'd let me know if I put too much butter in his mashed potato or too many capers in his bloody risotto. Not that we ever made anything that exotic.

'Does it matter?' Chloe asked. As she looked up at me expectantly, I waited for the barrage of questions to follow, only it didn't. I stiffened slightly, confused by her sudden taciturnity. Not to mention the turn the conversation had taken.

'Of course it matters,' I said. 'I want him to be honest with me.'

'But if him telling you Pongo's done something wrong will upset you, then you should know he's not going to want to do that. I think it's sweet that he'd hide it from you.'

'He's not going to hide anything from me!' I said, well aware that my voice was verging on a shout. 'Fine. I'll prove it to you.'

With everyone in the office, bar Bobby, currently looking directly at me, I picked up my phone, called Whip's number, and hit speaker.

Telephone calls weren't something we'd done much – we were more of a text conversation couple – but he generally responded pretty quickly. Though as the ringing continued, I found myself unreasonably worried that he wouldn't pick up at all. Not that that meant anything about Pongo. It was probably just because he was on a job. He was chief inspector of an entire paranormal island, after all. I was about to say as much to everyone who was listening in when he suddenly picked up.

'Hey you.' Whip's voice sent a flutter through me, though I couldn't help but wonder if it sounded a fraction tighter than usual. 'Is everything okay?'

'Yes, yes. I just wanted to see how you and Pongo were getting on,' I said. 'Make sure he wasn't causing you too much stress or anything.'

'Pongo?'

As his voice hitched, I couldn't help but glance at Diego. He was the only one who would be able to hear the nuances in tone as well as I could, and from his smirk, he'd caught the shift, same as me. Still, there could have been plenty of reasons his voice sounded strained. He had taken a weekend entirely off from work. The last thing he needed was me pestering him.

'No, no, we're getting on great. We're getting on *great*. Aren't we, Pongo?' Whip said. There was a rustling sound, almost as if Whip was scrambling across the ground. Like he was trying to grab the buttons so Pongo couldn't press a particular one. 'He can't reply,' Whip added quickly. 'He's too busy chewing his toy. He's very happy. *Very* happy. Right, boy? Anyway, I better go. Speak soon. Bye.' He hung up before I could say anything.

Silence filled the office. Until Dylan cleared his throat. I shot him my most venomous glare, which I then shared around every other person in the room.

'Do *not* say a word,' I said, my teeth well and truly gritted. 'Not. One. Word.'

For the next hour, I worked on my piece about Flo's shop, while constantly firing questions off to people.

'What kind of creature could've done something like this?' I said to Chloe, as we looked at the photos Diego had been down and taken. In true photographer style, he had chosen angles that showed the highest level of destruction and got some pretty shocking images. 'Any ideas?'

I'd opened my mind to the possibilities of the impossible, now that I was part of the paranormal community. Given how my first story involved an artist being killed by a newly hatched hydra, it felt like nothing was off the cards anymore.

'Surely that's too much damage for one person to have done,' Chloe said. 'Maybe it was a gang.'

'I hadn't thought about that.' In my head Henrik was still my top and only suspect, but that was hardly a solid journalistic approach. Looking for a group would definitely be a different angle to think of. As I pondered the idea, Theodora wandered over and looked at the photos.

'I could do that,' she said.

I twisted my neck up to look at her. 'You could?'

'Looks fairly straightforward. A few well-placed kicks. Easy damage. Whoever did this made more of a mess than they needed to. Very heavy-handed. Angry. Not effective. I could definitely have made more destruction than that.'

'Right...' I said, not sure how else I could respond to hearing that the woman with the desk on the other side of my office thought that she was capable of bringing down the front of a building. And as much as I liked to think she was exaggerating, I suspected that wasn't the case.

The thing was, I still didn't know what Theodora was. Or whether there were more of her type in Ravens Hollow. Just because she didn't have family here didn't mean there weren't plenty of paras like her. Take Whip, for example. He worked in the same station as another siren, yet he didn't have any relatives here. At least, not that I knew of.

'And are there many of your type on the island?' I asked, hoping I was being as subtle as possible, though her response caused me to jump in my seat. She let out a snort of laughter.

'Oh my goodness, Elodie, you are funny,' she said her voice lilting with her European accent. 'More of *me* on the island. Ha!'

She rolled her eyes, turned back to her desk, and resumed copy-editing.

Chloe looked at me.

'You don't know?' she whispered.

I shook my head. 'She's never said.'

Chloe opened her mouth, and for a second I thought I was finally going to find out, but then she shook her head and clamped her lips together.

'She'll tell you when she's ready,' she said. 'She's a private person, after all.'

So, great. I now knew that there *was* something capable of breaking bricks on the island, I just didn't know what it was.

I could always go home and grab the large book Chloe had given me when I first arrived on the island, which listed all the paranormal creatures known at time of publication. It felt like the most productive use of time, short of pestering Theodora until she finally told me what she was. And the fresh air would allow me a chance to clear my head.

I stood up, ready to tell Chloe where I was headed, but before I did, the door swung open and a blur raced towards me.

'Hey, boy!' I dropped to the ground, just in time for him to jump up onto my lap as if he hadn't seen me for months and months. 'I missed you, too. Did you have fun with Whip?'

From the way he was determined to cover every inch of my face with slobber, I took it as a yes.

'Yes, we had loads of fun, didn't we, boy?' I looked up to find Whip smiling at me, though before I moved to kiss him, I glanced at his shoes to check for any sign of teeth marks, but as far as I could tell, everything was alright. That was, until I noticed Raquel standing there. So this wasn't a casual boyfriend-dropping-of-my-dog situation then.

'What's wrong?' I said. 'I take it the pair of you aren't just here to bring me Pongo?'

'No, but thanks for letting us borrow him. I've been trying to convince Whip that we need a police dog,' Raquel said.

'Not gonna happen.' Whip replied, in a manner that

made me think he was less of a dog person than he'd been trying to convince me. Still, he hadn't banned Pongo from his house and that was what mattered.

'We were hoping to speak to you and Dad,' Raquel continued. 'It's about the shop. I suspect you're gonna find out about this sooner or later, and we need to make sure that you handle it as delicately as possible.'

Whip and Raquel had never come to the paper before with information. Whatever this was, it was clearly something serious.

'Sure. We'll go into Bobby's office,' I said, an unexpected flutter of nerves taking hold.

I gave Bobby's door one quick knock, before I opened it; I could already hear that he wasn't on the phone and he wasn't one of these bosses who insisted you waited until he said 'come in' before you entered.

'We've got visitors,' I said, stepping to the side so he could see Whip and Raquel.

'It's to do with the shop break-in,' Raquel said. 'We need to show you something.'

'I'll email it across to you now,' Whip said, taking out his phone.

A moment later, I was leaning over Bobby's shoulder, staring at a video.

A video of Flo's shop being smashed to pieces.

The violence. The anger. Theodora had been right about this person not being efficient in the way they attacked the shopfront. The absolute *feral* rage in the scene was unlike anything I had encountered before. I found myself wanting to back away from the screen, unable to watch it all.

But that wasn't the most shocking part. The most shocking part was who was doing the damage.

It was Flo herself.

A strange atmosphere fell over Bobby's office. The police had caught the culprit, and I had an even juicier angle to my story, but it didn't feel like we should be celebrating.

'I'm guessing it's some kind of insurance thing?' I said to Whip. 'Have you looked into that?'

He drew in a long breath. 'Thing is, Raquel and I spoke to her about it before we came here, but she has no memory of it.'

'She *says* she has no memory of it,' I said.

'No. She doesn't,' he said. 'I *spoke* to her. We both did.' He emphasised the word *spoke*, so I knew what he meant. They'd used their siren powers on the old woman, meaning she had to tell the truth, even if she hadn't wanted to.

'She didn't remember doing it. None of it.'

'She was in tears when we showed her, just as shocked as we were,' Raquel continued, taking over from Whip. 'More probably.'

As much as I went on evidence, gut instinct played a heavy part in what I did, too. My job allowed me that flexibility and had proved itself right more than one. At that moment my gut was telling me that Flo wouldn't do something like this. She just wouldn't.

'Could it be somebody pretending to be her? You can do that, right?' I said, thinking about my mother's elfish looks. 'Couldn't somebody have put a glimmer on them?'

'A *glamour*,' Raquel corrected. 'We thought that, too. But she's got cuts on her hands, and no recollection of where they came from. So it *looks* like she did it. The question is why. And how she could do it without knowing it.'

I leant back, still watching as the scene continued on a loop: tiny, angry Flo with a metal bar in her hand, crashing it again and again into her own shop. Spray from the bricks and mortar flying everywhere, included onto her. I remembered thinking when I saw her that the gloves could have been hiding something. Though I'd expected cloven hooves or excessive fur, I'd been right, nonetheless.

A wave of sympathy for the old woman rolled through me. I couldn't imagine how that must've felt. To find yourself in a position like this, with no idea how you got there. But then there was the other part of me in play, too. The part that knew this had just gone from a standard break-in to something much, much more. And that part of me, the part that lived for investigations just like this, was definitely excited.

'Well, we should go,' Whip said, with a nod to Bobby, before he glanced at me. 'Walk me out?'

'Of course.'

As I followed Whip out of Bobby's office and into the main area of the paper, I couldn't help but spot the way Pongo was lingering by my boss. Bobby had a definite soft spot for the pooch, which had only strengthened after Pongo had saved him from drinking hexed pineapple hooch. But the way Pongo was sitting, with his back to the door, it was almost as if he was avoiding looking at me. Or Whip.

'Do you want to take Pongo back with you for another couple of hours?' I said to Whip. 'Seems a shame to separate you, if you're getting on well.'

He ran his tongue over his bottom lip. 'Actually, I've got a busy afternoon,' he said. 'You know. Lots to do. Meetings and things. He'll probably be better off here with you.'

'Sure thing,' I smiled back. 'We've been missing him, anyway.' From across by Dylan and Diego's desks, I picked on up on several quiet snickers that I would glare at them later for.

'Well, I'll call you later,' he said. hovering slightly. This was unusual territory. Would he kiss me goodbye? Sure, he had come on official business, but that was over with now, and it wasn't like we would have a full make-out session in the middle of work, was it? This was a mature, adult relationship. Which was why I pushed myself up onto my tiptoes and kissed him lightly on the lips.

When I shifted back, there was a broad smile on Whip's lips and a familiar glint in his eye. Yup, that was the right decision to make.

'See you later?' he said. 'You guys are all still having drinks, right?'

'We are. See you there?'

'Wouldn't miss it.'

A moment later, he and Raquel were walking downstairs, and a chorus of 'Elodie and Whip, sitting in a tree K-I-S-S-I-N-G,' was echoing around me, led by Diego.

'You're complete idiots, the lots of you,' I said, yet I couldn't entirely suppress my grin as I swivelled on my heel and turned back to Bobby's office.

'So what could do something like this?' I said as I pulled out the chair opposite my boss and made myself comfortable. I got the feeling I was going to be there for a while. 'I was thinking a hex. Like with Diego and Theodora.'

'It's possible. Police'll look into it. Stupid fools if they're using hexes in Raven's Hollow again. 'specially so soon. Speaking o' which, we've got a council meeting comin' up next week.'

'A council meeting?' I didn't hide my surprise. 'I thought they were only once a month?' The last one had only been three weeks ago.

'After all that's gone on, they've decided to bump the forest issues up 'mongst other things. They don't want no one else getting hexed. That's for sure. Can't say I blame 'em.'

'Ines'll be pleased at least,' I said, only to wonder if she knew. From the impression Diego and Bobby had given me, she hadn't had a big circle of people around her to keep her informed, the way she had before. A long sigh rolled from my lungs, before I pushed the feeling away and focussed on the task in hand.

'So, if it's not a hex, what else could it be?'

'There's a lot of possibilities,' he said. 'Artefacts, obviously. Spells. Wards. Demon possession.'

'*Demon possession?*' I felt my eyes widen. 'That's a thing?'

He raised a single eyebrow at me. 'Everything's a thing. Now, what you planning on doin'? You heard what Raquel and Whip said. She don't need to be pushed.'

'I know,' I said. Yes, I wanted a story, but not at the detriment of an old lady's health. That wasn't who I was.

'Well, we could always talk to the nephews. She said she saw them for dinner, didn't she? Maybe they can fill us in on anything that might have caused her change. Not sure the best way to go about it. Any ideas?'

A slight glint shone in Bobby's eye. 'June,' he said, as if the single word – his wife's name – was the only explanation he needed.

'June? Is she friends with Flo?'

'June's friends with *everyone*. She was going to swing by with some food and things. You know, so Flo don't have to fret while she's dealing with all this. She'll be gentle. She's good like that.'

I couldn't help but wonder exactly how many things June'd been in the middle of over the years, what with her husband being the editor-in-chief and her daughter a member of the police force. I suspected she had a *lot* of Ravens Hollow's secrets at her fingertips.

I was about to ask Bobby if we should wait to hear from June before I questioned the nephews, when a voice from outside on the sidewalk caught my attention. Chloe's voice. But it wasn't her normal, chirpy, singsong tone. She sounded upset. Angry even.

'Is everything okay?' Bobby frowned.

'I'm not sure.'

Once again, I was forced to find out where that line – that boundary – was when it came to listening in on friends. I'd never listened in on one of Chloe's conversations before, but she'd never sounded like this, either. Deciding I'd hold my hearing just for a few seconds, to see if I'd got the wrong end of the stick, I listened in.

It turned out I hadn't.

'Why are you doing this again?' she said. 'We're all going out. Everybody. I said you were going to meet them. This is ridiculous, Mick.' I didn't hear what the response was, but hers came through as a stifled gasp, followed by several sobbing breaths. Well, if that's how you feel, why are you even bothering with this engagement? Why don't we just end it now?' I waited a moment longer, only to hear a slight tapping sound. She had hung up the phone.

'Elodie?' Bobby asked.

'I'll be back in a minute,' I said, then raced out of his office and ran down the steps, just in time to catch Chloe before she toppled to the ground, right next to a flaming waste bin.

CHAPTER
TWENTY

'You probably think I'm ridiculous,' Chloe said twenty minutes later as she struggled to catch her breath between all her sobbing. My first job had been to scoop Chloe up in my arms and run back upstairs, where I handed her over to Dylan, grabbed a fire extinguisher, put out the flaming rubbish bin, then went back to the office. I already knew that Pongo suffered from dizziness if I vampire-sped with him in my arms, but I'd never experienced it myself until that constant back and forth up and down the stairs.

Only when I'd caught my breath did I finally ask Chloe what had happened. I didn't want her to think I habitually listened in on her conversations. Turns out, it was hard for her to offer a succinct answer, when she couldn't even say Mick's name without dissolving into tears or setting something on fire. Thankfully, Diego and Dylan were in charge of the extinguishers, while Pongo and I continued to offer moral support.

'He *can* be real sweet, real loving. He was the one who wanted to get married, you know. He proposed. But maybe he just did it to shut me up. Because I kept mentioning it. But it's difficult when all your friends and family are getting hitched and you've been in a relationship longer than them, with no ring on your finger.'

She'd already got through the entire box of tissues that Theodora kept on her desk and had now moved on to using toilet roll to mop up her tears. I wasn't sure what would happen when that ran out.

'I know this is really hard, but just having a break, a little bit of time apart, might be good for you,' I said. 'It might make him see how much he really loves you.'

'And it might make you see you deserve someone a whole lot better,' Dylan muttered from behind her.

I shot him a look. I knew he was only trying to be helpful, but there was a slightly aggressive edge to the way he spoke. Still, I had to give him his due. If the subject of my unrequited love had just broken off their engagement and was in need of some serious TLC, I wasn't sure I'd have had the restraint to stay well back and simply hold a fire extinguisher. But then again, if he'd been in love with her as long as I assumed he had, this probably wasn't the first time he'd had to go through something like this.

'It just makes me so *angry*, you know?' Chloe continued. 'And I don't get angry. I don't.'

I maintained eye contact with Chloe the best I could, but it was hard not to look at the piles of ash that currently littered the office. Although she had a good point – if she had been an angry person, I couldn't imagine what the place would look like. Still, it was the most efficient way of dealing with unwanted paperwork that I'd ever seen.

'Would it hurt him to do something for me now and then?' she said, blowing her nose in the last scraps of toilet roll. 'Just to come for a drink?'

'So he cancelled on tonight?' I said, relieved at I'd finally got to the crux of the argument.

'Of course he did. I bet Whip's coming, isn't he? He said he was coming.'

Whip had been planning to join us for a drink at the pub to celebrate the un-hexing of my colleagues, but I was already drafting a hasty rescindment of that invitation. I'd explain later, but the last thing Chloe needed tonight was to see Whip and me together while she was going through heartbreak.

'He actually messaged me when he got back to the station. Something's come up,' I lied. 'It's just going to be us. Just The Oracle gang, okay? And we're going to have some drinks, some cocktails, and we're going to forget. You're going to have a great night, okay? You are going to have a great night without Mick.'

She sniffed again, but the tears had slowed to a mere meander down her cheeks, rather than torrents.

'Thank you,' she said. 'I really appreciate you. I appreciate *all* of you.'

A flicker of relief bloomed within me as Chloe moved to wipe her eyes and for a second I thought she was going to gather herself completely. But then her hand stopped just shy of her cheek, and her bottom lip began to tremble.

'I was going to get changed before we went out. Into something for goin' out in. But all my nice clothes are at his. Everything nice is at his.' She was descending again. I could feel it. From behind me came a creak of metal as the men raised the extinguishers, but I wasn't going to let it get to that state again.

'Well, then,' I said, 'why don't we get off early and go shopping?'

Her jaw wobbled.

'I've still got to write up the water polo match.'

'I'll do that!' Theodora practically shouted from her desk. 'I can do your work. You go. Go!'

No one liked a quiet work environment quite as much as Theodora, and I knew the offer was in no way altruistic, but I was grateful, nonetheless.

'There you go,' I said softy to Chloe while flashing the copyeditor a grateful smile. 'Bobby won't mind at all. Come on. I've yet to go shopping in Raven's Hollow. Let's see what we can pick out.'

As I stood up, a button beeped from across the room.

Go? Pongo looked up at me expectantly. He had tried his best to comfort Chloe, but the flames had scared him even more than the rest of us, so instead, he'd rifled through my bag and got his buttons cut, and had clearly found the one he wanted.

Go, he pressed again.

'Yes, come on, boy,' I said. 'Time to go and do some shopping.'

CHAPTER
TWENTY-ONE

L iving in Ravens Hollow required a big shift in wardrobe from my London days. For one thing, the weather was so good, I was living in shorts and T-shirts. I wouldn't have believed it, if you'd told me that a while ago. I was a professional investigative journalist. Living in London, I'd been the one always wearing a cute jacket and pair of heels. I never turned up to interview anybody in anything less than a suit, and as for jeans – let alone shorts – they were a massive no-no.

But it hadn't taken long at all for the ways of the island to creep into me. And even for somebody who didn't create their own body heat, it was way too hot to be wearing jackets and trousers. Now, the only time I used them was indoors for the air con.

As such, I'd been living in the same few outfits that were suitable for this weather, and I could probably do with a bit of shopping myself. Particularly with Whip and me dating. My scruffy attire had felt more than a little out of place in his show home at Peppers Bay, and I was sure at some point we would want to go for dinner together. Then there were nightclothes to think of. Yes, he'd slept in bed with me several nights now, but I'd opted for a comfy cotton T-shirt. Maybe splashing out on some expensive lingerie would show him I was ready to move onto the next stage of the relationship.

Unfortunately, there weren't loads of places to get clothes in Ravens Hollow. There were a couple of strip malls, mostly on the road which led towards the beach. But there were also several other little horseshoe-shaped clusters of shops off the main road into the island. Right now, I wasn't entirely sure where we were going. We were simply walking, with Chloe in the lead.

'Am I in the wrong?' Chloe said. It had to be at least the twentieth time. 'I don't feel like I am. I mean… I don't think I am. But he just says I'm blind to my own faults.'

'You just need to have some space apart,' I told her. 'Honestly, a night out with us, without worrying about him, will be great for you. And you can stay at mine too. Whip says the sofa's seriously uncomfortable,' I added, 'but you can crash in my bed. It's not like I actually need the sleep.'

'Thank you,' she said, turning and flashing me a smile. 'I really am grateful. I'm so glad you came here, you know. I've never had a girlfriend at work before. Theodora isn't exactly a girly girl who I can talk to about boys. There's Diego, obviously, and he's a massive gossip, and Dylan, well, Dylan's… he's just Dylan.'

A smile flickered on Chloe's face. Probably the first genuine one since she'd stopped crying. There was a moment where Pongo had hit – Cuddle Chloe – on his buttons and it was very sweet. But she'd been so overcome she'd accidentally set light to an entire stack of circulars that needed to go into the recycling. Considering I was the one who'd said they'd do it for the last couple of days, I wasn't entirely saddened by this. Even if Pongo hadn't got the appreciation he deserved for the gesture. But the smile that lit of Chloe's eyes when she spoke about Dylan was far from anything I'd ever seen when she spoke about Mick.

'You two get on well,' I said, sounding as casual as I could.

'We do.' Her smile remained in pace. 'We've known each other for a long time. He actually got me the job here. He's such a sweet guy. Although Mick *hates* him.'

'What a surprise,' I muttered to myself.

'Sorry, did you say something?'

'Don't worry,' I said quickly. 'Oh, how about in here?' Despite my reservations that Chloe had been walking mindlessly with no thought of direction, we had in fact found ourselves standing in front of a small row of shops that included at least two boutique clothing stores. 'You'd look amazing in that yellow outfit.' I pointed to a crop top ensemble in the window with matching flared trousers. I'd never have even considered wearing something like that in London. Andy would've said I looked like a banana, or banana boat or perhaps Banana Man – he was never particularly imaginative with his insults – and I would've felt way too self-conscious. But here, I could actually imagine it.

'I was thinking of something sparkly,' Chloe replied. 'Sparkly and short.'

'Sounds perfect,' I grinned. 'Come on. Let's go in. And we're not coming out until we've both got an outfit.'

I opened the door, and Chloe slipped through, though rather than following her into the shop, I looked down at Pongo.

'I guess we better check if you're allowed in, boy,' I

asked. 'They might not be a fan of dog fur on their designer clothes. 'Just wait here, okay? Sit. Stay. I'll be two minutes.'

If it turned out he wasn't allowed in, I would have to come out and tie him up properly, but I wasn't going to do that until I knew. I opened the door to the boutique for a second time, but before I could make a beeline for the shop-keeper, a voice spoke.

'Elodie?'

My stomach sank. I had my back to the person, but I already knew who it was, and the last thing I wanted was to turn around and face her. If I did, I didn't know what I'd say. And yet, could I really just ignore her and walk into the shop like I hadn't heard her say my name? I drew in a long breath. Sometimes, I hated being the better person.

Standing in front of me were the all-too-familiar elfish features of my mother.

Her eyes had shifted colour again since I'd last seen her. Was that part of the glamour, or her own vampire foibles? I wasn't going to ask, though.

'I don't suppose now is a good time for a conversation, is it?' she said.

I bit down on my bottom lip, suppressing all the rage burning through me. I was outside a shop, in the middle of the day, comforting one of my best friends who had just broken off an engagement. Of course, Amira didn't know that, but really. Out here, like this? This was how she wanted to talk? The woman had audacity, that was for sure.

'No,' I said. 'It's not.' With that, I turned on my heel and marched straight into the shop.

TWENTY-TWO

The moment I heard the shop door slam behind me, I realised my issue. I had left Pongo untied outside. Even if he was allowed in here, I would have to go back outside the shop to get him. And if he wasn't, then I'd have to spend even longer out there, tying him up. All with Amira standing there. Her sad eyes, boring into me. As I pondered what to do, the guilt flooded in.

That was my mother out there. Asking to talk to me. And I'd been horrible to her.

Then again, it wasn't as if she hadn't brought it on herself. And it wasn't like I hadn't thought of saying far worse to her over the years. After she'd written that letter, leaving us, I had imagined a hundred scenarios in which I would turn around and slam a door in her face. Where I would tell her that I had no need for her in my life. That I had coped better than she could have ever imagined. That I was proud of who I had become and that she could take zero credit for the woman I had turned into. I'd imagined bumping into her on the street, just like this. Or her turning up on my doorstep. And each time, my reaction had been the same. I didn't need her, and I didn't want her.

The issue was, in those imagined scenarios, telling my mother to beat it had come with a sense of pride. Actually doing it meant having to deal with the guilt, too.

'Look at this,' Chloe said, holding up a very sparkly, very short dress. 'Isn't it amazing? What do you think? Is it too bright for me?'

Considering the base colour could only be described as fluorescent, bright felt like an understatement.

'I think it'll look great,' I said, a smile flickering on my face, though I couldn't quite hold it in place. 'Sorry Chloe, I'll just be one minute. I need to pop outside.'

'Yeah, everything okay?'

'Yeah, I just left Pongo.'

I turned to the shop assistant, who had now stepped out from behind the counter and was watching us with an intent stare, as if he wasn't sure whether we were going to steal something or spend a fortune.

'Sorry, can I bring my dog in here?' I asked.

'Dog?' he said the word as if he'd never heard it spoken before. His lips pouted, although the rest of his face remained entirely motionless. Botox or magic? Who knew. 'Is it small?'

'He's only a puppy,' I said, aware that I was being choosy in my turn of phrase.

'You must carry him,' he replied.

'Right, no problem then.'

Carrying Pongo the entire time I was in there wasn't exactly conducive to looking at clothes, and it wasn't as if Chloe could take over while I was trying things on. He was already too heavy for her. So that meant tying him up there.

With a deep breath in, I opened the door. While Pongo

immediately bounded up to meet me, Amira remained at a distance.

'Elodie?' she said again. It was insane how much hope she could pack into three syllables. And how much it could tug at my beating heart.

'I just need to tie Pongo up,' I said, gesturing to my pup.

'Oh, yes,' she said. 'And I'm sorry. I know I said I'd give you time, and I was planning on it, I promise, but I saw you there and... I don't know. It was my fault. I shouldn't have come and spoken to you. I promised I wouldn't. I won't do that again.'

I nodded. 'I *am* going to need time,' I said. 'Quite a bit of time, I think, before I'm ready to talk about things. Do anything.'

'Okay. I get it, I really do,' she said. 'I'm sorry. And I hope you and your friend have a fun time shopping.' She looked at the yellow outfit in the window. 'I think you'd look fantastic in that,' she said. 'You know, if you were thinking about it.'

She smiled at me, and I tried to offer a smile in response, but my face just wouldn't respond. Instead, I focussed on securing Pongo's leash to the railing.

'I *will* be in touch,' I said. 'Just not yet, okay?'

'I get it,' she said. 'Take care of yourself, Elodie. And I love you. You know that. I love you so much Elly Belly.'

A moment later, she turned around and was walking away again and I was dealing with a very dense lump that had lodged itself in my throat.

'You and Amira seemed to be having an intense conversation. Everything okay?' Chloe asked when I came back into the shop to find her holding up several outfits in the mirror.

It had slipped from my mind that Chloe knew Amira, if

only in passing. My mother masquerading as a fae meant she'd had to integrate with others of her assumed type, on some level anyway.

'Oh, she was just asking what type of breed Pongo was,' I replied, only for the man behind the counter to clear his throat and flash me a narrow smile, complete with canine fangs. A vampire. A vampire who had been listening in on my conversation.

No wonder gossip spread so damn fast on this island.

TWENTY-THREE

They were undoubtedly the best cocktails I had had since moving to the island. And possibly before *then* too.

'Why have I never had one of these before?' Chloe said, lifting up her drink.

'This is exactly the same as the last cocktail you had last time,' Dylan replied. 'And the one before that.'

'But this one tastes so much better,' she said. 'It's delicious.'

'I have to agree,' I said, aware that my words had the slightest slur to them.

'You know what? It's nice drinking something without mango hooch in it as well. That's all we ever drink. I'm like, "Let's get a nice wine," and Mick's like, "Oh no, let's have a mango hooch," and I'm like, "What about a cosmopolitan?" and he's like, "Mango hooch, mango hooch!" I don't *always* want mango hooch!'

She raised her voice, her tone tipping into a flash of fury. A large pile of paper napkins sat on the table in front of us. Slowly, Dylan pulled them away from the fire fae as he placed a hand on her shoulder.

'We get it. No mango hooch tonight,' he said.

Despite both Amira and Chloe's suggestion that I try the complete yellow outfit, I had opted for just the top, which I paired with a denim miniskirt, while Chloe had purchased the fluorescent sparkly dress. And she looked amazing in her outfit.

She was determined to make the night a party and had downed her first drink, and with the entire group together socialising for the first time, it really felt like a celebration. Although that hadn't stopped work creeping into conversation when we'd first arrived here.

'Why do I recognise the barman?' I'd said to Diego as we'd turned up at Betty's Beach Bar. The man looked to be in his late thirties, with widely spaced eyes and a narrowness to his face that was strangely familiar.

'That's Fritz Hoffman,' he said.

'Hoffman, as in Henrik Hoffman?'

'Yup, that's his brother.'

'Flo's other nephew,' I said, more to myself than Diego.

So that was why I recognised him. He looked more than a little like Henrik. In fact, the pair could have passed as twins.

'Does he want Flo's store too?' I said, lowering my voice to a volume that I hoped only Diego could hear.

'Prob'ly more than Henrik. He's got another bar, like this, on the mainland, and I think he wanted to open a small little tapas place where Flo's is. That family are like vultures, if you ask me.'

I was torn. It was always hard for me to switch off from a story, but when there was a potential lead sitting only feet away from me? That was close to agony. But tonight was meant to be about spending time with one another outside of the office. So I fought the urge and focussed on enjoying my cocktails.

Betty's was a great location for a celebration. Sand slipped between our toes and lights twinkled in the wooden roof. But while the view out over the water was phenomenal, I couldn't help but think about the view from Whip's house in Peppers Bay. Not to mention the things we had done while looking out at it. It would have been nice to have had him there, but at the same time, I appreciated tonight for the chance to bond with my colleagues over drinks, rather than traumatic events.

While Diego and Bobby drew Chloe into a conversation about baseball, I pulled out my phone and fired off a quick message to Whip.

Sorry again about tonight, I said. *See you tomorrow.*

Absolutely, he replied.

'Put away your phone,' Chloe said, smacking my arm lightly. 'We're celebrating, remember? That we're all healthy and well and unhexed. The Oracle Octagon!'

'There ain't eight of us,' Bobby said.

'No, it would be The Oracle Hexagon,' Theodora replied.

'It's eight with Pongo!' Chloe protested as she threw the cherry under the table for him.

'No. That would be The Oracle Heptagon,' Theodora corrected.

'Although that might be your eighth drink,' Diego joined in with a nod to Chloe.

'You know, I couldn't imagine ever working anywhere else, could you?' Chloe continued. Drink definitely made her loquacious, and it wasn't like she was quiet before. 'You're just such an amazing bunch. I love you all, do you know that? Don't you? I love every one of you. I love you and your big eyepatch, Bobby. I love you and your werewolf feet and blue eyes,' she said to Diego. 'And I love... I love...' She looked at Dylan, suddenly struggling to work out how to finish her sentence. 'I just *love* you.'

'I love you too,' he said, the words slipping from his lips with sadness.

'Well, I'm guessing it's going to be a fairly late start tomorrow,' Bobby said. 'Fingers crossed we have nothing major on.'

'I have got to write an article on a golf tournament,' Chloe groaned, dropping her head down to her straw and taking an exceptionally long draw from it. 'I *hate* covering golf tournaments. I just stand there for hours. You know that some people actually pay to watch people play golf? Why would you do that?'

I had to give her her dues. I wasn't going to run out and spend my hard-earned salary on a trip to the local golf club. Let alone watch other people play. But I wasn't the island's sports journalist.

'I'll come with you,' Dylan said. 'If you want. I've just got to take some phone calls, but I don't have to be in the office to do that.'

'You'd do that for me?' she said, her eyes widening.

'Of course I would. I'd do anything for you.'

Two very unsubtle comments from Dylan in a row? I glanced at the table and noticed that Chloe and I weren't the only ones who were getting through our drinks at an impressive rate. Chloe put her hands on either side of Dylan's cheeks, cupping him lightly.

'I'm so lucky to have you as a friend,' she said. 'I'm *so* very lucky.'

'I will always be there for you,' he whispered back.

While her expression was soft and affectionate, a look

of absolute adoration washed over Dylan. Chloe was drunk. Just saying whatever she needed to keep herself feeling upbeat. But Dylan, this was all too real and raw for him.

Deciding that maybe it would be good to give the pair a little space, I stumbled out of my seat, when a voice growled out behind us.

'Get your hands off her.'

All our heads spun around to the bar area, where a bulk of a man stood in oil-covered clothes, his greasy hair slicked back.

'Mick? You came!' Chloe wobbled as she pushed herself onto her feet. 'I can't believe you came!'

Mick didn't even look at her. Instead, all his focus remained locked on Dylan.

'You're going to regret that,' he growled.

TWENTY-FOUR

As great as vamp speed is, it doesn't help you see things before they're going to happen. The moment Mick lunged for Dylan, I was on my feet, grabbing Pongo and moving him out of the way.

As we crashed into the table and chairs next to us, Mick barrelled into Dylan's chest. I gasped. That kind of force should have knocked someone flat on their back, yet Dylan didn't move so much as an inch. Whereas Mick? Mick bounced off him like he'd slammed into a brick wall.

'That is some stance,' I muttered to myself.

Mick clutched his head, swaying with dizziness, or drink, or perhaps a mixture of both. But rather than backing off, as anybody sensible would've done in such a situation, he let out a low growl.

'You need to stay away from her!'

This time he sent his hand swinging up towards Dylan's jaw. Whether he was drunk or not, his aim was perfect, and perfect stance or not, Dylan wasn't going to withstand a strike like that unscathed. That's what I thought until Mick's knuckles collided with the skin of Dylan's cheek.

The moment was near-instant, a flash in which Dylan's flesh turned to hard stone before returning to its normal state. The stone had taken the impact. Dylan was a freaking gargoyle! I'd read about them in the book Chloe had given me, but I hadn't thought I'd met one, let alone been working with one for the past two months. I had so many questions, though now was definitely not the right time. As Mick's hand struck, I heard the crack of his knuckles against Dylan's cheekbone. They had to have been broken.

'Mick! Stop it. Stop it! What are you doing?!' Chloe shouted. 'You need to stop this *now*!' Around us, paper napkins were going up in flames. With all my attention on the fight, I hadn't even thought about Chloe and her power triggers. But now I had, and it needed to be dealt with ASAP.

'Elodie!' Bobby shouted.

'I'm on it! Where's the fire extinguisher?' I yelled at Fritz, who was looking on at the fight with a mixture of trepidation and anger. Clearly, he didn't want his bar trashed by an angry whatever-the-heck Mick was, but he wasn't about to intervene either. Still, I had a tough time believing that a place serving alcohol in a town full of shifters and other paras hadn't seen its fair share of fights.

'It's... it's...' he pointed down the edge of the bar, apparently not getting any closer to the fray. In one leap, I jumped over, grabbed it, and pointed it at the various napkin fires Chloe had started.

'Please, please, Mick!' Chloe was sobbing as she tried to reach him, but Diego was holding her back. Whether Mick couldn't hear her or wouldn't listen to her, I didn't know. He didn't stop. Instead, he tried again, this time aiming his elbow at Dylan's neck, his knee towards his groin. Every time, the same thing happened: his body met stone. As far as I was aware, Dylan hadn't thrown a single punch. Mick was breaking his own bones left, right, and centre. It was a miracle he was still standing, not rolling on the floor in agony.

'This stops now!' Bobby yelled above the ruckus. 'Mick, that's enough!'

With one hand, Bobby grabbed Mick by the grubby collar of his shirt, lifting him a clear foot off the ground. And yet Mick kept swinging. His attention was divided now. He wasn't willing to let the Dylan issue rest, but he was also trying to free himself from Bobby's grip.

'Why won't he just stop?' I whispered.

That was when I caught the scent in the air. A sharp, hot tang, like chilli and metal, somehow fused together.

I looked at Diego. 'That smell, that's an emotion, right?'

'Yeah. Anger. Crazy anger.' As if speaking had helped make up his mind, Diego moved in to help his colleagues try to subdue the crazed Mick.

'You won't get away with this. *Any* of you,' Mick spat, still swinging and kicking in every direction. 'You won't get away with taking her from me.'

'What are you on about?!' Chloe cried 'No one's taken me from you. I'm right here! I'm right here!'

'You won't get away with it,' Mick growled.

'Please Mick, this isn't you.' Chloe was sobbing now. 'What are you doing? Why are you doing this?'

'Enough of this,' Theodora roared.

She had remained seated at the table the entire time, rather than running for space like the rest of us. Almost as if it wasn't worth interrupting her drink for. Now, though, she'd clearly had enough. Still, she moved with a casual lethargy. As if she were taking a stroll down the beach, not across to a veritable war zone.

She walked over to where Mick was currently battling both Diego, Dylan and Bobby, and lifted her skirt.

There were legs under her skirt, yes. But not normal legs. These were thick. Muscular. They could've belonged to a bull. And they were covered in the same bristly fur that you would have expected to find on the animal, too. Having seen that she was now involved, the three colleagues dropped back, leaving Mick snarling in her direction.

'Sorry, this will hurt,' she said, before twisting slightly, raising one of her legs and powering it straight into Mick's stomach. Even though he'd seen it coming, he didn't stand a chance; he flew through the air and into a wooden post behind him. For a second, his body hovered there, as if it had been permanently imbedded into the wood by the force, until, with a thud, he fell to the ground.

With a long exhale, Theodora brushed down her skirt and turned to our party, catching my eye as she did so.

'Part Minotaur,' she said with a smirk. 'So now you know.'

TWENTY-FIVE

I hadn't expected to see Whip at all that night, but he turned up at the bar only a few minutes after Theodora had knocked Mick unconscious. And he wasn't alone. Alex was with him.

A knot formed in my stomach. It was the first time I'd seen Alex since he'd turned up on my doorstep before the weekend, and at some point, we would need to talk to one another. Even if it was just about what we were going to do next with our investigation into The Guardians.

While he got on with sorting out Mick with a pair of runed cuffs, Whip came over to me.

'You okay?' he said.

'Believe it or not, I actually stayed out of the trouble.'

He grinned. 'Heard it was pretty bad. Fritz rang up, said there was a brawl. Thought I needed to step in. Should've known you lot could handle yourselves. What happened?'

I gestured to where Chloe was still sobbing. Pongo had placed himself between her and Alex, his head on Chloe's lap, as he tried to comfort her, though his tail gave involuntary wags as Alex scratched behind his ear. It was an absentminded action on Alex's part as he continued to listen to Chloe.

'He was just so angry,' she said between her sobs. 'I've never seen him like that. He was furious. He just wouldn't stop. And he's not like that. He's not. Mick's a good man. Honestly.'

'I should take her back to mine,' I said to Whip. 'She was going to stay there anyway, but after that... well, I think it's safe to say she won't want to go back to Mick's anytime soon.'

'I don't think Mick's going to go home himself for a while,' Whip replied. 'I'm no doctor, but it looks like he's got at least a dozen broken bones. And you're saying he just kept fighting through the pain?'

'It didn't even look like he was in pain,' I said honestly, before nodding my head over towards the bar and indicating our need to move a little further away from the group. Diego was likely to listen in. And Alex too, but they weren't who I was worried about. I just didn't want Chloe to overhear us.

'What are you thinking?' Whip said, moving as if he was going to place his hand on my waist, only to draw it back to his side.

I chewed on the inside of my cheek, offering Mick and Chloe quick glances before I spoke.

'The way Mick was when he was fighting... it reminded me of Flo in the video. It wasn't like he could see anything, hear anything. He was just *so* furious. Fighting was all that mattered.'

'Do you think it could be the same thing? Whatever caused her to smash up her own place could have done this to him?'

'That's exactly what I'm thinking. Maybe another hex,

perhaps. Though I was talking to Bobby about it earlier. He mentioned it could maybe be a demon. Do you think that's possible? I've never seen anyone possessed before, but I could believe it.'

Whip nodded as he bit his bottom lip.

'It's definitely not impossible,' he said. 'But demons aren't normally something we've had to worry about. Even with the portal.'

'The portal?'

It didn't matter how many times I thought I'd got to grips with all the secrets this island had, it never failed to throw up more.

'The Scorched Circle. That's what it is. A portal. But demons only come through when someone summons them.'

'The Scorched Circle?' I had indeed heard of it. Sophia had been hunting near there when she'd come across the wood sprites that had taught her how to make hexes. Clearly, nothing good came from that place. I would definitely keep it off my list of places to visit on the island.

'I can't believe there's a portal to the demonic realms, and nobody thought to *tell* me,' I said, with just a hint of petulance.

Whip shrugged, as if he hadn't just told me something simultaneously ridiculous and headline-worthy.

'Honestly, it doesn't really impact us in town. People know to steer clear of it. I mean, once you've seen what a demon can do, you really don't want to bring one into your world.'

'But somebody *could* have,' I said. 'If they wanted to.'

'Maybe,' he nodded. 'But Fritz just said that Mick looked drunk. We can't rule that out either.'

'No,' I replied, though my mind was already in full

investigative mode. Henrik had had dinner with his aunt the same day she'd seemingly been possessed. And now this happened to Mick in his brother's bar. That didn't feel like a coincidence.

'Do you need a hand getting home?' Whip asked. 'Walking Chloe back and everything?'

I shook my head. 'We'll be fine. I'm sure Dylan will help.'

Whip pressed his lips together, then placed his hands on my shoulders.

'I know you hate me saying this, but if there *is* a demon on the loose—'

'Then you don't want me to go chasing after it. You want me to be sensible and stay close, et cetera, et cetera,' I said, raising an eyebrow at him.

'You've got it.' His lips twisted into a slight smirk.

'Same applies to you, okay? Unless you can just tell a demon what to do? Can you do that?'

He hesitated, and a flicker of contemplation crossed his face. 'I can't be possessed. But I can't do anything to stop them either.'

'You can't?' Whip's power was so strong I sometimes forgot that it had limits. Not that he ever used it unless it was necessary.

'No. The only person who can control them is the person they're possessing, but the problem is, the person being possessed doesn't usually know that they've got a demon trying to control their actions. It's a complex thing.'

'So you've faced a few?' I asked, partly out of journalistic interest. Partly to learn more about this man I was falling for.

'More than a few. The one who cursed me wanted to

know exactly how strong my powers were. They made me go through an entire series of tasks.'

'Tasks?' My throat tightened. Whatever he had gone through, I was sure it couldn't have been pleasant. Anyone who tried to make another person, especially a para, into a weapon didn't sound like a great guy to be around.

'There were a lot of things,' he said. 'Werewolf bites, vampire bites. I probably faced a dozen demons, but none of them did anything. Other than seriously piss me off. Mermaid venom was also fine, but if one of those basilisks had bitten me? Let's just say it was a good thing I only got a very small dose of that when she was testing that theory.'

She? I'd always assumed the shit bag that cursed him was a man, but clearly not. My heart throbbed so deeply imagining everything that Whip had suffered, I could barely find it in me to speak.

'I'm so sorry,' I said finally.

I let out a long sigh and wrapped my arms around his waist. Then, in an easy casual motion he planted a kiss on the top of my head.

'It was a long time ago.'

'Still, I'm sorry.'

I stayed there for a moment, wishing I could take away just a fraction of all the pain he had suffered. Yet as I stood there, head against his chest, I became aware of the figure standing beside us.

As I broke away from Whip, the knots in my stomach reformed at the sight of Alex. His attention was solely on Whip, as if he couldn't even bear to look at me. I didn't know whether it made me angry or sad. Though it was most likely a bit of both.

'Mick's cuffed up. He's healing pretty fast, but I'm

gonna take him to the hospital. No point taking him to the station till he can talk. As long as you're okay with that?'

'Sure, sounds good.'

Alex turned around, and for a split second, I thought he wasn't going to acknowledge me at all, but then he twisted back, and his eyes met mine.

'Glad you're all okay, Elodie,' he said.

Elodie. Not Evergreen.

My chest tightened.

'Did something happen between you two?' Whip asked as Alex and Bobby worked together to manoeuvre Mick onto a stretcher. 'Something I should know about?'

Was that jealousy in his voice? I didn't think so, but I wasn't sure.

'No,' I said, shaking my head. 'Just difficult Guardians stuff. Him wanting to question Amira more, you know. Me not wanting to go there.'

I hadn't planned on lying to Whip, particularly when Alex hadn't even mentioned going to see Amira again, but there was no way I could tell him the truth.

'Well, if you need me to tell him to back off, I can.'

'It's fine,' I said, honestly wishing I'd thought of a better response. The last thing I needed was to be caught out lying. That wasn't going to help the jealousy issues at all. 'You don't need to do that. Honestly, it's probably best if you don't say anything.'

As he nodded his head in the most miniscule motion, I couldn't help but be momentarily jealous of his power. If Whip told someone not to do something, he didn't have to worry they'd go back on their word. They had to do what he'd asked of them. Then again, if I was worried that Whip would do that, it didn't say much about the state of our new relationship, did it?

With a slight shudder, I shook my worries away. I was just projecting, that was all. Projecting, because if anyone was going to screw this thing up, it was almost certainly going to be me, not Whip.

'Will I see you tomorrow night?' I asked, only to smack my tongue on the roof of my mouth. 'Crap, I forgot. Tomorrow night's the council meeting. I've got to be there.'

'You're covering council meetings now?' Whip frowned.

'No, it's still Bobby's remit, but they're bringing the hunting rights forward. I feel like I need to be there too. For Ines now.'

'Guess I'll see you there,' he said, kissing my forehead again. 'Until tomorrow Elodie.'

TWENTY-SIX

The sofa wasn't half as uncomfortable as I'd thought it would be, but that was possibly due to me spending most of the night sitting up reading, rather than sleeping on it.

The moment Chloe and I had stepped into the house, Pongo'd made it abundantly clear he wasn't going to be left out of the bedroom the way he'd been all weekend at Whip's. He launched himself onto the centre of the bed, only shuffling to the side when Chloe climbed up next to him. Within five minutes, she was fast asleep, cuddling him like he was a giant teddy bear.

'So much for loyalty,' I muttered as I scanned the room and removed any books and other paper objects that could prove unwanted kindling if Chloe's powers sparked in the middle of the night. Then, leaving the door ajar, just in case Pongo changed his mind and wanted to spend the night with me rather than on the mattress with Chloe, I got to work researching.

A scarily large chunk of the book Chloe had given to me

was on demons, or Portal Entities, as the chapter was titled, although the information found within those pages was annoyingly sparse. 'No known corporeal form' appeared several times, indicating that no one had any idea what the demons looked like. Some had images, but included such unhelpful lines as 'abilities unknown'. In the end, I did all I could, which was focus on those that had decent descriptions and see if they fitted with whatever it was we were encountering, which automatically ruled some out.

Gossip demons were known to stir up trouble in small-town communities by starting rumours, though posed no physical threat themselves, while FOMO demons tended to get their hosts in trouble by trying every crazy exploit available to them, from skydiving to free diving and everything in between. It was difficult not to get drawn into learning all about the different types, while simultaneously wondering which ones Whip had been made to face. Sure, a laughter demon might sound like a great thing to encounter. Until you read how the side effects could include laughing until you passed out, wet yourself, or worse, when you couldn't stop. You had your standard temptation demons and demons loyal to particular lords. Then you had ones that were attracted to lust, to greed, to grief, to vanity. So many bloody demons. It wasn't helpful.

I had just eaten my third red-velvet cookie from Whip – and was incredibly grateful for the extra dose of blood to keep me awake – when I accepted this approach wasn't going to work. We still had too many unknowns. Still, I suspected portal entities –I had no intention of calling them that in public – were like the hexes. You needed to know *what* you were dealing with to trap it, banish it, or whatever the hell you did with demons.

Which was when the idea struck.

The next morning, while Chloe was still asleep, I headed to the office, where I brought my idea to Bobby.

'No. Not a chance.' His response was succinct and to the point. And exactly the opposite of the response I'd hoped for. But it wasn't the first time an editor-in-chief had told me no, and I'd done it anyway.

'We might be able to find some clues.'

'In the Scorched Circle? No. You are not going there.'

'Well, I wasn't planning on going on my own,' I stressed. 'I thought we'd go together.'

If I'd thought my suggestion would appease my boss, I was very wrong. His single eye bugged so wide I thought it would pop out of its socket.

'You have to be joking. I'm not going near there, and neither are you. That is an *order*. And trust me, I'm so serious about this I'll get Nyrah to undo your ward so Whip can control you if that's what it takes. You are *not* to go near the Scorched Circle. Do you hear me?'

Undoing Nyrah's ward? That was a threat he hadn't made before and if he'd hoped it would scare me, he was right. Bobby wouldn't have made it unless he was scared. And if Bobby was scared, it meant that I should probably be scared, too.

'Really? What's that bad about it?'

'What's *that bad*?' he echoed, incredulously. 'It's a *portal*, Elodie. A portal to a demonic realm.'

'Which means?' I said.

'Which means nothin' good comes outta it. Period.' He let out a long sigh. 'Demons do just fine in their own realms. Eatin', sleepin', terrorisin'. Whatever it is they do. But if they wanna come to our world, they gotta hitch a ride. Possess someone. Ain't no other way they gonna get out of the Scorched Circle. The only way we keep Raven's Hollow safe is by not going near it. Simple as that. Which is why I can't believe that a demon is what we're looking at here. I can't imagine *anyone* on this island would be stupid enough to go near it.'

My jaw locked.

'You were the one that mentioned demons in the first place!' I realised my voice was raised, but it was hard to stay calm. 'And if it wasn't a demon, how do you explain Mick? The way he kept fighting through the pain?'

This time, Bobby pursed his lips as he fiddled with the strap of his eyepatch.

'I know what I said, but we were spitballing ideas.'

'And what about the wolf packs?' I questioned.

'The wolf packs? Has there been an incident with the wolves?'

'No,' I shook my head, annoyed at myself for not explaining my thoughts properly. But it was difficult when I had so many of them running through my head. 'I mean they go to the Scorched Circle, don't they? I thought it was in Wraith Woods. Where Diego lives.'

As Bobby drew in a breath, there was a knock on the door. When I turned around, Diego was there, leaning against the doorframe. Damn supernatural hearing. I should have known he'd be listening in.

'Sorry, you were pretty heated there. Could hear you two arguing all the way up the road. An' in answer to your question, *no*. Every wolf knows to give the Scorched Circle a very wide berth. And not just us, animals too. Squirrels, foxes, badgers; nothing goes near it. That place is bad news, Elodie. You don't want to go there.'

I wanted to keep going. To keep defending my point, but Bobby spoke again.

'Listen kid, if – and this is a big if – this is to do with the Scorched Circle, then you need to leave it be,' he said. 'And if you don't, then I'm afraid you're going to find yourself looking for a new job.'

TWENTY-SEVEN

It was officially the angriest I'd ever been since working at The Oracle. I wanted to throw something, hit something, but even in my fury, I was well aware that wasn't a good idea. The last thing I needed was to break my desk or put a hole in the wall. I wasn't broke, but I wasn't exactly flush with cash either, and I wasn't in the mood to pay for repairs. But it didn't stop the anger from rolling through me.

The office was still only half full. Theodora and Dylan weren't yet in, and I'd left Pongo at home with Chloe, just so she wasn't entirely on her own. Though, as I headed downstairs, hoping that a Weirdoughs cappuccino would erase my urge to put my job in jeopardy, I spotted her walking up from the main road, Pongo on his lead, a take-away cup in her hand.

I always thought Chloe dyed her hair. It had been a vibrant array of colours since I'd moved to Raven's Hollow. But as she stood there in front of me, it was a drab grey. Entirely different from the pink it had been the night before, and far more muted than any colour I had ever seen her with. Was her hair colour linked to her emotions, perhaps? Did it change while she slept if she had a particularly emotional experience? It definitely looked like that, but it wasn't the right time to ask.

'I'm so sorry about last night, Elodie,' she began.

'What are you on about?' I said. 'You don't have anything to be sorry for.'

'Well, Mick turning up and ruining the entire night—'

'Was because of Mick, nothing else,' I said, cutting her off. 'Do not blame yourself for this, you understand?' She tried to nod, but her head barely moved. 'I mean it, or I'll get one of the sirens around here, and you won't be able to ignore them.' Yes, it was basically the same threat Bobby had given me, in regard to Whip using his powers to stop me from heading to the Scorched Circle, but it was a good one. It seemed a waste not to reuse it. 'What happened was not on you, okay?'

She nodded. 'Thank you. You're a good friend. Oh, and if you're going out for a drink, there's no need...' She gestured to her hand, which was when I caught a whiff of the drink. As the waft of the O-negative cappuccino hit the back of my throat, I wondered how the heck I hadn't noticed that was what she was holding. 'I thought you needed this after a night on the sofa. I'm ever so sorry for doing that to you.'

'Don't be silly, it's fine. But thank you for this. I need it. And not because of the sofa.' One gulp was all it took for me to feel slightly calmer, though I was aware that it probably wasn't a good thing that I got all my blood infused with caffeine or sugar. Still, it was a habit I wasn't planning on breaking. After a second, even longer gulp, I moved the cup away from my lips, only to find that Chloe was still staring at me intently.

'Are you going to be looking into what happened?' she said. 'I know the others think Mick was just drunk, but it wasn't that, I promise. It's something more.'

'I agree,' I said, locking my gaze with hers, just so she knew I wasn't lying. 'I'm going to look into it. I promise.'

'You are?' The relief on her face was palpable as something close to a smile actually flickered onto her lips. 'Thank you ever so much. With you and Bobby on the case, I know you'll get to the truth in no time at all. I guess we better get back to work then?'

As encouraging as Chloe's words should've been, all they did was increase the sense of guilt and hopelessness that I felt when I returned to my desk. The Scorched Circle had been my one lead, but with a visit out of the question, I wasn't sure where to start.

A tiny reporter part of me was itching to ignore everything Bobby had said. It was like a physical sensation beneath my skin, begging me to go to those woods and find out what was there. Would he really fire me if I found out what type of demon – assuming it was a demon – was behind the outbursts, before any more happened? Then again, I had gone into a forest one night, having been told explicitly not to, and look where that had got me.

Dead.

'Chloe, does Mick know Flo at all?' realising I would need to go down the standard question route to find my leads. 'Have they ever, I don't know, worked together?'

'I don't think so,' she said. 'Why? What are you thinking?'

'I don't know. But if they had been in contact somehow, maybe when and where could be a link. Maybe she took her car to him and it happened at the garage.'

'Can't drive,' Bobby interrupted, from where he was

standing over by Diego's desk, assumedly looking at pictures.

'Sorry?' I said.

'Flo can't drive. Never has. Her nephews take her everywhere she needs to go.'

Her nephews... I still hadn't ruled them out of my suspicions yet.

'Maybe she gets hooch,' I said, thinking of another possibility. 'Maybe Mick delivered some to her and that's how they both came into contact with the demon.'

I opened up my phone and looked at the picture I'd taken at Mick's garage; the list of people in Ravens Hollow who had hooch delivered, but there was no sign of their names on there.

'You know there's going to be a link in there somewhere,' I said. 'There's *got* to be.'

The thing was, with paranormal issues like this, I'd already learnt that if the source wasn't found, the problem could escalate *fast*. When Wren Belkin had died and we hadn't known the cause, the hydra had gone on to kill two more people before it was stopped. Of course, that had been a fairly specific situation, given that those two had been trying to catch the hydra, but still. Then there was the hexing when Sophia had targeted people from The Oracle to make her point, but who knew how many others she may have hurt if she hadn't been caught.

If this was a demon we were dealing with, then it had currently taken two victims. And even though no one had been seriously hurt – aside from Flo's shopfront and that one wooden post at the bar – that didn't mean the next incident wouldn't be the one where something irreversible happened.

We needed to find out who or what was behind all this beforehand.

'I'm going to go talk to Flo,' I said to Bobby. 'See if I can find a link that way.'

I felt like I'd get a better reception from her than I would from Mick.

'Do you want any company?' Bobby asked.

'I've got Pongo. I'll be fine,' I said, revelling in how he was now actually allowing me to go out and talk to sources on my own.

'Alright. Just—'

'Just stay safe.' I rolled my eyes. 'Yes, I get it.'

CHAPTER
TWENTY-EIGHT

I used the opportunity to walk to the shop and give Pongo his first decent walk of the day, and from the way his tail wagged constantly, he was glad for a little one-on-one time.

'I know, it's been busy lately,' I said. 'But you were the one who decided to sleep in with Chloe, rather than me, remember?'

He cocked his head to the side like he had no idea what I was talking about, but I wasn't convinced.

As we reached the main strip of beach, I glanced up towards Amira's flat. She'd been a vampire for a lot longer than I had, meaning she likely had her senses finely tuned. Did she know that I was walking past? Did she think I was coming to see her? After the conversation we'd had the day before, it seemed unlikely, but I kept my gaze straight ahead and quickened my pace, just in case she decided to appear.

'Yup, it seems as though I'm scared of seeing my own mother,' I muttered to Pongo. 'It's a strange old world, that's for sure.'

The shop had been boarded up, but I could hear someone working away inside. Creaks of wood and clattering of plastic, as if someone was rearranging the mess inside. From the slow, shuffling footsteps, I was willing to bet that the person was Flo, rather than one of her younger, fitter nephews.

'Flo,' I said, knocking on the MDF board that replaced the door. 'Are you in there? It's Elodie Evergreen, from The Oracle. I just wanted to have a word with you about what happened.'

The movement stopped, though I heard her pulse kick up a notch, as if she were fearful of what I might say or do, or more likely, what I might write.

'I don't think you're the only person this has happened to,' I said, speaking to the door, fairly certain she was listening to me. 'I think it's happened to someone else, too. And I'm hoping we can find a way to stop it. I just want to talk to you, ask a few questions about where you went the other night, see what you can remember.'

Again, my words were met with silence, but as I stood there, debating what to say next, the footsteps started up again, and this time they grew louder. I was debating whether I should say something else, when the sheet of MDF shifted to the side.

'I've told the police all I know,' Flo snapped at me. Once again she was dressed in a dirndl, though she had opted for plastic Marigold gloves, no doubt to help with the cleaning, rather than to hide the scratches on her arms. 'I don't know what happened. It's a trick. Somebody doctored those tapes. That's what I told them, and I'll tell you the same. It's a trick. You think I would not know if I broke my own shop?' Her face scrunched up tightly as she rapidly shook her head. 'I would know.'

'I understand,' I said. 'Honestly, I do. I've spoken to the police. But like I said, there was another incident yesterday. Someone else got angry. Very angry. And he doesn't remember what happened, either.' I was on dodgy grounds, given that I had no idea what Mick did or didn't remember, but I was a journalist, not the police. I could be a little more fluid with what I said. Besides, I believed it was the truth.

I was telling my first, not insubstantial lie in the last twelve hours. I couldn't help but think back to Alex. Would Whip have asked him about Amira? Questioned him about putting pressure on me? I hoped not, but maybe it would be worth giving him a call. Though I wasn't exactly sure what I was going to say to him. *Please could you lie to Whip, so he doesn't find out I lied to him?* I certainly wouldn't be convinced by that. And after how our last conversation had gone, I couldn't imagine he would be in any hurry to help me out.

'Someone else?' Flo's voice brought me back to the conversation, though a sceptical frown line remained between her brows, as if she wasn't quite sure whether I was winding her up or not.

'Yes. Yes,' I said, perhaps a little too enthusiastically. 'I mean, we think it is the same. And I could be wrong, but I have a hunch.'

'A hunch?' The frown deepened.

'Yes. I think there might be a demon at play.'

I waited for her response. There was a good chance she'd reply like Bobby and tell me that no person in Ravens Hollow would go anywhere near The Scorched Circle. Maybe she'd even laugh the idea off. Those were both reactions I would have expected. But instead, she simply remained there, motionless, waiting for me. Not that I had much to give her. 'I...I'm not sure what sort it might be,' My voice cracked as I tried to think what else I could say to persuade her to talk to me. 'I'm not very knowledgeable about that kind of thing. I'm quite new to the para world, actually. But I'm not new to journalism, I've been doing that for a long time, and I know a hunch doesn't sound like much, but it can be. So I thought maybe if I asked you a couple of questions, we could see what we could come up with?'

I sucked in a quick breath. I sounded more like a babbling newbie on the job, rather than an experienced reporter. And as her brow furrowed, I could feel it was fifty–fifty whether she was going to slam the door in my face or agree to talk to me. But then she stepped outside and pulled the large plank of MDF over the door.

'You can buy me a coffee,' she said. 'Or something stronger. I think I could do with it.'

TWENTY-NINE

Given her nephew was the owner of a bar, I assumed that's where Flo would want to go, but instead, ten minutes later, we were sitting on the veranda of a small eatery and bar called Hex on the Beach. I'd passed it countless times since moving to Ravens Hollow, and even sent a photo to Donna. (As a witch who loved cocktails, I figured it was right up her street.) but I'd never gone in. My loyalty was very firmly tied to Weirdoughs, and the last thing I wanted was to feel swayed about where to get my beverages.

Thankfully, there was no option of the extra shots on the menu, meaning my loyalty didn't have to be tested as I made do with a standard cappuccino.

'You really think it's a demon?' Flo asked as she took a sip of her black Americano.

'Well, you're certain it wasn't you.' I replied.

'I know what it looks like. What people are saying. They think it was me. That I went crazy and am pretending. But it's not true. I didn't do. I couldn't. I love that shop.'

'I know. I know you do,' I said. 'And for what it's worth, I think the police believe you, too.'

'They do?'

While the community obviously knew Whip was a powerful para of some sort, very few people actually knew what he was. No one was going to assume that he was a male siren. They were so rare that, on average, one was only born every two hundred years. It was important that knowledge of his powers remained confined to his close circle. His talent was exceptionally useful at dissolving conflict and keeping life on the island running smoothly, but if the general population found out what he was – and thought they were being manipulated by him – well, that could cause a whole load of trouble.

'They've spoken to lots of people,' I said, racking up my lie count for the week. 'Everybody's mentioned that it would be incredibly out of character for you to do something like that.'

'Yes, yes, absolutely,' she said. 'It would, because I did not.'

Relieved that she'd bought my explanation as to why the police believed her, it was time to see if I could learn something useful.

'I wanted to ask you a couple of things that might help us put together a timeline of what happened, if that's okay.' I asked.

'I can try,' she replied with an impressive roll of her r's.

'Great, thank you.' I pulled out my phone, ready to take notes. 'So, where were you last Sunday night?'

'Sunday, I eat roast at my nephew's.'

'Henrik?' I questioned. 'Or Fritz?'

'Both,' she said. 'We've done it for years. Henrik married

a Brit, like yourself. He loves a roast dinner. Very good cook. It's become a tradition. Reminds him of home.'

'I can believe that,' I said. 'I really miss my roast dinners, too. Parsnips are my absolute favourite vegetable. Not to mention cauliflower cheese.'

A line of wrinkles formed on her forehead. 'Cauliflower cheese with a roast?'

'Don't knock it till you've tried it,' I said with a grin.

Flo managed a fleeting smile in response, but it was clear she was struggling.

'So,' I continued, 'after the dinner, what happened then? Assuming the dinner was normal, that is,' I added, realising I might have missed something there.

'If by normal you mean the boys stick their noses into my business, then yes, normal. They say I waste money. Say I'm irresponsible. Huh! I work to the bone. Money's not everything. Course, they say they care about me. I'm old. I know the truth. They just want me out the way.'

The way her teeth ground together made it clear this was a bone of contention in her relationship with her nephews. But while I could see how much she loved the shop, I could also understand that it could be difficult for her nephews, watching their aunt toil away in a job that made her no money, when she could turn it into an up-and-coming enterprise. That had to be frustrating.

'So what happened then? Did you drive home?'

'Drive? No, dear, I don't drive. Don't have a car. Never have.'

Damn it. I knew what Bobby had said, but I'd secretly hoped he'd made a mistake. Obviously, linking the two incidents wasn't going to be that easy.

'So, did one of your nephews take you home instead?'

She crinkled her nose, as if trying to remember.

'No. I walked home. I always walk home from there. It's only ten minutes, and you can see the ocean most of the way.'

'That sounds lovely. So you walked home. You've got a flat above the shop, right?'

'Yes,' she replied, although her voice was distant, as if she were only half listening. 'I think. I must have done. I was in my bed when I woke up the next morning, but, I said this to the police, and I'm not lying. I can't remember! Not any of it!'

'You can't even remember walking home?'

She shook her head. 'I don't think so. No.'

'What about leaving their house? Can you remember that?'

Her nose crinkled again. 'Yes, but it is fuzzy. Like too much hooch. But I did not drink.'

'Flo,' I said, placing my cup down and holding hers in my hands, 'have you been to the Scorched Circle recently?'

I watched as the colour drained from her face, only to rush back again in a hot flush of pink as her pulse simultaneously spiked.

'Me? There?!' A sound somewhere between a growl and a goat's bleat rolled from her throat.

A flicker of nervousness swept through me. Every now and again, I understood why Bobby didn't want me going out and talking to the locals on my own. Because I would do something stupid like this.

'I'm sorry,' I said hurriedly. 'I didn't mean to offend you. I've only recently learned about the Scorched Circle. About that being a place where, perhaps, one might come into contact with demons on the island.'

'There is no, *perhaps*,' Flo said through gritted teeth. 'I know exactly what happens to people who wander into that part of the woods. Saw it myself. I was only sixteen years old. That's why you'll never get me into those woods.'

'You've seen one?' I said, unable to quash the hint of excitement that quivered in my voice.

'Once in a lifetime, and believe me, that was plenty.'

Whatever she had seen, the woman was clearly still shaken by the incident. I could hear it in the erratic rhythm of her pulse, not to mention the shallow unevenness of her breath.

'Flo,' I said, trying to ignore the pang of guilt already hitting me, even though I hadn't asked her the question yet. 'Is there any chance you'd tell me what you saw that night? If you can remember, that is.'

The last part of my comment caused the old woman to let out a snort so loud that Pongo jumped up from where he was sitting.

'Remember? Like I'd ever be able to forget,' she said, only to glance down at the dog, and then the dregs of her drink. 'We're going to need something stronger than this, though. Much stronger.'

THIRTY

I hadn't expected to have my first mango hooch just past midday, with a source I was questioning about a story, but it did give me the opportunity to bring up another line of questioning I'd wanted to go down.

'Do you drink this a lot?' I said. 'Do you know if you would've had it with your roast the other day, for example?'

She shook her head.

'No, no. I love it, but Henrik likes wine. Sometimes beer. But hooch? Not with dinner.'

Well, there went that idea. But that was fine. I was done with questions for the next few minutes. I needed to listen and find out everything she knew about demons. And from the way she was leaning forward on the table, clasping her hands together, it was a story she enjoyed telling.

'Like I said, I was sixteen,' she said. 'Dating a member of the Onyx pack.'

'The Onyx pack,' I said. 'They're the ones that live in Wraith wood, right? With the Lapiz Wolves?'

She shrugged. 'Then it was different. No Peppers Bay. And Ravens Hollow was so small. Just a little town and lots of trees. But not so many wolves either, mind.' She let out a melancholy sigh as she shook her head. 'Development. Nothing you can do about it. It's the same all over the world. Makes me sad. Those wolves who did the hexing? I'm not saying they were right, but I understand. You know?'

I nodded, but stayed quiet on the matter. Of course I understood. Even though my friends had been two of the people who'd been hurt, I knew why Sophia had felt she needed to act. But as a voice for the paper, I had to appear impartial and that included during conversations like this too.

'So, you were in Wraith Woods,' I said, wanted to get her back on track to talk about the demon she had seen. 'Were you there alone?'

'Huh.' She let out a scoff. 'Kimberly Brown was the reason I was there. She was in the year above me. Always a bully. Told me that Alfred, my wolf boyfriend, had been doing a dirty dance behind my back with a mermaid from town. Ach, I know what you're thinking. What mermaid would date a wolf, when they hate water and mermaids hate land? But my parents were different, and they loved each other. So I believed her. Went to the wood to catch them myself. Only I got lost. Ended up somewhere bad.'

'The Scorched Circle?' I said quietly.

'Yes. The Scorched Circle.' Her voice was so low I could have sworn the temperature of the air dropped by at least a couple of degrees.

'And what happened there?' I said, desperate to get to the crux of the story. 'What did you see there?'

She drew in a long breath, building the anticipation to a point that I could feel myself swallowing repeatedly. What the hell had she seen that left her so spooked she struggled to think about it decades later? I leaned in as Flo whispered the word.

'Shadows,' she said, her voice airy and distant.

'Shadows?'

I didn't mean to sound mean, but she'd just told me that she'd gone to a forest late at night and seen shadows. It didn't feel particularly earth shattering.

'These were shadows that moved by themselves,' she said. 'Nothing created 'em. No trees, no branches, and they swept around in that circle, back and forth, like they were talking to one another. And that's not the only thing. They were whispering.'

'Whispering,' I said. Okay, that was definitely starting to get creepier.

'They wanted me to come to them. I know they did. I could feel it. That's what they were saying, but I didn't. I didn't. I ran all the way out of that forest. And I've never been there since.' She paused, picked up her glass of hooch and took a long gulp. 'Believe me, if you're saying that something come out of that well, well, then we need to find it. We need to find it before things a lot worse happens than my shop broken up,' she said.

I tended to agree.

CHAPTER
THIRTY-ONE

I didn't need to get a second glass of hooch with Flo – I wanted to get writing up all the details from the conversation – I could see that the old woman wanted some company. Company that wasn't in the form of her nephews, trying to convince her to sell her beloved business. And given the time she had taken out of her day to talk to me, it felt like the least I could do. Besides, as much as I hated to admit it, the drink was good.

'Do you know Mick, up at the auto shop?' I said, unable to stop work-based questions filtering in the conversation. After all, I was unlikely to get an opportunity like this to talk to her. 'He and his brother are the ones that make it.'

'Is that right?' she said, taking another sip. 'No. I don't. But if you do, thank them for me. This is my favourite tipple. My Fritz always makes sure I've got a steady supply in.'

Fritz again. I didn't want to jump to conclusions, but there were only so many times you could call matters a coincidence.

'If I see him, I will let him know,' I replied, clinking my glass against hers. As I enjoyed yet another sip of the annoyingly tasty hooch, I contemplated whether I should mention Mick being the other possible victim of the demon. I wasn't police, meaning there weren't the same confidentiality issues that Whip and the others had to deal with, and as I had been there when Mick got angry and attacked, I would be perfectly within my rights to raise the comment as a concerned citizen. Witness even. But it didn't feel quite right.

Instead, I was about to probe more about her nephews, and in particular Fritz, when my phone buzzed in my pocket. Bobby's name flashed on the screen.

'Hey, boss,' I said as I picked up. 'Everything okay?'

'All good on my end,' he said. 'I just wanted to check if we were headin' over to the council meeting together or you were going to meet me there.'

'The council meeting—' I glanced at the time on my phone, only to be struck by a surge of panic. Somehow it was already five-thirty? I had been talking to Flo for over two hours. I still needed to get across town for the council meeting at six. And it wasn't like I had Maureen. Which was probably a good thing, considering I'd had a couple of drinks. From what I'd seen, mango hooch bottles didn't come with proof values on the label, for very good reason. And while I didn't feel particularly drunk, the last thing I wanted was for the alcohol to hit when I got behind the wheel. 'I'll see you there,' I said, finishing the conversation with Bobby while standing up.

'I'm ever so sorry, Flo,' I said as I grabbed my bag and hung up the call. 'I completely forgot I'm meant to be somewhere. I'm so sorry. But I'm ever so grateful for you taking the time to talk. It was incredibly useful.'

'You will let me know what happens, yes?' she said. 'If it is a demon, you will tell me when they catch them?'

'You have my word. Come on boy,' I said, grabbing Pongo's leash. 'It's gonna be a fast walk, I'm afraid.'

THE COUNCIL MEETINGS happened at the town hall – a small but stately building that reminded me of a school hall back in the U.K.. And just like my memories of school assemblies, the space had been filled to bursting with plastic chairs. The last time I had come, I'd arrived with plenty of time to spare, and Bobby and I had sat near the front, where we could record what people were saying, just to make sure we didn't misquote anyone. Now though, the place was rammed, people already finding standing places at the back.

I searched the crowd, grateful for Bobby's impressive height, as I spotted him in one corner. An empty place next to him, where he had dangled his press badge on the seat. Gotta love a boss who saves a seat for you.

As I squeezed my way through to get to him, a hand brushed against my waist.

'Hey!' I said, spinning around on the spot, ready to give whoever it was a lesson in keeping their hands to themselves, only to find myself face to face with Alex.

'Sorry,' he blushed. 'I was just... I just wanted to say sorry about last night. I was off with you, and I'm sorry.'

'Oh, right, it's fine.' I replied. Yes, Alex and I needed to talk, but the last thing I wanted to do was to have that conversation here, surrounded by half the town. 'You were at work. Look, I better go. Bobby's got me a seat.'

'Sure, yeah. Me too. Work, that is.' Despite what I had

said, neither of us moved. It was like we were waiting for something to happen. What. I wasn't entirely sure. 'Looks like Bobby's not the only one waiting for you,' he added, motioning to the centre of the hall, where a very familiar pair of eyes were looking straight at us. Whip.

Without another word to Alex, I squeezed my way over to him.

'Everything okay?' he asked. I felt my mouth open, not sure what to say. It wasn't like Alex had said anything bad, and Whip could hardly be jealous of a two second interaction, could he? 'You're later than I thought you'd be. Nothing happened, did it?'

'Oh, no.' A flood of relief washed over me. He wasn't talking about Alex at all. 'Well, yes, but no, not really. Just talking to Flo. That was all.'

'I can see. And looking incredible, as always.'

As a grin flittered onto his lips, I was struck with the sudden urge to push up onto my tiptoes and kiss him, only before I moved, his hand squeezed gently on my shoulder.

'Working professionals, remember?' he said.

What? Oh crap, he was right. I had actually been about to kiss him in public. And while he was wearing his uniform and everything. Though in my defence, he did look damn good in it.

'Sorry,' I said, feeling my cheeks flush with embarrassment. 'I'm not sure what got into me.'

He tipped his head to the side as he observed me quizzically.

'Have you been drinking mango hooch, Ms Evergreen?' he said. 'I'm pretty sure I can smell it on you.'

That wasn't a good sign. Whip's para powers didn't include super senses, although he was standing close to me. I'd have to avoid talking to people for now.

'I just had one,' I said. 'Well, two. But it was for work.'

His eyebrow arched.

'Is that right? How very rebellious of you.'

The way his lips twisted into a smirk made that desire to stretch up and kiss him almost unbearable. And had it not been for the way Pongo tugged on his lead to pull me away, I might have ended up doing exactly that. Thankfully, the yank on my arm brought me back to reality.

'Catch you later?' I asked, flashing him a smile.

'I hope so.'

With my mouth now sealed shut and breathing solely through my nose, I tried to reach my boss. The aisle that should have been free to move through was entirely blocked, and so I decided to try my luck down one of the rows. The first few people shifted in their seats, either standing upon sliding their legs to the side, but some weren't so helpful.

'Excuse me. Sorry, could I... Thank you. Thank you. Sorry. Excuse me...'

I finally reached a complete standstill next to a short gentleman, twisted fully around in his seat so that I was facing his back. I cleared my throat and tried again.

'Excuse me,' I said, using my most polite and professional voice, while hoping all my talking wasn't filling the air with mango hooch fumes. Judging by the way neither of them acknowledged me, I guessed that was the case.

'Excuse me,' I tried again, a little louder. 'Could I get past please?' Still nothing. Even when Pongo offered a short sharp bark, to try to help me out, the man merely tensed a little, then carried on his conversation. There was no way around it. He had to be deliberately ignoring me now. I was sure of it. They were just rude. And I didn't like rude people. Especially not when I'd had a couple of drinks.

'Can you just move out of the damn way?!' Whilst I had intended my voice to come out louder, I hadn't expected it to be quite such a shout.

The man swivelled around in his seat, fixing me with his most narrowed glare.

'You. I know you...' I'd planned on keeping the words in my head. But apparently, the hooch was kicking in. A moment later, I realised why the face was familiar. 'You're one of Flo's nephews.'

There was no mistaking the goatlike features, though whether it was Fritz, or Henrik, I couldn't tell. Either way, he was dressed smartly, and for someone sitting down, did a very good impression or looking down his nose at me.

'Is there a problem?' his voice was narrow. Bleat like.

'I was just hoping you can move so other people could get past?'

Flo's nephew – whichever it was – sniffed a little, before shuffling a miniscule amount in his seat, making barely half a foot of space for me to squeeze through. He was being deliberately difficult. Well, two could play that game.

'Gonna need a little more room than that,' I said. 'Unless you want my boyfriend to see you trying to get uncomfortably close to me. I don't think he'd take kindly to that.'

I cast a glance over to where Whip was standing, watching me in the exact way I suspected, or at least hoped, he'd be doing. The nephew slipped back a little further.

'That's better,' I said, before continuing my way until I finally reached Bobby.

CHAPTER

THIRTY-TWO

Somehow, the walk across the hall had been even more exhausting than the jog from the bar.

'Looked like you were busy making friends there.' Bobby smirked when I slid into the seat he'd saved for me. It wasn't right at the front this time, but it was close enough that we'd be able to hear everything that said.

'I was talking to Florence,' I said, ignoring his comment as I took Pongo's lead and dropped it beneath my chair. 'She had lots of things to tell me.'

'And you needed to drink hooch while you spoke to her, did you?'

Damn it. Both Bobby and Whip had spotted it straight off. Meaning Alex had probably smelt it too. But I wasn't going to think about that. Alex was already judging my relationship choice. He might as well judge me for after-noon drinking, as well.

'Actually, yes. She insisted,' I said.

'Learn anythin' interesting?'

'Actually, I did. She told me—' Before I could finish my reply, my attention was stolen by someone sitting on the front row. Internally, I cursed myself for not spotting the horizontally angled ears before I'd sat down, but it wasn't like she was the only elf here. Not that she was an elf at all. Still, I was even less pleased to see her than I had been to see Alex. Though hopefully, she wasn't going to try to make conversation the way he had. Somewhat unsuccessfully.

'You all right there?' Bobby asked. 'Cat got your tongue?'

'Sorry,' I muttered. 'Kind of wishing I'd had another shot of hooch. I didn't realise she was going to be here.'

'Who?' Bobby asked.

I tilted my head forward and nosed towards my mother.

'You know Amira?'

'Oh, I know Amira.'

'Sound ominous. Wanna talk about it?'

'No. Yes. I dunno,' I replied truthfully. I needed to sober up and focus on the work I was there to do. Thankfully, the thought had barely formed when Mayor Hillary Hilliard and the rest of the council began making their way towards the small stage at the front of the hall. 'I'll explain it to you soon,' I added, making a note that I definitely needed to talk to him about it. Generally speaking, Bobby was great at giving sound advice, and when it came to Amira, that was definitely what I needed.

When the council members had all filled their seats, Mayor Hilliard banged her gavel on the table in front of her.

'Ladies and gentlemen,' her nasal voice cut through the noise of the crowd. 'I would like to call to order today's meeting.'

The conversation began to die down, but rather than continuing to silence, a burst of noise rattled out from the back of the room.

'You have no place here!'

'I've been cast out of the pack, not Ravens Hollow! I have every right to be here! To listen to what they're going to do about—'

'It's Ines,' I said, turning to Bobby. 'Ines is here.'

Here was a loose term. By the sound of it, she hadn't yet got all the way into the building. Still, if I knew Ines, she wasn't going to take kindly to being told where she could and couldn't go.

'You need to leave here,' a male voice growled. 'I'll let you know what the outcome is...'

'Dad, please, don't do this.'

Her dad. The big Alpha of the Amber Wolves was finally gracing us with his presence. I moved to stand up, just so I could get a glimpse of the arsehole who had done this to his daughter, but Bobby grabbed me by the arm.

'This ain't your fight, kid.'

'It's Ines,' I said, my voice pleading. 'She's a member of Ravens Hollow. Part of the community. She should be allowed, shouldn't she?'

'That's not our call,' he said.

The man next to the mayor leaned in and whispered something into her ear. He was the vampire who'd been in the clothes shop, I realised. Which meant he was probably hearing everything being said and was busy relaying it to the mayor, who stood and hammered her gavel. Had I had any sense, that was what I'd do too. Listening in. But there were more voices than Ines and her father. The entire back of the hall was falling into disrepute.

'This meeting will come to order,' she said, 'or it will be adjourned and matters for discussion postponed.'

Raised voices dimmed slightly, but it was far from silent. I, and everyone else, knew exactly what she meant. Postponing the meeting would mean postponing a decision about the hunting grounds. But as much as I wanted to hear the mayor's ruling, I also wanted to make sure Ines was okay. And I wasn't the only one.

'Can you hear?' Bobby whispered to me. 'What's she doing? Is she going to go?'

I listened in. There was no sign of Ines talking, or of her father, though one voice was now making their presence known.

It was a low, gravelly voice. One that I recognised all too well.

'I know this isn't what you want, Ines,' Whip said. 'And it won't be like this forever. But right now, things are just a little raw.'

'A little raw?' she scoffed. 'How do you think they are for me, Whip?'

'I can't imagine. Truthfully, I can't. But coming in here now, getting all riled up, isn't going to make matters any better.'

'Getting riled up?' she said. 'I won't get riled up, as long as the mayor makes the right decision.'

'Please Ines. Trust us on this. You know we're on your side.'

This time it was Alex who spoke, and despite his lack of siren powers, his words seemed to get through to her, as she let out a long sigh.

'You'll let me know?'

'Of course I will,' Whip replied. 'Just stay away for tonight.'

A deep thorn rattled in my heart for Ines. I wasn't sure where she was living, but I was going to make it my goal to seek her out at some point this week. I couldn't be her pack, I already knew that, but I could be her friend. And maybe that would be worth something.

'I think she's going,' I said, holding my breath to see if any other noises came. The vampire next to the mayor nodded, having deduced the same thing.

'Now,' the mayor said, tapping her gavel again, 'As long as there are no more interruptions, the meeting will commence.'

THIRTY-THREE

While several issues that arose in paranormal town meetings that didn't arise in standard one – like reminders that shifters should only return to human states in places of discretion (i.e., don't suddenly transform back to human form buck naked in the middle of the high street), and that any creatures who could produce flames should only do so outside, or in controlled and designated areas. I couldn't help but think of Chloe. Had the Mayor ever seen an emotional fire fae? Telling her when and where she could have set fire to things over these last twenty-four hours would have been on par with telling a vampire to see how they got on with a vegan diet.

But along with para aspects on the agenda there were also a lot of the standard boring parts you'd expect to hear at a typicals town meeting. Sure, it might have been the drinks that lowered my patience, but honestly, I can't imagine there's a world where anyone finds hearing about parking fines, road resurfacing, or budgets for a new skate park interesting. Okay, maybe younger me would have found the skate park parts interesting, but now there were bigger issues to deal with. Bigger issues I wanted to hear about. And I wasn't the only one.

Every time the mayor moved to a new agenda point that wasn't the forest, a series of grumbles would go up around the room. After a while, the general notices had been going on for so long that my eyes were beginning to sag, and more than once, Bobby had to elbow me in the side.

I made a mental note that I needed extra blood to get through these things. Extra blood and maybe less alcohol. Finally, after close to an hour in the very cramped hall, the mayor's demeanour shifted and her pulse stuttered ever so slightly.

'I think she's going to tell us now,' I whispered to Bobby, just as she continued.

'Now, to the main point of us gathering today. Hunting rights in the parklands.'

My eyes were fully open, and it was as if all the effects of the hooch had evaporated. I was back, focussed. Ready to hear the – hopefully good – news. And I wasn't the only one. It sounded as though every heartbeat in the room had upped its pace, although none was going quite as fast as the mayor. Was that a good thing or not? I didn't know.

She waited for the murmurs to die down before she spoke again.

'Having reviewed the information given to us,' she said. 'And after careful discussion with a variety of experts we have decided that we will re-open Forlorning Forest for hunting—'

A cheer went up at the back of the room, so loud that the Pongo let out a loud bark. I on the other hand, looked to Bobby. The Mayor wasn't done speaking, yet.

'Order! Order!' She banged her gavel down in front of her, though it had little to no affect. She looked to the vampire behind her, who promptly stood up, put two fingers between his lips, and let out a high pitch wolf whistle that shot through the room.

'Thank you,' he said, as he sat back down. 'Now, if we could all let the mayor finish.'

Why did I get the feeling that this wasn't going to be quite such good news as everyone thought?

She cleared her throat, as a smile flickered on her lips, though it was gone by the time she started speaking.

'Forlorning Forest will be open for hunting on a rotation, with one wolf pack per full moon allowed to use the land on a schedule set up by—'

The uproar was instantaneous.

'That will make no difference!'

'There'll be nothing left to hunt elsewhere!'

'You want us to starve, that's what you want to do.' I wasn't sure that was fairly accurate. At least not for wolves like Diego. I was fairly sure that the rabbit or two he hunted on a full moon added no caloric sustenance to his diet compared to the endless donuts and banana cake, but I got what they were saying.

'You're deliberately trying to weaken the werewolves. You've been trying since you got that position and we won't have it!'

Now that was interesting. I didn't know anything about how the mayor had come into power or even where her politics lay. But that was something I was definitely going to look into.

'Is that true?' I said to Bobby. 'Does she have a thing against the werewolves?'

'They certainly think she does.'

Now that felt like a story. I needed to get evidence. Substantiate points to explain why the wolves felt that way, and obviously I'd have to give the mayor a chance to respond to them all before I went to print, but maybe there was more here than just the hunting rights story.

I tuned to Bobby to ask if he could give me any examples of things she may have done, only for a shriek to cry out across the hall.

'Watch out!'

An object was hurtling through the air towards the mayor. A bottle of mango hooch. I jumped to my feet at the same time as another half a dozen people did the same, though it was the vampire next to the mayor that caught the bottle with their right hand.

A moment later, all hell broke loose.

THIRTY-FOUR

'Do we stay out of the way, or do we get involved?' I said, turning to Bobby, just in time to see him slipping off his jacket and rolling up his sleeves.

'I guess that's a "get involved" then,' I muttered.

He shot me a look. 'Just make sure they don't get to the Mayor,' he replied. 'Even I don't wanna write that up. No matter how many copies it'd sell.'

Stop the riot reaching the Mayor. I could help with that, couldn't I? Absolutely. Only first there was one other issue I had to deal with.

There, next to my feet, Pongo was letting out low whimpers. I swear, the bigger that dog grew, the more of a scaredy-cat he became. He'd been happy to face off against a mermaid while a basilisk was on the loose when he was tiny. But now? You sneezed too loudly and he was running for cover.

'You're going to be fine, boy,' I said as I tried to work out somewhere I could put him. He was already too big to just sit under a chair and wait it out, and I didn't want to risk moving him anywhere else in the room. It didn't leave many options. Actually, it didn't leave any. 'Just don't move, okay? Stay. Are you listening? Stay. Do not move.'

He might not have had his buttons to press to tell me he understood, but from the way he dropped his head between his paws, I was pretty sure he got it. With Pongo sorted, it was time to do as Bobby said. Stop the chaos from getting to the Mayor.

The various council members on the dais had all taken very different approaches to the fray. While the Mayor had ducked below the table, she was still banging her gavel on the ground like it might contain magical powers. Unfortunately, it was useless against the ball of fire that shot through the air and turned it to ash in her hand.

'No fire indoors!' she shrieked. 'No fire is to be used indoors!' I turned to see where the flames had come from, just in time to see Alex snap a pair of runed cuffs on a woman. Not that having one less magic user in play made much difference.

A group of burly shifters were trying to push their way to the front. Though thankfully, it was so damn packed that it was difficult for anyone to move at all. For the first time since moving to Ravens Hollow, I was reminded of the London Tube during commuter time. It didn't matter how many of you wanted to get off at the station, you could guarantee there'd be one person going the other way, stopping the rest of you going anywhere.

Amidst all the swinging fists and flying objects, there were still a couple of people trying to do the right thing, hands in the air, pleading.

'Please, can we all just discuss this sensibly?'

'We all need to calm down.'

'Deep breaths people. In through the nose, out through the mouth.'

Their voices were lost in the screams, cries, and crashes all around. Shoes were hurled. Phones were flying. Something that looked suspiciously like a mottled ferret launched across the room.

'Meeting's over, folks! Go home! Go home!' It was Whip's voice calling out above the crowd. He wasn't asking. He was telling. Siren power in full force. And yet the ruckus continued.

When a flash of blue soared through the air in front of me, I jumped up and caught it before it could hit anyone, though when I looked into my hand it was with a pleasant sense of surprise; I'd just caught a large plastic takeaway mug. Easily big enough for two standard cappuccinos.

'I think we'll keep that,' I said, dropping it next to Pongo. It was time I switched out all the disposables I was getting from Weirdoughs, anyway. And if someone was foolish enough to throw it, they clearly didn't deserve to keep it. I'd just get Nyrah to check it wasn't hexed or cursed before I took a drink from it.

Amongst the people happy to get involved in the brawl, there were still those trying to make their way to the exit.

'Is there not another door out back people can use to get out?' I asked Bobby, who, by the looks of things, had just knocked out several men and one bear shifter. I was reminded never to get on his bad side.

'Nope,' he said, as his fist flew again.

'Maybe they need to spend the next meeting thinking about fire safety protocols for this room,' I muttered, blocking a random elbow that was swung in my direction.

'Hey! I'm on your side here!' I said, despite having no

idea whose side the person who had tried to hit me was on at all.

It was difficult to tell how many people had actually left, or how many more, who'd been outside during the meeting to lack of room, had managed to get in. As I scoured the space, debating if there was any practical solution to the situation, my eyes fell involuntarily on Amira. Her face was tense, though she remained crouched down tightly, a scared expression on her face. And I suspected I knew why. Fae weren't known for brute strength, nor for crazy speed, reflexes, or reactions. But vampires were. Situations like this were likely much harder to blend into than a casual stroll through a coffee shop. If something flew straight at her, natural instinct would cause her to react, which meant risking exposure. She was next to Fritz, who had also crouched down and was clutching his knees. No wonder he'd called Whip to help with Mick during the fight at the bar. He clearly wasn't about to help himself.

As I thought of Whip, he made his way to the centre of the crowd, still bellowing commands.

'This ends now,' he said. 'We're done. Go home. Go home.'

There was an edge of panic in his voice. Something I'd never heard before. I glanced at Bobby, caught the cyclops's eye, and knew we were thinking the same thing.

Why wasn't it working?

Bobby and I were both warded against Whip's powers. As were a couple of other people, like Alex, Raquel, and Nyrah, the witch who performed all the wards. And there were definitely some people his power was still working on. Including Amira. She and Fritz were now desperately battling to make their way to the front door, as were the council members who had crawled out from beneath the table. But countless bodies, particularly the wolves who had come in from the back of the hall, were ignoring him altogether. I could understand a few people being unresponsive to his particular type of magic. But this many? It didn't feel right.

I watched on, a sense of terror grasping at me.

I had never seen Whip in a fight before. He'd never needed to be. While he was certainly a large man, and God knows with all those muscles, I was sure he could handle himself, he'd never needed to. Normally, his power was enough to de-escalate any situation before it got this far. But now it wasn't. There were too many people not responding to him. And if all those that were suddenly now immune to his powers turned on him... I shuddered. That wasn't something I wanted to think about. He needed something else. Someone else.

Could I help? I wasn't the only vampire in here. Between me, Bobby, and a couple of others, maybe we could bring this to an end slightly more quickly if we got our hands a little dirtier. Yet before I could even try to get my suggestion out to him, Whip's voice rose again.

'Alex!' he yelled. 'End this!'

Alex? How was Alex going to end this? Surely he would be at just as much a risk as Whip. A moment later, the blond-haired police officer was pushing his way to the front of the hall, unbuttoning his shirt as he went. And with a mixture of fear and excitement, I knew exactly what Whip meant for him to do.

THIRTY-FIVE

One thing's for sure certain. Lions get people moving. Fast. Especially lions that looked like that: fully grown, wild mane, and teeth bared. He launched himself from the dais.

All the anger that had been directed towards the council was suddenly transformed into undiluted fear. People bolted for the door, leaving everything from coats, bags, and even one rather miffed looking elderly grandmother in a mink stole in order to make a swift exit.

'They can't really think he's going to hurt them, can they?' I said to Bobby as several grown adults cried out as they bundled to the side of the room. Unfortunately for me, I timed my question at almost exactly the same moment as Alex let out a roar so primal and deafening that it rattled the light fittings and caused an unexpected loosening around my bowel.

Okay, I understood why people were scared. Common sense struggled to play a part when the primal part of your body took over. Though, while the hysteria continued around us, Pongo crawled out from the mess of chairs and nuzzled against my knee.

'Right. You're afraid of fighting, but not of the big scary lion?' I said, picking him up and allowing him a quick lick of my face before I put him back down. In his defence, he had seen Alex in this form once before. And it was an impressive form. The pure muscles. The obvious strength. It was easy to see how the blond police officer transformed into such an imposing creature, and the more I saw of him in this state, the more in awe I was.

Sure, it was still chaos, but it was chaos in the right direction. Everyone trying to get out of the hall.

Not wanting to get caught in the stampede, or make it even worse, Bobby, Pongo, and I slipped further in, making way for all those who wanted to get out. Which, unsurprisingly, was everyone. It took only a few minutes before the only people who were left in the hall were those who were in no fit state to move. Including several who seemed to have met my editor-in-chief's fist.

'Think we're good now, Buddy,' Whip said to Alex, throwing the lion a pair of boxers that he caught in his mouth. With a dip of his chin, Alex turned around and sauntered over to the corner of the room, my eyes following him every step. Would it be very, very wrong of me to watch my friend turn back into human form, knowing he would be, for a moment at least, stark naked?

Yes, yes, of course it would. I shook my head, hoping it was the after-effects of the hooch that were making me have those thoughts. Alex was my friend. Not to mention my equally attractive boyfriend was still in the room with me. As was my boss. Although considering the mayor had brought up issues with shifters changing in public spaces only an hour ago, he would have to shoulder part of the blame if people did sneak a quick peek.

'Hey,' Whip strode towards me from the back of hall, where I suspect he'd been stopping people trampling over one another. 'Looks like we'll have to take a raincheck on dinner tonight.'

'It's fine,' I said, locking my eyes on his and hoping he hadn't noticed the way I'd been watching Alex. Then again, he'd said it himself; seeing Alex in his lion form never became less remarkable. 'Is there anything I can do to help?'

He shook his head. 'Called Raquel. She's outside now, moving everyone on. We'll get a cleaning crew in to sort this out. You just get home. Safely.' he shifted his attention to Bobby. 'You okay to get her back? I'm gonna be locked in meetings with the mayor all night.'

A frisson of annoyance fluttered through me. He might not have seen, but I did a perfectly good job of holding my own, stopping flying objects and deflecting punches, all whilst making sure I didn't hurt anyone else. Then again, he'd had bigger things to worry about, and his fears when it came to me weren't unfounded.

'Got my truck,' Bobby said, looking at me as he spoke. 'Wanna lift?'

'Sounds good.'

As I went back to grab my bag and newly acquired drinks cup, Alex had just begun buttoning up his shirt, meaning his entire bare chest was still exposed. His eyes met mine, and I was struck with a sudden urge to say something. And not just so it didn't look like I was staring.

'Good job tonight. You know, with the lioning.'

'The lioning?' he smirked, still working on the unfeasible number of buttons. 'Good on yourself. And nice catch with that, by the way.' He nodded to the blue drinks cup.

'You saw?'

'Maybe,' he said, before he reached down and picked up his jacket. The conversation was over, but we'd had a conversation. Sort of. That was progress.

THIRTY-SIX

'How often do people leave these things with broken bones?' I said to Bobby as we headed out toward his truck. Diego had been standing by the doorway waiting for us, having attended both as a member of The Oracle and a wolf. Apparently, he'd taken photos of the record attendance at the start of the evening, and then tried to get a few of the fight in too, before he became an active participant.

'You okay?' I asked. 'From a wolf point of view?'

He drew in a long breath, which he let out as a sigh. 'It's not gonna be easy. But we'll work through it. Probably be late in tomorrow though, boss,' he added to Bobby. 'Need to help Carlotta patch up some of the pack.'

'No worries.' Bobby replied, placing a hand on his shoulder. 'Take all the time you need.'

While Diego was the beta for the Lapiz pack, his wife Carlotta was Alpha and so the pair had more than a little responsibility between them. He liked to play the office clown, and more than once he'd joked that being hexed was the only time he'd got some proper rest in years, but I wasn't sure how much of a joke that was.

As Diego headed off, we climbed into Bobby's truck. Even with all the questions rolling around in my head, I waited until he had started the engine, put on the music, and was a good thirty feet away before I started speaking. After all, I was far from the only one on the island with supernatural hearing.

'So how often do people leave those meetings with broken bones?' I asked. It might have sounded like a perfectly innocuous question, but Bobby knew exactly what I was asking. Just as I'd known he would.

'I know what you're thinkin', but you'd be hard pressed to prove there was anythin' demonic at play there,' he said. ''cept maybe good old-fashioned greed, if you was lookin' too closely at that council.'

'You don't think it's funny Whip's powers suddenly stopped working?'

'Bit of an exaggeration. He still got half o' them out of there.'

'And is fifty percent a normal average for how many people his abilities work on?'

'No,' he muttered. 'It ain't.' He let out a sound somewhere between a groan and a sigh. 'Look, I spoke to Raquel before the meetin'. Said Mick's up and talking.'

'And...?'

He groaned again. 'Looks like he's struggling to remember what happened before he showed up at the bar.'

'Struggling to remember, or can't remember?' I questioned, feeling that journalist scoop taking hold. 'Because the two are very different. He might've been struggling because he was drunk. Or it might've been some sort of demon that stopped him from remembering at all.'

'Look, maybe I was wrong in ruling it out altogether, but that still doesn't change how we ain't going anywhere near the Scorched Circle. If this is demons, you need someone who can actually deal with that kind of business. Not reporters poking their noses in.'

'And are there?' I asked. 'Are there people who deal with them? People who live in Raven's Hollow?'

'Not sure. Maybe. But the police will be looking for it. I ain't saying you can't write this up when we're sure. Go to town. But not if it's gonna put you in danger.'

'Sometimes I don't know who's worse. You or Whip.'

I hadn't expected the words to come out quite as harshly as they did, but from the silence that swept through the car, I'd obviously made Bobby feel awkward. And that wasn't an easy thing to do.

'How 'bout we talk about something different,' my boss said, as he took a turn opposite the station, towards my house. 'Like what's goin' on with you and that old elf, for instance? Didn't even know you knew her.'

Of all the subjects I hadn't wanted Bobby to shift to, that was one that was right at the top of the list. I bit down on my bottom lip.

More than once, I'd thought Bobby's perspective on things could help. He was a parent, after all.

'She's my mum,' I said after a pause.

'Your what?!'

'Amira is my mother, who abandoned us on a holiday twenty years ago.'

He blinked several times, as if he wasn't quite understanding what I was saying.

'Amira's an elf,' he said slowly.

I couldn't help but laugh. 'No, Amira *looks* like an elf,' I said, 'because for the last, oh I don't know, fifteen plus years, Nyrah's been warding her to look like an elf. But that's because she didn't want to be found by the people who turned her.'

'Turn her. You mean...' He gasped. Seemingly unable to get the rest of his sentence out.

'An illegally sired vampire. And I don't have any evidence yet, but I've got a suspicion that she was the starting point for The Guardians. A test subject, even, so they saw if it was possible to get new vamps in under radar.'

'Jeez.' He stretched the single vowel sound for an unfeasibly long time. 'How long've you known?'

'Since last Friday. When Alex and I went to speak to the sireless he found.'

Bobby nodded, as if the movement was helping him put the pieces together one by one. 'So he knows? That why stuff's weird with y'all, or's that some messy triangle thing I don't want to know about?'

'Triangle thing?' I had to laugh. 'No, there's no triangle thing,' I added, although I couldn't help but think of the way Alex and Whip were, now that Whip and I had got together. To use Bobby's words, there was definitely something messy happening, but that wasn't something I was going to go into. Certainly not with Bobby.

'From a story point of view, this thing with Amira could help break the whole thing with The Guardian's wide open,' I said instead, trying to move as far away from the emotional aspect of things as I could. 'Yet she says she doesn't know the name of the vampire that sired her.'

'And you think she's lying?' He asked.

I shrugged.

'I don't know. If she is, and I find out, she's got to know it ruins any chance of us having a relationship.'

Bobby let out a low whistle.

'That's a delicate line there, Elodie. Just be careful, okay? I know you want your stories, but you put yourself first, okay?'

'I will. Don't worry.' The problem was, I didn't know what that meant. Was putting myself first by prioritising a relationship with a mother who had abandoned me, or the career I'd worked my arse off for. Had you asked me six months ago, I would have known exactly what answer I'd have given. But now, after seeing her, speaking to her, it wasn't quite so easy.

'I'll write up the piece on tonight's meeting in the morning, if that's alright?' I said, refocussing on things in the present that actually needed addressing.

'Sounds good.'

'And don't worry, I'll use lines like enthusiastically assertive, rather than needlessly violent.' Raven's Hollow residents were unlikely to take too kindly to the paper describing them as mindless thugs. Even if that was how several of them had acted.

'That's why you're damn good at this job.' Bobby grinned back at me. 'You take care of yourself, kid. It's one long life you've got now. Plenty of years for regrets. Trust me.'

'Thank you,' I said, before calling into the back of the car. 'Come on boy, it's time I got you some food. It's been a long day.'

THIRTY-SEVEN

Maybe it was because I'd spent the night before flicking through the book of paranormal creatures, maybe it was the fact that I'd spent the weekend staying up late each night, talking to Whip or perhaps it was the mango hooch, but my body was heavy with a need for sleep. So, in an unusual state of laziness, I didn't even bother taking my makeup off before crawling under the duvet.

'Hey, one pillow only. That's the rule,' I said, pushing Pongo over onto his side. How the heck normal humans dealt with having Leonbergers was a mystery to me. I sometimes felt I was using vamp strength getting him to share the duvet as I had been fighting two werewolves. And he was a long way from fully grown.

Still, it was only lying there, next to his oversized furry paws on the comfort of my own mattress that made me realise how much I had missed our evening cuddles these last four days. I didn't begrudge him choosing to cuddle Chloe, given she'd needed a little TLC, but Whip and I were going to have to come to a better sleeping arrangement than me sneaking out onto his sofa to be with Pongo every time I stayed at his. And as for staying here... I wasn't sure how much longer there'd be room for three of us on this mattress. But love me, love my dog. That was the deal.

When I woke up the next morning, I was surprised to find there was room to stretch out. It was hardly the first time Pongo had woken up before me, yet normally he reappeared as soon as he heard I was up. Either to ask for food, or to be let out, or just to give me a slobbery morning-breath lick. This time, though, I was all the way downstairs, and he'd still not come to greet me. When I reached the kitchen, I discovered why.

'What have you done?'

I stood in the doorway, staring at the sight. The white tiles of my floor were obscured by hundreds and thousands of small brown pieces of kibble.

'Pongo!' It wasn't just a case of them being on the floor. They were under the counters, inside the drawers, even in the dishwasher. If I hadn't known better, I would've thought Pongo had thrown the dog equivalent of a foam party in the kitchen. Only, unlike foam, the kibble hadn't simply dissolved or disintegrated. No, it was absolutely everywhere.

In all the chaos, it took me a couple of moments longer to find the culprit. Having fled the scene of the crime, he was huddled in the corner of the living room.

'Pongo...' I used my sternest voice possible. 'Have you seen what you've done? Have you seen the mess you've made?'

I waited for him to skulk over to me, and hit his Sorry button, the way he normally did when he'd done something he shouldn't have done, which included, but was not limited to, chasing after chipmunks, using the laundry basket to relieve himself when it was wet outside, and stealing food from the kitchenette when the rest of the office were in a team meeting. Yet rather than crawling over to me, or even reaching for his buttons, he remained exactly where he was. Head down between his paws.

'Pongo?' The anger shifted from my voice as I took another step closer to him. The saddest sounding whine I had ever heard rose from his lips. 'Can you get up? Can you move?'

He tipped his head to the side slightly, causing my stomach to tighten. This wasn't the normal way he responded when he was feeling guilty about something, like chewing through a light cord. He looked genuinely ill.

'How much did you eat?' I asked. This time, his whimper was even louder. 'Stay there, boy.'

I skidded across the room, grabbed the buttons, and placed them down in front of me.

'How are you feeling? Do you feel poorly?'

He gingerly lifted his paw, then placed it delicately on the first button: *Pongo*...He lifted it again, then hit the next one. *Sad*.

'Yeah, Pongo, sad. I get it.'

I looked back at the mess. It was impossible to know how much he'd eaten. It was a thirty-pound bag, and I'd only bought it a couple of days ago. The way it was all spread out, it was impossible to tell how much was left. Could dogs make themselves properly ill by eating too much? Did I need to get him to the vets? Was there even a vet in Ravens Hollow?

I had always assumed that, if I ever got my dream of

owning a dog, I would be the most sensible dog owner possible. And in so many ways, I was. He was always walked properly. Fed properly. And was now trained to follow a whole heap of commands, or at least I thought he was. But other than the first night when I'd found him, when he'd been covered in dirt and desperate for a good feed, he'd never needed taking to a vet. And of course, I was planning on getting him chipped, only I hadn't got around to it.

I was a hundred percent sure that Pongo had been dumped because people who had left him outside, coated in dirt and angry at the art's festival, had wanted rid of him. But there was still a small part of me that worried if I went to the vets, to get him chipped and registered to me, I might find out that wasn't possible. That just maybe, there was someone out there who wanted him. Someone else, who, legally anyway, had far more claim to him than I did. And that wasn't something I could cope with. And so I had just kept putting it off. Now, I realised, that had been a stupid thing to do.

As Pongo let out another whine, I grabbed my phone, hoping that a quick internet search would tell me what to do, only to stop. The last thing I wanted to do was send myself into a spiral of medical jargon I didn't understand. Heartbeat or not, I could feel the palpitations in my chest, nausea wafting through me. I needed someone to help. Someone to tell me what I should do.

My first instinct was to call Whip. But as my thumb hovered above his name, I hesitated. He'd said he'd be in meetings all night after the events with the town council. The last thing he was going to want, after spending all night with Mayor Hillard and the council, was me being a nervous wreck over my dog that I wasn't yet a hundred percent sure he even liked.

So who did I call? Chloe? No. I dismissed that idea immediately. Finding out something could be wrong with Pongo was likely to push her over the edge. It was the last thing she needed. So who did that leave? Who could I ring that wouldn't find me, and my Pongo-related drama, hysterical? One name sprang to mind. One who I knew was the best option, yet still I tried to think of alternatives. Bobby would come and help me. He loved Pongo. But he had a family. And other responsibilities, like a paper to run. And with the news the wolves had just got, it wasn't fair of me to ask Diego.

Half wishing there was another option, I scrolled back up to the top of my contact list and hit the name at the very top.

THE KNOCK at my door came less than ten minutes later.

'How's he doing?'

'Still not moved,' I said, leading Alex into the living room, where Pongo was still curled up in the same corner he'd been in since I arrived. When he saw Alex, his tail gave one small wag before dropping back down.

'I've rung a buddy of mine. A vet. They'll be here in about ten minutes.'

'Thank you. Thank you. And I'm sorry for calling you, it's just... I knew Whip had the council things, and with everything—'

'You never need to apologise for calling me, Evergreen.' His hand hovered by my arm, like he was about to comfort me that way, only to change his mind. 'It's fine. Honestly, it's fine.'

He glanced through to the kitchen and the blanket of kibble I hadn't even thought about cleaning up.

'How are you doing? You had breakfast? Anything to drink?'

I shook my head. 'Not yet.' I'd spent the entire time waiting for him to show up sitting next to Pongo. Trying to get him to sit up. Even offering him free rein of the sofa to jump on. But the furthest he'd got was to lift his head, then flop back down.

'You got blood bags in the fridge? Why don't you grab something, then go sit with Pongo while I clean up in here.'

I went to reply, only to find a lump in my throat and heat prickling behind my eyes. No matter what was going on, Pongo had been the one constant in my life since the move, and if something happened to him because I hadn't thought to check his food bag was sealed properly... I couldn't bear to think about it.

'Hey.' This time, Alex didn't hesitate. He pulled me into his chest and held me there. 'He's going to be alright. I promise.'

It wasn't a promise he could keep. I knew that. And yet, his heartbeat was strong and steady. He believed what he was saying. That would have to be enough for now.

His hand moved to the top of my head, stroking down my hair. Was this the first time Alex had ever hugged me like this? I couldn't remember another time he'd held me so close, but it felt so unbelievably normal. Comforting. Easy. It was everything I needed, and in that moment, I couldn't help but wonder why I had been worried about calling him. Then I remembered. Whip. Whip and his jealousy over this friendship.

I shifted away from him, wiping my eyes as I sniffed away the tears that had escaped down my cheeks.

'Thank you. Thank you for being here.'

As his eyes met mine, the slightest smile glinted within them. 'That's what friends are for, Evergreen. Now, let's get this mess sorted before the vet arrives.'

THIRTY-EIGHT

While I did have blood in the house, it wasn't in the fridge. Having discovered Weirdoughs after a few days living in Ravens Hollow, I had happily given up drinking the raw stuff in favour of my caffeinated, coffee-flavoured shots, and had taken the blood Chloe had generously stocked the fridge with prior to my arrival, decanted it into ice cube trays and frozen it. My idea had been that, if the situation called for it, I could make my own Weirdoughs equivalent with my home coffee maker and a couple of defrosted cubes. This was my first time testing that theory.

'How is it?' Alex asked, watching me crinkle up my nose as I took my first sip.

'Bearable,' I replied.

'Good. Now get out of the kitchen and keep an eye on that dog of yours. I need to clean this all up.'

I didn't need telling twice. While Alex began sweeping up the mess, I took a seat next to Pongo and ran my hand over his head.

'Why did you do this?' I said. 'You should've just asked

me for more food if that's what you wanted.' Another whimper followed, without even an attempt to hit one of his buttons. 'It's okay. Alex's friend's a vet. He's coming now, okay? Any minute. He'll make you better, okay?'

By the time I'd finished my drink, Pongo had shuffled forward enough that he could rest his head on my lap, and was fast asleep. I was debating whether I should get up and see if Alex needed help when there was a knock at the door.

'I'll get it,' Alex called from the kitchen, before making his way into the hallway.

As the front door clicked open, I had no intention of deliberately listening in. That was until I heard Alex speak.

'Thank you so much for this. I owe you.'

'You do. Dinner. Wine. The whole hog. It's been one heck of a night.'

For no particular reason, other than the use of the term 'buddy,' I had assumed Alex's vet friend was a man, yet the person speaking was a woman. She sounded a similar age to me, if not younger.

'Name your place,' he said. 'Patient's through here.'

Before I knew what was happening, Alex was in the living room with quite possibly the most beautiful woman I had ever seen. Her hair was a coppery auburn, and her eyes the palest of blues. There was no chance she was a typical, not the way she looked. But what she was, I couldn't guess. She was dressed in a pair of Daisy Dukes and a plain white top, and could have stepped straight off a runway.

I, on the other hand, had unbrushed hair and teeth, yesterday's makeup smudged on my cheeks, and was wearing a pair of creased cotton pyjamas that had a variety of unidentifiable stains on them, not to mention a fair amount of dog drool.

'So here's the boy that's causing all the worry,' the vet

said, crouching on the ground next to us. 'What's happened to you, then? Woke up feeling poorly, did you?'

'Um, not exactly,' I said. 'He got into the bag of kibble.'

'Oh...' Her lips pursed as she ran her hand down his back, then switched to rubbing his belly. 'Well, that's never a good thing to do. Leonberger, right?'

'I think so. I'm not exactly sure. He was a stray. Well, dumped.' My nerves tightened as I contemplated how much I wanted to tell her about me picking up a random dog and claiming them as my own. Was that something I should have done? Then again, I could hardly leave out details if I expected her to help me. 'I found him as a pup a couple of months ago, at the art festival. I've been meaning to get him chipped, but... well... I just haven't got around to it.'

Her face hardened, and for a second I thought the aggression was going to be directed at me. 'Dumped? God dammit. Bet it was one of the damn Ansell twins.'

'The Ansell twins?' I was getting more familiar with the well-known names in Ravens Hollow, but that wasn't one I'd heard of. Still, it felt as though a weight had shifted off my shoulders when I realised she wasn't going to give me a lecture, or worse still, say that she was going to take Pongo away from me.

'Snake shifters. Got a couple of barns out on the outskirts of town. Call themselves farmers, but not the type of farmers you want. Got shut down for running a puppy mill about six months ago. Bet this one slipped through the net.'

'A puppy mill?' I considered the implications of what she was saying. 'You mean they might still have Pongo's mum?'

My chest throbbed. I had been so concerned with Pongo

that night, I hadn't even thought about his mum. But if she was still out there, living in the same conditions I'd found him... it was too much to bear thinking about. I would have to find her. I needed to.

'One issue at a time, Evergreen,' Alex said. 'Let's get the little guy sorted first. Then you can go chasing down another vendetta.'

He flashed me a smile, but my attention was stolen by the vet, whose perfectly proportioned face was currently sporting a single, infuriatingly sympathetic frown line.

'So you're Elodie Evergreen,' she said. 'No wonder Alex was so insistent I came. He talks about you non-stop.'

'He does?' I questioned, my previous nerves shifting to a different, more butterfly orientated type. 'Sorry, what's your name?'

'Of course he wouldn't mention me. I mean, bringing up your ex is hardly a good way to win over the girl you're trying to woo.'

'You're Alex's ex?' I felt my jaw hang open. Alex had called his ex to come and help me.

'I wasn't trying to woo Elodie, thanks Jenna,' Alex interjected, his cheeks taking on a decidedly pink hue. 'She has a boyfriend. She's seeing Whip.'

'You do?' Jenna looked at me in surprise. 'Whip... wow. Okay. Well, he sure is pretty to look at, and I bet he's not half as snarky as this one either. Poor Ally, though. That must've been a blow to your ego.'

It was a lot to take in. Not that Alex had an ex. Of course he did. And why wouldn't she be the most attractive woman I'd ever seen in my life? He was one of the most good-looking guys. But the friendship between them. The way he'd been able to call upon her to help me. And the way she was ribbing him now. Not to mention they'd said about having dinner together. Did that mean they were looking at rekindling the relationship? But then he had told her about me. Or had they really just ended things is such a healthy mature manner that they could still consider each other friends? That felt even more unlikely than living in a world with lion shifters and killer basilisk.

'The dog, Jenna.' Alex said, offering her a withering look. 'You're meant to be looking at the dog.'

'Sure, right.' After flashing him the slightest grin, Jenna turned her attention to Pongo.

'I'm guessing you don't know exactly how much he ate?' She said.

I shook my head. 'The bag was pretty full, but it was spilled all over the place.'

'But it's just kibble?'

I nodded.

'What about vomiting? Any uncontrolled sickness?'

'Not since I've been up with him.'

'There was a mess in the kitchen, but I cleaned all that up.'

My eyes sprang up to look at Alex.

'You did?'

'Yeah, no biggy. Just dog sick.' I wouldn't have thought it possible, but my gratitude for him flicked up yet another notch.

'So he's been sick, but nothing crazy. And he's mostly been lying down like this? Like he's comfortable? He's not been squirming around, looking like he's in pain?'

I shook my head. 'No. I mean, he told me he was sad, but that's it.'

'He told you?'

I gestured to the buttons on the ground. 'But he often uses sad when he's done something wrong. I'd not thought to get one for hurting. I guess I'll need to move onto that next.'

Her smile quirked. 'Impressive. Well, by the feel of his stomach, he's just bloated, but he's been lucky. Eating too much can cause some real issues, but I think he's avoided the worst of it. Still, I'm happy to take him to the surgery and keep him for the day if you want? Do an x-ray just to make sure he's not caused himself any serious damage.'

'You'd do that?'

'Of course. Though I warn you, things are a little chaotic there at the minute. Cliff, the kid whose been training with me for the last six months, decided it would be fun to let all the animals I'd got in overnight for observation loose.'

'What?'

Alex and my reactions were simultaneous and near enough identical.

'Yup. Birds, cats, hamster, a damn iguana. You name it, they were all running loose. Took me over an hour just to get them back in cages. Then I had to check they were in the right ones, meds and all that. Gonna have a pissed-off owner later today when she sees her rabbit that came in to get fixed has got four stitches on his ear.'

'Why would he do that?' I asked. Feeling even more grateful that Jenna had come out to see him. 'Was it some kind of protest?'

'No idea. I don't think so. He's the type of guy who loves animals more than people most of the time. Wants to rehabilitate injured mammals back to the wild, and he's been a great worker.'

'And you're sure it was him?' Alex asked.

She nodded, and weariness rolled off her. 'Yeah, CCTV and he used his card to login to the building. I rang him up this morning, told him not to come in, obviously, and he sounded completely confused. Like he had no idea what he'd done. Said he was in bed all night.'

For the first time since I'd woken up, my attention shifted away from Pongo – who was now edging towards Alex with his nose twitching like he was hoping for a treat – and on what Jenna had told me.

'You're saying he acted completely out of character, did something reckless and potentially dangerous, and he has no recollection of it?'

'Pretty much.'

I glanced at Alex.

'Why do I have a feeling I already know where you're going with this?'

THIRTY-NINE

There was no doubt that Jenna's compassion extended beyond the animals that she treated. She was clearly a good boss too, and the guilt she felt over giving us Cliff's details was clear by the amount of time it took to persuade her.

'You should have called the police straight away,' Alex started, as she began telling us about confronting Cliff that morning. 'What he did was criminal damage. Not to mention reckless endangerment for those creatures.'

'I know. I know, but his life's already been derailed by this. And he's a good lad. I didn't want to cause him any more trouble. He won't be able to finish his training now that he's not with me, and there's nowhere else he can do it in Raven's Hollow. And he won't leave here. Not with all the animals he's already adopted. Losing the chance to follow his dream felt like punishment enough. I swear. If I hadn't spoken to him myself, I would have sworn someone had tampered with the videos.'

'So what happened when you spoke to him?' I said, grateful that my journalistic head was helping to keep me distracted from thinking about Pongo, who was now awake and listening, but still lying on the floor. 'How did you know it wasn't a glamour?'

'He was wearing the same clothes as in the video and had pink feathers all over it. And one of the birds we've got in for observation is—'

'A flamingo?' I suggested

'A rose breasted cockatoo,' she corrected.

Alex snorted a laugh that I skilfully ignored. Though had I thought about it properly, a flamingo didn't feel like the type of bird you'd keep in an indoor cage at a vets.

'Gallah, the cockatoo, she's pretty fiery, and she's started pulling out her feathers. I think it's some kind of stress thing. That's why she's with us. I'm the only one who's meant to deal with her. And Cliff knows that. Cliff knew exactly what animals he should and shouldn't handle. And he sure as heck knew better than to let them out of their cages. I just don't understand what he was thinking.'

'I don't think he was thinking,' I replied. I could feel Alex's eyes boring in. Whether he was trying to tell me to keep my ideas to myself or that I could trust Jenna, I wasn't sure, but I didn't look at him, just in case it was the former. 'There've been a couple of incidents over the last few days, people acting out of character and having no memory of it. Maybe if Cliff can remember anything from before he let the animals out, it might help us get to the bottom of it. And... it might mean he's allowed to carry on with his training, even if you don't want to be the one to train him any longer.'

Jenna's lips pursed slightly as she looked from me to Alex, then back again.

'Okay,' she said after a pause. 'Just be gentle with him, okay? I was pretty harsh with him earlier.'

'I DON'T WANNA TALK. Can't y'all just let me be?'

Cliff was a young man, in his early twenties with a tattoo stretching up the side of his neck; a collage of different animals. Big cats, insects, fish. Jenna wasn't joking when she said he was an extreme animal lover.

'I'll just take five minutes of your time,' I said. 'And trust me. You'd much rather talk to me than to him.'

I nodded to where Alex's truck was parked behind me. Alex had insisted on coming with me, and given that I wasn't sure how to reach Cliff's and the Pongo incident meant I wasn't a hundred percent on my game, I'd agreed. Still, I'd asked him not to follow me in with the hope of coming across as a gentle journalist, seeking the truth, as opposed to the big bad cop who wanted to throw him behind bars. 'You know that Jenna's within her rights to press charges,' I continued. 'The owners too, if what happened got out.'

It wasn't the kindest tactic, and I felt more than a little guilty when the fear flashed across Cliff's face, but I quashed that guilt with the knowledge that I was actually trying to help him. If I could prove that this was a demon possession, then maybe Jenna wouldn't have to sack him at all. Not that I was going to tell him that.

'I don't understand what happened,' he snivelled, wiping his nose.

Despite assuring him we'd be fine to discuss matters outside, once Cliff agreed to talk to me, he insisted I come in to his house. If you could call it a house. Sure, it looked like one from the outside, but inside? It was what I imagined it had looked like when a hurricane hit a zoo decades ago, and they'd had to put all the rescued animals in whatever shelter they could find. And this was what happened when one person volunteered to have way more animals than they should.

As he moved a quail with a neck cone off the sofa, I counted six domestic cats, three lizards, a bobcat and what appeared to be a condor perched on the banisters. Two dogs had claimed an armchair, while the dining table housed over half a dozen cages, one of which definitely held chinchillas but as for the others, I had no idea. A large python had made its home lying across the mantelpiece and there appeared to be a nest in his light fitting. And the chaos wasn't limited to this room. There were several bangs and growls from upstairs that sounded remarkably like a bear.

'From what Jenna said, you have no recollection of letting all the animals out last night.' He may have cleared the quail off the sofa, but the gifts the bird left behind remained, and so I opted to keep standing. 'What do you remember?

Great, bulbous tears were rolling down his cheeks as he snorted in another breath. I probably should have checked with Jenna exactly what Cliff was before striding in here. His stockiness reminded me of a troll, not that I'd actually met one in real life. I was once again grateful that Alex had insisted on coming with me. He was probably listening in, making sure I didn't get into too much trouble. But at least he had the confidence in me to let me do my job without hovering over me. I appreciated that.

'I don't remember any of it,' he said. 'I know Jenna

thinks I lied, but I swear, the last thing I remember was having a hooch at Betty's.'

'Betty's. Fritz's bar?'

'Right. Was gonna head to the council meeting, you know? Was hoping they'd make the right decision, keep those wolves and shifters out of the forest. Mayor needs some people on her side.'

'You're against them increasing the hunting areas?'

'Too right, I'm against it. Bad enough how big town's got now. And it's not like any of them need to hunt. It's fun for them. This island don't belong to us. If I had my way, I'd make the whole damn island a nature reserve.'

Other than the mayor, Cliff was the only person I'd met who didn't think opening up the hunting areas was a good idea. And had it been another time, I would have loved to get his opinion on it for the paper. Not to mention myself. I knew Ines had done extensive research into the ecosystems on the island and the harm that the current regulations were causing, but it didn't hurt to hear other people's opinions. Still, I had a bigger story to cover right now.

'Betty's, that's the last thing you remember?'

'That's what I said, weren't it?'

'Sorry, yes.' He might have said he was willing to talk, but clearly this wouldn't be the type of situation where he suddenly relaxed, opened up, and let every little detail spill from his lips. Instead, I suspected he was quickly going to get aggravated with my presence. Which meant working fast. 'What about who you were with? Was anyone there with you? And how about serving behind the bar?'

The young man pinched the bride of his nose. 'Fritz was there. Yeah, but he went off to the council meeting before me, I think. Meeting a buddy maybe. I dunno.'

'But what about you? Were you with anyone?'

'I don't remember, okay! Don't you get that? I don't remember. I had a bad day. Marvin didn't make it, and I needed a drink.'

'Marvin?'

He gulped in a long breath. 'Bobcat. Hit by a car by some bastard. I needed a drink, and that's all I remember. That's it. Okay. Are we done? I can't help you. Maybe I just drank too much. I dunno.'

A loud squeal came from upstairs, followed by two loud squawks. Cliff marched towards the staircase.

'You need to go,' he said, though as he started to climb the bottom step, he stopped and turned to look at me. 'If you see Jenna, tell her I'm sorry. I really am.'

'She knows,' I said. 'I promise she knows.'

Alex was still sitting in the truck when I reappeared out of Cliff's house. I had no doubt had it been Whip with me, he would have appeared by my side the second Cliff raised his voice. But then Alex had seen me battle werewolves. That was bound to have given him more confidence in my ability. So maybe that was what I needed Whip to do; see me get myself out of danger. Maybe then he'd relax a bit. But then it was unlikely I'd ever get into any trouble with him around.

'So, what are you thinking?' Alex said, as we drive toward town. 'Still on the demon idea?'

'Yeah, and I think it's linked to Fritz.'

Alex turned his head from the road to look at me and frown. 'Fritz? The guy's a goat shifter.'

'And?'

'I don't mean to be funny, but us shifters aren't exactly known for any other sorts of magic, and if they are, well, they tend to be stronger types than, well... goats.'

'You mean like you.'

He let out a laugh. A warm rumble that filled me from

the inside. 'Oh no, I'm very ordinary. Lion, human, and nothing else. Sure, I'm the only lion shifter on the island, but I'm just grateful none of my brothers are here. I'd lose all my kudos if they found out I'm basically the runt of the family.'

I couldn't help but laugh. 'I don't believe that for a second.'

'Which is why none of them are ever invited here.'

He looked at me with a glint in his eye, and an involuntary smile spread to my lips. Things may have only been awkward between us for a couple of days, but only now we were back to being us did I realise how much I'd missed it.

'I'll send you Jenna's number, so you can check on Pongo,' he said, breaking the sudden silence. 'Though I suspect she did the x-ray as soon as she got to the surgery. She'd have already rung if anything was wrong.'

'She's lovely,' I said, already feeling the next questions burning on my lips. I wasn't sure how much I should pry, but then again, if we were friends, there was no harm in doing a little digging, was there? 'So how come you split up? Was it recent?'

A deep throat chuckle rattled in his throat. 'No, not recent. 'bout a year ago.'

'Did something happen?'

'You mean, did I break her heart, or did she break mine?' He flashed me another grin. 'Nah, not that exciting, really. We were together a couple of years, but we were best mates, that was all. Pizzas, films together. My favourite person to spend time with, but we kinda lost that spark. If we ever had it. I think people were trying to set us up for so long we just kinda went along with it.'

I found it difficult to believe that two people who looked as perfect together as them could not have had a spark, but then, I knew there was a lot more to relationships than how they looked on the outside.

'You going home or to the paper?' Alex asked, interrupting my thoughts.

We were coming up to the T junction I walked and drove down several times a day. A left turning took me toward home, straight on was towards the paper, the station and, most importantly, Weirdoughs.

'I should probably go straight to the paper.' I replied. 'I've still got to write up a piece on last night's meeting.'

'No worries. But in that case, I'll drop you just up here.'

He flicked on the indicator and pulled up next to the sidewalk, still a hundred or so yards from the turning to the paper. It wasn't that I minded – it was hardly a long walk – it just felt like a strange thing to do, considering he was going to drive straight past to get to the station, which was where I assumed he was headed next.

'Everything okay? Are you going somewhere else?'

'No, it's just—' he hesitated. 'It'll make sense. Stay in touch about Pongo, okay?'

I wanted to hug him, the way I would've done only a couple of weeks ago, before Whip came back and he I were officially a thing. Or the way I had that morning, when I had so desperately needed someone to hold me. But now it felt... wrong. So instead, I unclipped my belt, stepped onto the sidewalk and watched him drive away.

It was a minute or so later that I realised why Alex hadn't dropped me in front of the paper. There, walking towards the building with a takeaway coffee in his hand, was Whip.

Damn these shifters and their hearing. As a vampire, mine should have easily been as good as Alex's, but perhaps he had simply been listening for Whip. Or maybe, after years working with him, he recognised the sound of his boss's footsteps in a way that I didn't yet. Either way, I was surprisingly grateful. The reason I hadn't rung Whip was out of genuine desire not to cause him more stress, and the fact that Alex had an ex-girlfriend who was a vet meant I'd definitely made the right call. But I still wasn't sure how Whip would feel about it. Though it was difficult to pretend I'd had a normal morning, when I was walking to the office, missing one very notable, furry accessory.

'Hey you,' Whip pulled me in for a kiss before breaking away. 'You're late to start today. Everything okay?'

So much for thinking Whip would immediately notice the issue. 'Not exactly. I had a bit of an incident with Pongo. He's at the vets.'

'Crap. Everything okay? You should have rung me?'

'It's fine, I think. And I didn't want to bother you. I knew you'd had a rough night.'

He let out a long stream of air, like the word 'rough,' wasn't even close to cutting what he'd been through.

'Yeah, it wasn't ideal.' Shrugging off the weariness with a lazy smile, he handed me the takeaway cup he was holding. Unlike when Chloe had brought me a drink, I'd already clocked the O negative in this one, and unless Whip had another vampire on the side, I assumed it was for me. One sip later, and I knew my homemade monstrosity hit none of the spots this one did.

'I was hoping that after cancelling on you last night, you'd let me make it up to you. Take you for lunch.'

The fact that bringing me a morning coffee wasn't part of his 'making it up to me,' was just proof of how good a guy I had got in Whip. And it wasn't like he'd had a choice in cancelling on me.

'Do you have time?' I said, well aware that last night

would have probably had repercussions that spread well past the evening.

'I can make time,' he said, slipping his hand around my waist. Sparks ignited where he touched me. Sparks that only grew as he leant in and placed his lips against mine. Sometimes it was hard to believe that Whip's power came from speaking, because there was nothing remotely typical about his kisses. When he broke away, his eyes had a familiar glint in them.

'Weirdoughs at one,' he said.

'Sounds perfect.'

'It will be, as long as you're there.'

UNLIKE WHIP, who had been happy to accept that Pongo was at the vet's and didn't feel the need to discuss it anymore, it hadn't been the same in the office. As I could've expected, Chloe burst into tears, while Bobby told me to take whatever time off I needed, but I assured him it wasn't necessary and got to work. Just as Alex had said she would, Jenna had sent me a message only five minutes after I'd arrived at the office, saying that the x-rays were all good, but she'd keep Pongo in until I was ready to pick him up that evening. In terms of favourite people in Ravens Hollow, Alex's ex had just risen to one of the top spots on my list, and I made a mental note to pick up a bottle of wine to thank her. Although I knew a hefty vet's bill would be waiting for me too.

With my mind substantially more at ease, I sat and wrote out the article about the council meeting in a couple of hours, focusing on the key things that had been covered, but obviously I put extra attention on the hunting rulings, and how people who had actual knowledge of the ecosystem knew there would be no positive effects from interference. As much as I valued Cliff's idea to turn the whole island into a nature reserve I had the feeling his was the response of an extreme animal lover, rather than someone with scientific evidence.

With that done, it took longer than I had hoped to get all my wording correct, not to mention sort out the quotes, so it was just gone twelve thirty when I was finally finished. Which meant there was still time for me to discuss other matters with Bobby.

'There was another case of this possible demon acting up last night,' I said as I took a seat in his office.

'Really? Who?' he replied.

'Cliff, the trainee vet with Jenna. She doesn't want it becoming common knowledge, so we can't write about it or anything, but he let all the animals out of their cages last night. No memory of doing any of it.'

'Lettin' animals out of cages?' Bobby raised his singular eyebrow. 'Hardly the same as tryin' to beat someone up or smashin' up your buildin'.'

'No, but it was still acting completely out of character. And he has no recollection of it.'

'You speak to him?' Bobby asked. 'Find out where he'd been?'

It sounded a little like a trick question. If I said yes, he might well have a go at me for following up with sources on my own, and without his approval. But even if the latter bit had been true, I hadn't been on my own.

'I did. He'd been to Betty's. This is back to Fritz again. Fritz is involved in every case...'

Bobby pursed his lips, and I knew his response was going to be almost identical to Alex's.

'You can't think the goat shifter's involved.'

'Why not? People thought werewolves couldn't do magic, until the tree sprites helped Sophia make those hexes. Who's to say a demon couldn't possess Fritz?'

'But you've spoken to him at the bar. We've all seen him. I don't think demons work that way.'

'You don't think? Since when did we work off speculation?'

Bobby exhaled heavily, though I could tell he wasn't actually cross with me.

'Look, have a talk to Nyrah and Vincent. They're not experts, but they've probably got more knowledge than most of us. If it is a demon, maybe they can tell us how to start looking. Safely.'

'Thank you,' I said.

I checked my watch. Only twenty minutes until I was due to meet Whip and there was still another person in the office I wanted to talk to.

Unsurprisingly, Diego was already in the kitchen, munching through an empanada.

'How's Carlotta after last night?' I asked him.

He sighed. 'As you'd expect. Not great, but can't say it weren't expected.'

I remembered what had been shouted at the meeting the night before, about the mayor, having it in for the werewolves, and I was tempted to ask him about it. There was definitely a story there. But I didn't want to ask him about work. I wanted to ask him about something personal.

'Did you see Ines at all?' I said. 'I'd really like to speak to her, if you know any way of getting in contact.'

'I'll ask around for you, but last night she was gone pretty fast. Think it was all a bit humiliating.'

'She has no reason to be humiliated,' I said. 'None whatsoever.'

Diego knew far more about wolf politics than I ever would, and disagreed with my opinion on things, but that wasn't going to change my mind that I thought the way she'd been treated was abysmal.

'If you can get a message to her, or if you know anybody who could, I really would like to speak to her.'

He nodded. 'Aye. You're a good friend, Elodie.'

My thoughts suddenly shifted from Ines to Alex. To how I had treated him, and yet how he'd still been there, without hesitation, when I needed him. Was I really a good friend? As much as I liked to think I was, at times, I wasn't so sure.

'Can I put the kettle on? D'you want a drink?'

'No, thank you, though. I'm meeting Whip for lunch.'

'Best make tracks then. Don't wanna keep him waiting. And I'll keep my ear out for Ines for you.'

'Thanks Diego.' I flashed him a smile. 'You're a good friend too.'

FORTY-ONE

I was hardly surprised when I got to Weirdoughs before Whip did. Sure, he was incredibly punctual and organised, but I knew what my job was like, getting sidetracked, time running away from you; I could only imagine how much worse his was. But as I stood in the queue for a table, I wished I'd stayed outside.

'An embarrassment to the wolves, that's what she is. You know, I heard the mayor was going to agree to open all the forests up, until what her sister did.'

'But at least Sophia had the decency to stay clear of the meeting. I mean, turning up like that. Why would she do it?'

I bit the inside of my cheek and forced myself to stay silent. I had no idea who the women in front of me were, gossiping like that about Ines, but whereas in the human world I would've happily called someone out for unsubstantiated remarks, para life was a bit different. For all I knew, they could've been powerful warlocks who'd conjure a stake and punch it through my heart before I could even get my fangs out. All I could do was stand and wait.

Thankfully, it was only a couple of minutes later when Whip showed up.

'Hey, you don't need to queue,' he said. 'I've reserved us a table at the back.'

'I thought you couldn't reserve tables at Weirdoughs,' I said.

'I can,' he grinned.

At that exact moment, Omar spotted Whip and waved him into the restaurant area, where an empty table was waiting for us in the corner. Thankfully, away from the gossiping women.

'It's always a lot quieter when you sit down I'd expect, considering how busy it is,' I said to Whip as I handed the waitress back my menu. I'd done my normal order, shakshuka with an extra dose of blood and chorizo. It was my favourite. And that, with my usual dosed-up cappuccino, meant I'd be good to go on the blood front for a fair amount of time now.

'They put sound wards on,' Whip told me.

'They do?' I asked.

'Not to completely mute things or anything, but just to keep the volume down, and I guess to stop people eavesdropping too much. It's a nice idea. Means you can always enjoy a conversation, even when there are other people around.'

'That is a nice idea,' I said, recalling lunches in London where we had to shout across the table to try to hear each other, because the place had been so packed.

'Any news on Pongo?' he said. 'What happened to him? I'm sorry, I should have asked you earlier. I was just distracted.'

'He's okay,' I replied, grateful that he had brought him

up. 'The x-rays came back from the vet and he'll be fine. I just need to lock the kibble away from now on.'

A laughed croaked from his throat. 'That was why you called the vet, because he ate too much?'

'There can be all sorts of complications, when dogs overeat,' I said, hearing the annoyance in my own voice. 'It can be life threatening.'

'Wow, I'm sorry. I didn't know.' His hands had been holding mine since we sat down, but he lifted them up and kissed my knuckles. 'I'm sorry if you thought I was being cruel, I really didn't know.'

'Neither did I, until this morning,' I admitted. 'But Jenna says he's going to be fine. So that's all that matters.'

'Jenna, as in Alex's Jenna?' Their tiniest inflection clipped his voice, though his smile remained perfectly in place.

'Yeah, Pongo's with her now.'

'That's good. I hear she's great at what she does. A good person to be friends with.'

As he looked into my eyes, I couldn't help but wonder if I'd been wrong thinking he'd sounded tense at Alex's name. Maybe I was just trying to read into things. After all, if my hearing was that well trained, then I would have heard him outside the paper when Alex did, wouldn't I?

'I saw Amira at the meeting last night,' Whip said, causing a sudden and direct change in conversation. 'Did you speak to her?'

I felt my cheeks suck in as I pursed my lips.

'No, I didn't. I'm just not sure how to handle it.' Our hands had dropped back to the table, but I found myself squeezing his ever so slightly. 'She said she's fine taking time before we talk and things, but I'm not sure what that means. She's been a vampire a lot longer than me. Years probably don't feel as long to her as to me. I don't think I've even got used to the fact that I'm immortal in any way. It's only been a couple of months, so the idea of waiting years to speak to her... it just doesn't feel right.'

'So you want to speak to her?' Whip's gaze bored into me. 'It's sounds like you do.'

As we sat there, hands still interlocked, I considered the question, just like I'd considered it a hundred other times since I'd found out my mother was here.

'I don't know. I think so. I guess I should, but I don't know where we'd start. I don't even know where I'd do it. I don't want to go back to her house. I don't want to be out in the open talking to her, because that'll raise questions. I already told Bobby yesterday, because he was asking how I knew her. I don't need more people doing that. But I'm not bringing her into my home. No chance.'

'Well, bring her to mine then,' he said.

'What?' I said.

'Whichever one suits you. You could bring her to the apartment above the station if you'd like. I can do a few nibbles and then it's up to you. I could stay with you for support or I could leave you two to chat on your own if you'd prefer.'

'You'd do that for me?' I said. This wasn't a small deal. This was a big personal trauma that I was dealing with. But he was there with me. If I'd doubted that Whip was fully invested in this relationship, said doubt was now fully erased.

'Of course I would. In case you haven't noticed, you've got me a little bit smitten, Elodie Evergreen,' he said.

My cheeks ached as I smiled, my lips twitching into a grin. 'You've got me rather smitten too,' I said, leaning forward and kissing him, before leaning and in and whispering in his ear.

'I'm starting to wish I never showed you that passport,' he laughed, shaking his head. 'Look, just let me know when you want to do it. Any night this week works for me.'

'This week?' The thought of speak to Amira so soon, caused my stomach to churn.

'It's up to you, but once you've done it, you can stop stressing about it.'

He was right. Of course he was right. He was Whip. 'You're amazing. You know that, right?'

'I try. For you.'

I leant forward, kissed him again. It was the first public display of affection I could remember being involved in; Andy definitely wouldn't have kissed me out in the open. And he'd convinced me that I felt the same. Like displays of love were meant for private only. Not that he would do them there, either. Still, as Whip's lips pressed against mine, I would've quite happily not stopped for hours, had there not been a loud tut from behind us. As I pulled myself away from him, I noticed the waitress standing by the table, a tray in her hand and a scowl on her face.

'Two cappuccinos, one with AB negative? Nice to see you, Chief Inspector Whip.'

I blushed as I moved further apart, ignoring how the waitress's scowl seem only fixed on me.

'So, I guess we're not keeping this relationship low-key,' I said, when she'd finally moved away.

'Not unless you want to,' Whip said, then kissed me again.

'I think I'm happy with how things are,' I grinned.

'Good, me too.'

FORTY-TWO

H alf an hour later, Whip and I both needed to get back to work, but there was another surprise in store for me as we walked out of Weirdoughs. Walking towards us were Chloe and Dylan, and for the first time since the incident with Mick, Chloe was actually smiling.

'Hey guys. Everything okay?'

Chloe sniffed a little and looked at Dylan.

'He's making me get some food,' she said. 'I agreed, as long as he paid, that is.'

'Sweet,' I said. 'Well, have fun,' I added, trying to hold my smile in. No matter how much I tried to ignore it, the pair really were an incredibly cute couple.

'I know what you're thinking, and you need to give them space,' Whip said as soon as they were out of earshot. 'I've known those two since I moved here. There'll get there. They don't need you pushing things along.'

'As if I'd do something like that?' I said innocently, only for him to shake his head before kissing me on the forehead. 'Let me know what day you want to speak to Amira. We can sort it out.'

'Have I told you, you're the best boyfriend?'

'Well, I have a pretty remarkable girlfriend, so it would make sense.'

Girlfriend and boyfriend. Whip and I were girlfriend and boyfriend. I didn't care how childish it sounded. It was exciting. I was excited. And Alex and I were friends again. It was really as much as I could have hoped for.

Back at the office, I sent my copy of the council meeting over to Theodora before looking at another load of lesser stories I had to cover. I needed to do more on the woods. Pieces from different angles. I was considering ringing the mayor's office, when the door opened and a furry figure came pounding through.

'Pongo!' As he bounded into me, I dropped and buried my head in his fur. When I looked back up, Jenna was in the office. 'Thank you,' I said, mopping up my tears, as I stood up and walked across to her. 'Thank you so much.'

'Honestly, I didn't do anything. Just took a bit of time for the food to go through him, that's all.'

'Well, I'm still so grateful. And you really didn't have to bring him back. I would have come and got him.'

'Yes...' A muscle feathered in her jaw. 'Well, when I saw he was looking a bit better, I gave him his buttons. He hit the Elodie one about a hundred times, so I figured he wanted to come back to you.'

'You missed me, did you?' My eyes were blurred with tears as I scooped him up in my arms. 'I missed you too, buddy. I missed you too.'

I glanced back at Jenna, and she was staring at us intently. 'You okay to walk me out?' she said.

A knot formed in my stomach. This was where she hit

me with the astronomically big bill. But it would be worth every penny, cent, whatever it was.

'You stay here, okay boy?' I said placing Pongo back on the ground. 'Theodora, can you make sure he doesn't eat anything while I'm gone?'

'It will be my honour,' she replied, striding over on her Minotaur legs and picking Pongo up, leaving me to follow Jenna down stairs.

'So,' she said when we stepped outside. 'This is a little bit awkward.'

I drew in a deep breath. I wasn't exactly flush with cash, but I could cope with paying a vet bill. Couldn't I? Then again, I'd heard how much medical bills were on this side of the pond. Maybe it was the same with pets. But even if it was, I would find a way around it. It wasn't like I had a choice.

'It's fine, honestly. I'm prepared. Just hit me with it. How much?'

Jenna tilted her head to the side. 'How much? Oh! You think this's about a bill.'

'Isn't it?' It was my turn to look confused.

'I was just gonna charge you for the x-ray. That's it... now, I wanted to talk to you about Ally.'

'Ally? You mean Alex?'

She pressed her lips tightly together. 'He'll kill me if he knew I was saying this. But he likes you. Likes you likes you.'

I felt my jaw hang open. Suddenly I wished I was being smacked with that bill instead.

'I'm with Whip.'

'I know. I do. But I also know that it wasn't Whip you rang this morning, when you needed help with Pongo, was it?'

'No... but—'

'I get, there are reasons. And Ally will always be there for you. That's the type of person he is. But, maybe, if you've got a boyfriend, then don't treat Ally like he's a spare. He's worth more than that. A lot more.'

I hadn't thought my jaw could have gone any lower. And yet there it was. On the ground. When I picked it up, a flurry of anger rippled through me.

'Alex and I are friends. And I don't know your history, but I have been very clear with him from day one where I stand. Friends, that's it.'

Sure, he and Ines were the only people who knew my biggest secret; that my blood could heal werewolves, but she didn't need to know that. And it was not as if I'd chosen to tell Alex that secret. Just like I hadn't chosen for him to know about Amira. If Whip had been there, he would have been the one to know. At some point, I would tell Whip about it. There just hadn't been the right time yet. No, Jenna the vet had definitely dropped down my list of people I wanted to be friends with in Ravens Hollow.

'Thank you for all your help with Pongo,' I said stretching out my hand. You can email the bill to me at the paper.'

With that I turned on my heel and headed back upstairs.

FORTY-THREE

I couldn't believe her nerve. Sure, she had done me a favour, coming to my house in the early hours of the morning, after a very busy night, not to mention giving me Cliff's address so I could talk to him about his actions, but did she really think that gave her the right to stick her nose into my friendship? Because it didn't. No way. And I had half a mind to tell Alex what she'd done. Not that I thought he'd be surprised by it. After all, Alex had thought nothing of telling me how he thought I should handle my love life, either. Perhaps the two of them were better suited for one another than they realised. Or maybe... maybe... No, I didn't want to think about it. I wasn't stringing Alex along.

Sure, when Whip had been away, I had spent more time with Alex than anyone else, but we'd been researching The Guardians. If something was going to happen between us, it would have happened then, wouldn't it? I mean, I wasn't exactly sure how I would have explained the situation to Whip, given how much we were texting, but I would have found a way. I'm a grown adult, after all. But the way Jenna had spoken to me, like I was some... some siren. No, I wasn't having it. I had been straight with Alex about my feelings for Whip. But did that automatically mean I couldn't have feelings for him too? Argh! When the hell did life get so complicated?

As I dropped down at my computer, I started hammering away at my keyboard with such force I was surprised the keys didn't split.

'Interesting conversation?' Diego said. I looked up to find him standing over me.

'You know it's really bad manners to eavesdrop, don't you?' I glowered at him. 'Even if you do have supernatural hearing.'

'I wasn't eavesdropping. No idea what you two were talkin' about. Only you went down smiling, and now you've come up and made a dent in your desk.'

'I have?' I glanced down. Sure enough. The keys were still in place, but the actual keyboard was embedded a full centimetre in the desk.

'Dammit!' I tried to pry it out with my fingers, before twisting my neck around and offering Diego another glare. 'Did you want something? Or did you want just to want to make my bad mood even worse?'

'And here I was, hoping to give you some good news. I just spoke to a buddy of Ines's.'

'You did?' I pulled my nails out from underneath the keyboard. 'What did they say?'

Diego's nostrils flared a little before he spoke. 'They said you might wanna give her a bit of space. A bit of time.'

I let out a groan. I should have known better than to expect something useful.

'They also said, she'll probably be avoiding the woods – too many memories – so you'll be looking at somewhere deliberately un-werewolf-like. Maybe somewhere with a bit of a sea breeze. Where she could grab a cold one.'

'You mean she's at one of the beach bars?'

'I'm just passing on what I heard.'

'Thank you, Diego,' I said, grabbing my bag and Pongo's leash. 'I really appreciate it.'

'No worries. Just... be careful with her.'

Weirdly, I'd been told this countless times since I moved to Ravens Hollow. Be careful. Be careful when talking to werewolves, be careful when talking to mermaids. But the thing is, with Ines I wasn't actually worried. Her life had been thrown upside down in a way she'd never imagined. And maybe – even though I wasn't a werewolf – I could understand what that was like. To have your future stripped from you in a way that you hadn't thought possible.

'Bobby, just going to head out,' I yelled as I passed his office. 'Trying to track someone down.'

'Okay, stay—'

'I'm not even listening, Bobby,' I said, before that last word could come out.

Every now and then, I would take stock of how different my life was here, to how it had been when I lived in London. And not just because of the lack of pulse, hot boyfriend, and potential love triangle. Just the location itself was mind-blowing. I was hunting down a source – not to mention a friend in need – while staring out at glittering blue water and pristine sands. I really did need to pinch myself.

Pongo's tail wagged at the sight of the water. He really was a thousand times better than he'd been that morning, and I knew, begrudgingly, that I'd always be grateful to

Jenna for that. Even if she had dropped substantially in my estimation during the last half an hour.

'I'll be honest, boy, I'm not sure you'll like England. It is a lot colder and greyer there,' I said. 'Then again, you've got thick fur. Maybe you could be okay with the cold weather. And it's not like it affects me anymore. I'm a vampire and everything. And Dad would love to meet you.' Thoughts of my dad caused a pang of guilt. I couldn't keep Mum from him. I wouldn't be able to live with myself if I did. The question was how and when I was going to approach it. Although that wasn't a question I was going to worry about at the moment.

After checking we were on part of the beach that allowed dogs, I unclipped his leash, at which point he barked and careened towards the water, only to stop. With his tail frozen in the air, he turned back to me and tipped his head to the side.

'It's okay boy, I'm watching you,' I said. 'You're fine.'

Yet he didn't move. That was when I realised he wasn't looking at me, but past me. With a flutter of hope, I turned around, hoping that perhaps Ines had heard I was looking for her, and sought me out instead. Unfortunately, it was a different para I found myself looking at.

'Really?' I said, making no attempt to hide my annoyance. 'I should have known.'

CHAPTER
FORTY-FOUR

I'd always thought that I was nothing like my mother, but maybe that had just been wishful thinking. The way she was pursuing me, even when she'd said she'd stop, reminded me of the way I behaved when I got my teeth into a story and didn't want to let go. Still, that was my job. This was my life. And I wasn't appreciating her constant presence.

'I wasn't going to say anything,' she said. 'I just saw you and I... I...' She gulped in a breath. 'I just wanted to watch you. You loved the beach ever so much when you were little. I wish I'd taken you more.'

'You would have had a chance if you'd stayed.' The words spat from my lips before I'd even considered them and hurt flashed across her face, and a flicker of guilt stung behind my sternum. But it wasn't like the words weren't true.

'I know you don't believe me, but I haven't been following you,' she said. She remained exactly where she was, her voice a low whisper designed for only me to hear. Though, I wasn't sure that was any less suspicious. I was pretty sure that anyone passing would find an elf and a vampire standing ten feet apart, staring at one another in apparent silence, a far stranger sight than if we'd just been having a conversation. Still, I wasn't going to move any closer.

'Raven's Hollow is a small town,' she continued. 'I often come down to the beach. But I can do my best. If you tell me the places you go regularly, I can try to avoid them. And I could ask Nyrah to change the glamour on me so that you didn't recognise me anymore, if that would make it easier for you?'

I tried to hide my surprise at her suggestion. That was one hell of an offer. She had built up a life as Amira. That was how people knew her. It would mean starting her life from scratch. Not that she hadn't done that before.

I shook my head. 'You don't need to do that,' I said. That wasn't just because of her. I had a weird suspicion that I would recognise her, in whatever glamour she put on. Now that I could see it in her eyes and the way she looked at me. Yup, Amira, Maria, whatever name and visage she chose next, I would know it was her. Aware that Pongo was now standing by my side, like some overly fluffy bodyguard, I took a deep breath in.

'Look, you're right,' I said, slowly. 'We do need to talk. And Whip said we could use his flat above the station as a neutral location.'

'Chief Inspector Whip?' she said. 'You two are friends?'

'We're more than friends,' I said.

Her eyes widened. 'Oh, well, that's interesting. I wasn't aware that he had relationships with people in Ravens Hollow.'

I wasn't sure why her words grated on me so much. Maybe because of the surprise in her voice, like she couldn't fathom Whip dating someone as ordinary as me. Or maybe because this was the first time she'd ever known anything about my private life, and she was already criticising my choices.

'I'm sure there are lots of things you aren't aware of,' I said.

'You're right, you're right, Elodie, I'm sorry. I didn't mean... I wasn't judging. I wasn't. I was just surprised, that's all. He seems like a very lovely man. And very handsome too. Very attractive.'

She offered me a flash of a smile, which was clearly meant to be warming, but had the opposite effect. If I didn't get this invite out soon, I'd back out of it.

'Tomorrow night.' I couldn't deal with speaking to her twice in one day. 'Come to the station tomorrow night. Seven-thirty. Then we can talk then.'

Thank you. Thank you Elodie.' Her eyes filled with tears, and she reached out her hands, as if she was going to step forwards and take hold of mine. But before she could I spoke again.

'Don't be late,' I said. 'You probably might not remember this about me, but I don't like it when things – or people – are late.'

With that, I turned to Pongo. 'Come on, boy. We need to go. I'll take you for a swim later.'

CHAPTER
FORTY-FIVE

F or the next three hours, I tried my best to hunt down Ines, but had no luck. I went to all the places I thought were anti-werewolf as possible, the beach shack that sold coconuts, the one next to the skatepark that was mostly full of teenage witches, trying to spell themselves to do tricks, and even Betty's. At every place I asked if they'd seen her, giving her description as well as her name, but my questions were always met with the same answer. Sorry, but she'd not been there.

'Maybe she's headed to one of the other beaches,' I said to Pongo.

Ravens Hollow may have been the only town, but there were plenty of other beach areas. And not just Peppers Bay. There was Calypso Cove at the very north of the island and several small inlets adjacent to the various woodlands. But was there really any point in trying them? I could have gone around in circles for hours, always missing her. And considering less than twelve hours ago, Pongo had been lying on the floor, unable to move, I didn't want to keep him out any longer than necessary. And so, at just gone six, I headed back home to find a paper bag on the doorstep.

Pongo's tail immediately started wagging furiously.

'Hey, let me get to it,' I said, leaning down to pick it up, and noticing the note on the top.

Not for tonight.

Glad he's doing better,

A

Inside were a range of Pongo's favourite treats, from pig's ears to bones and a couple of other unidentifiable meaty specimens. With any trace of his sickness now gone, he was jumping at my side, and he was already so tall his paws were on my waist.

'No chance. He's right. You need to take it easy for a couple of days. Come on, let me put these somewhere you won't be able to reach.'

After placing the snacks on the top shelf in the kitchen, I poured Pongo a tiny dish of kibble, then resealed the bag and shut it in the cupboard, before picking up my phone to text Alex and say thank you, only for Jenna's voice to pop into my head. Thanking him for doing something nice wasn't leading him on, was it? No, it wasn't. It was what friends did. And not doing so was just rude. I typed out a quick thanks and hit send when my phone rang. A flash of fear rushed through me. Did I want to talk to Alex? Should I talk to Alex? My mind whirred in a frenzy, when with a flood of relief that a different name was on the screen.

'Hey, Chief Inspector.' My voice came out breathier than expected.

'Hey yourself.' Whip's low, gravelly voice caused a shiver to cascade down my shoulders in the nicest possible way. 'So I'm just stuck at the station and I found myself thinking about you.'

'Is that right?' A smile formed on my cheeks. 'And were there any particular thoughts you were having about me?'

'Oh, plenty. But not that I would say aloud where people could hear.' I let out a chuckle. 'I was hoping I'd get a chance to see you tonight,' he continued. 'But I'm bogged down with paperwork. I wondered if you might want to have dinner tomorrow instead. We could go out, or I could cook at yours, if you want?'

'You know, the way you say that, it's like you don't even want to try my cooking?' As I put on my most wounded voice, I could almost see him roll his eyes down the line.

'Do you even know how your stove works?' he replied.

'I could work it out.'

As he let out another laugh, a thought entered my mind. It was all very well us talking about who would cook dinner, but as much as I wanted to forget the plans I'd made, that wasn't going to happen.

'Actually, about tomorrow...I've invited my mum to yours. You know... to talk. Hope that's still okay?'

'Of course, absolutely.' His immediate response was followed by a slight pause. 'How are you feeling about it?'

'Nervous. Angry. Simultaneously looking forward to it, but also dreading it? Worried I might wring her neck, but also might turn into a blubbering wreck. Does that answer your question?'

'It'll be fine, it will. You don't have to listen to anything you don't want to, okay? And I'll be there as long as you want me to.'

The smile that formed on my lips this time was different to the grin from when he had first rung. It was something that went far deeper.

'Thank you, Whip. For everything. I really do appreciate you, you know that?'

'I appreciate you too,' he said.

There was another word, one that could easily have replaced 'appreciate', but that would've been ridiculous. We'd been together less than a week. That couldn't possibly happen. And it didn't help that my mother's voice was in my head. Her words about Whip not dating people in Ravens Hollow. I knew I shouldn't let other people's response to us dating affect my thoughts. But it was difficult. Especially when that person was my mother.

I moved to say goodbye, hang up the phone and let Whip get back to work, only to stop and change my mind. 'Whip, have you dated anyone in Ravens Hollow before?' The question escaped my lips before I could stop it.

'Sorry?'

'It's just, someone said something to me, how they didn't think you dated people on the island.'

'Someone?' His voice lifted at the end, like a question.

'My mother, actually. But I just wondered. Am I suddenly going to find myself randomly bumping into your exes when we're out for dinner?' Jenna's image popped into my head, but I immediately pushed it down.

'No,' Whip laughed. 'You don't have to worry about bumping into any of my exes.'

'You haven't dated anyone, in all the time you've been on the island?'

As a slight paused filtered into the conversation, I found myself trying to guess what he looked like. Had he just shrugged nonchalantly? Or had his face hardened at all the questions? No, that didn't seem likely. And he could hardly think badly of me for having a twinge of jealously after the way he acted around Alex. And it wasn't like anything had even happened between us, anyway.

'I guess it's one of those immortal things,' he said eventually. 'You know, not having to worry about time to meet "the one". And then the whole curse thing... it makes things more complicated. Not to mention my position. People need to know that I'm impartial. That I treat all the sects the same. I guess I worried that if I started dating someone – particularly someone who wasn't a siren – it could affect that.'

A sparkle of fear struck within me. Was he going to say that I'd made him question this? That he'd remembered why dating in Ravens Hollow *was* a bad idea, and that this was a mistake? Damn my mother. Still, I'd asked it now. There was no point chickening out.

'So what changed with me?' I said.

'What changed with you?' he let out a laugh. 'Everything Elodie. Everything changed with you. I thought I was this almighty siren, with the ability to control everything and everyone. And then you came along. You and your stubborn journalistic streak. Who staked a vampire when they were a tip, and I knew for the first time in many, many years, I'd found someone with the ability to break my heart,' he said. 'I guess that's the first time I've ever seen that in somebody, and it was an opportunity I couldn't give up.'

I was speechless. He hadn't said the L-word, but it had been implied near enough, and it lodged like a lump in my throat.

'I shouldn't have told you, should I?' he said. 'That was too much, and I know—'

'No, it wasn't. Thank you for telling me. And just so you know... I think you have the ability to break my heart, too.'

'Well, then, let's promise not to do that to each other. How does that sound?'

'That sounds pretty good. I should let you get back to work now. I've distracted you long enough.'

'I'll cope. You get some rest. And don't stress about tomorrow with your mum. I'll be there.'

'I'm trying not to think about it. But who knows , maybe she'll remember a few more details about the young vampire woman that sired her.'

Silence followed. Such complete silence that for a second I thought Whip had hung up, though before I checked my phone to see, he spoke again.

'You didn't say a female vampire sired her.'

'Didn't I? Does that make a difference?'

'No... no,' he mumbled. 'No, of course not. Well, I should go. Speak tomorrow, Elodie.'

For a split second, I was fearful that maybe he was going to say those words. Or that he wanted me to say them first. A strange tightening squeezed around my throat. Could I do it?

'Speak tomorrow,' I said instead, then hung up the phone before anything else could slip out. Then I dropped down on the sofa, not even bothering to object as Pongo jumped up next to me and snuggled into my side.

'I think I might have got myself into a pickle, boy,' I said with a groan. 'This isn't good. It isn't good at all.'

FORTY-SIX

After the shock I'd had that morning, I should have used the quiet evening as an excuse to get an early night. That was definitely the sensible thing to do, but I needed to ring Donna. There was no way she would forgive me, what with everything that had happened, with Whip, Alex, Pongo, and Jenna. Besides, there was also the other issue I still hadn't told her about. My mother. Keeping it from her this long was ridiculous, but it wasn't the kind of thing I could simply fire off in a late-night text, which was how so much of our communication happened nowadays.

But this time, I messaged first to ensure she had a chunk of time free for me to catch her up on things. And when she immediately called me back, I let it all out. Ten minutes of nonstop blabbering on my part. It was another advantage to being a vampire, I discovered; I no longer needed to pause for breath.

'That's insane,' she said when I finally stopped. 'I thought you meant your mum, not Whip and Alex,' she said. 'Of course they're both into you. You're absolutely incredible. But I'll be honest, I'm kind of in awe of Nyrah.'

'Nyrah?'

Of all the people I'd mentioned in the previous fifteen minutes — Amira, Jenna, Alex — Nyrah wasn't the one I'd expected her to mention.

'Hell yeah. Her powers must be phenomenal to put on a glamour like that. And no one suspects Amira of being anything other than an elf?'

'Not that I know of,' I said. 'I mean, Chloe's a fae, and she said that Amira used to look after her when she was younger. I'm sure the other Fae wouldn't have done that if they thought she was dodgy.'

Donna let out a low whistle. 'Yup, that's some serious glamour. More than just the physical. She must have altered her auras, too. Her whole energy profile. When I come and visit, you have to introduce us. I need lessons.'

I found myself notably surprised by the remark. Donna was the first witch I had ever met, and in my mind, she was capable of doing everything, but obviously, that wasn't the case. Still, I hadn't rung her to talk about Nyrah, as lovely as she was.

'But the stuff about how she was turned,' I said, shifting the focus back onto my mother. 'Do think it could be linked to The Guardians?'

'I don't know. It's not a lot to go on. I'm sure there are plenty of sireless vampires linked to The Guardians.'

'I know,' I replied, wishing I didn't agree with her so much. 'It's just a feeling that I can't shake.'

'Well, when you get those niggles, they do have an annoying habit of being right. I just don't want you to get even more hurt by her.'

'I don't think that's possible,' I said. 'I've just got to wait and see what tomorrow is going to bring.'

'Tomorrow night at Whip's. So you're just going to ignore whatever this is with you and Alex?'

'There isn't anything going on with Alex,' I said forcefully. 'Other than us being friends.'

'Hmm.' Donna's humming sound caused an annoying prickle on the back of my neck.

'What?' I said, knowing it was probably better that she just spat whatever it was out, rather than making noises for the rest of the call.

'Well, it's just, I agree with what he said. And what Jenna said. You did rush into this thing with Whip and not give yourself a chance to see if there was anyone else for you. And you did call Alex when you needed help with Pongo.'

'Because Whip had had a late night working!' I practically shouted down the phone at her. To which she offered only the slightest sigh.

'Look, I'm not saying you and Whip aren't the real deal. All I'm saying is keep your guard up, okay? With your Mum. And with the swoony siren.'

'He is very swoony,' I grinned slightly. 'And don't worry. We are taking things slow.'

'Okay, just take care of yourself.'

I was about to add a remark about her and Bobby being cut from the same cloth when another voice joined in the conversation.

'Hey El. How's life on the west coast?'

'Hey Jules,' I said. 'What, are you at the office?'

I was used to having conversations with Donna and Jules being in the background. Or normally asleep in the bed beside her. But it was nearly midday in the UK. And they definitely weren't weekday nappers.

'What do you think I'm doing?' Jules replied. 'Bringing her a damn lunch, because you know she'd work all day without a bite to eat if I didn't.'

'You're a great wife, Jules,' I chuckled.

'Yes, yes, I am.'

For the next five minutes, I proceeded to chat to Jules and Donna together, almost as if it was old times. Not long after, I was yawning. I'd had three doses of blood today, but it seemed like I was getting used to it. My body had developed a steady rhythm based on the amount of blood I consumed, and that rhythm was telling me it was time to get to bed.

After saying goodbye, I clicked off my phone and curled up in bed. My eyes had just fluttered closed when the phone started ringing.

It was one of those weird sensations where it felt as if I hadn't even properly fallen asleep. As I picked up my phone to answer, I saw that it was, in fact, three a.m., and an unknown number was ringing me.

I hesitated. It was an American mobile, meaning it was likely to be someone on the island, but I had all my work colleagues' numbers in my phone, along with Whip's, Nyrah's and Alex's. There was only one other person I could think of who would have a reason to call me.

That was my mother. Did I want to speak to her? No, but did I think she would ring me unless something was urgent? Also no.

Still, my thumb hovered above the red button, ready to end the call before I'd even picked up, but instead I took the call.

'If this is what you mean by giving me space, you're really not doing a great job,' I said.

'Well, that's strange.' The voice on the other end was not the one I expected to hear from. 'Because I heard you were looking for me.'

FORTY-SEVEN

'Ines?' I said, hearing the question mark as I spoke. I had Ines's number in my phone from the meetings we'd had about the article written in the paper and I had tried calling it and leaving at least half a dozen messages since I'd heard how she'd been cast out of the pack, but they hadn't even gone through. I guess now I knew why.

'I changed my number,' she said. 'It was easier that way. It's true, right? You've been looking for me.'

I nodded. 'Yes. Yes, I have.'

'Because you wanted to know how I feel about this absolutely ridiculous change to the hunting rules the mayor's put in place?' Of course, I expected her to sound bitter and angry about the matter, but there was a coldness to her tone. One that I'd never heard before.

'Partly,' I said, 'but also because I wanted to see how you were. Mainly because I wanted to see how you were. I was worried about you.' I paused, so that I could sit up properly, and shuffled Pongo across so that he was back on his half of the bed. 'How are you doing?'

She scoffed. 'How do you think I'm doing?'

I knew it was a rhetorical question, but I didn't answer it that way. 'Truthfully? I reckon you feel as if you no longer have any purpose. You're furious because the entire future you'd seen for yourself has just been stripped from you, and trying to reimagine another one is so painful that your entire body rebels in response. That it feels like you don't know who you are anymore, or even what you are. You don't know what you're capable of, in good ways and bad ways, and you don't want to find out because you just want to close your eyes and wake up to discover it was all a terrible dream. But every time you fall asleep, you wake back up, and it's like the nightmare has started all over again. How does that sound?'

Silence, and I was wondering if I had said too much when she spoke again 'That's what transformation was like for you?'

'Transformation and having my fiancé tell me that he could never be with me now that I was a monster,' I said.

'I'm sorry. I didn't know about that part.'

'It is what it is.' I shrugged. 'And I'm getting used to it now, but let's just say that's not the only massive U-turn that's happened in my life these last couple of months. And the second one... that's a biggy too. So I get it. I get the frustration, the confusion. The anger.' A bitter laugh cracked in my throat as I thought about Amira. 'Trust me, I get the anger. And, in my opinion, you have every right to be angry. So if you want someone to talk to, or just someone to sit next to you when you have a drink so you don't feel so alone, then I'll go there.'

Another pause followed. This one so long I had to check my phone to make sure she hadn't hung up, but when she spoke again, her voice crackled. As if she was holding back tears.

'Thank you, Elodie. Genuinely. I really appreciate that.' She sniffed. 'It's difficult, with the pack. I know that some of them want to be there for me, but they can't. And as for others... well, so much for blood being thicker than water.'

It was hard to know who she was talking about. Her father was the one who had kicked her out of the pack, but none of that would have happened had her sister Sophia not rebelled against her. Sometimes, being an only child felt like a blessing.

'Well, I'm not a member of any pack, and I can do what I like,' I said. 'Why don't we meet up tomorrow? I was thinking we could do lunch.'

There was a pause, during which I wondered if she'd nodded or shaken her head, but then she spoke again. 'I've got to go somewhere at lunch,' she said, 'but how about a bit later? Five-ish? Would that work?'

I considered the time in my head. I'd just said to my mother earlier in the day that I would meet her at Whip's place at seventy-thirty, but I didn't want to rush Ines. I'd had friends who'd been down before. And for longer periods than me after my transformation, when I'd had the move and the new job to keep and Donna to help keep me up. I knew what it was like when simply arranging something took so much effort it felt like a miracle to even manage, and how any disruption could have you running for the duvet. I didn't want her to do that.

'I could do a couple of hours then, but I've got to be somewhere else in the evening. Would that be okay?'

'Not sure... only if you can manage it. I don't want to put you out.'

'Honestly, five-thirty is fine,' I said. 'Do you want to

meet at Weirdoughs?' The moment I spoke I realised that the chance of her wanting to meet somewhere as public as that was unlikely.

'There's a little shack at West Beach. Betty's. Would you be okay with that?'

'I know it. Sounds good. I'll see you there. Five-thirty. And Ines?' I added before I hung up.

'Yes.'

'Take care of yourself, okay?'

FORTY-EIGHT

The next morning at the office, I had to stop my workmates from spoiling Pongo rotten.

'You know the whole reason he was ill was because he overate,' I said, as he hit the snack button again and Chloe immediately sprang up to get a chew from her jar. 'He does not need that,' I added, placing my hand on the lid. 'He now needs to learn some restraint.'

'Sorry, boy,' Chloe said, before Pongo hit his sad button.

'I'm getting another button,' I said, glaring at him. 'It's called "greedy". And another one called "healthy". I still don't know how much that extra vet visit of yours is going to cost me.'

After the way Jenna and I had finished our conversation, I expected an email with an excessively high number waiting in my inbox, but, as of yet, it hadn't come.

Although a different delivery arrived at the office.

'I'm looking for Elodie Evergreen?'

I didn't actually see what the person was carrying at first, given that my attention was stolen by who, or rather what, was speaking. Torso of a man, bottom half a horse. A centaur? Had I actually met my first centaur? And how the hell had he climbed the stairs to the office? They were narrow and steep enough that I struggled some days, and I had legs designed for staircases.

'Elodie Evergreen?' he groaned. 'This is the address I have for Elodie Evergreen.'

He didn't sound like a man who was enthused by his career, as what I assumed was a speedy delivery boy. Only then did I notice what the creature was holding; the most enormous bunch of red roses I had ever seen.

'Those are for me?' I said, finally finding my voice and standing up.

'If you're Elodie Evergreen.'

'She is,' Chloe said excitedly as I took the bouquet and slipped the note from the top.

Just because I know tonight's going to be tough. I'm proud of you. W x

'They're from Whip,' I said.

As the centaur headed back down the stairs, I put the flowers back down in front of me.

'Whip sent you *roses*?' Chloe said, eyes wide. 'I can't remember the last time Mick even bought me flowers. That's... not fair.'

'Are you guys still not talking?'

'Not talking,' she confirmed. 'Though a part of me feels terrible. It wasn't like it was him; there's this demon on the run who's been doing all these things. But maybe it just made me see a side of him I didn't want to admit was real. He had to have had it in him to *be* like that, didn't he?'

'I don't know,' I said honestly. My thoughts flickered to Flo. She hadn't seemed the type to have that much rage inside her, to be capable of tearing a house apart. But then again, who knows what's really going on beneath the surface?

Could *I* do something like that if I were possessed by a demon?

I liked to think the answer was no. But maybe you didn't know until it happened.

IT WAS A FAIRLY quiet afternoon at *The Oracle*. Diego was rushing around, trying to get photos sorted, one thing after another. There was an opening of a new pet hotel and an enchanted furniture studio, which – because everyone else was busy – I had to cover. Definitely not my usual type of journalism, but it filled the time. I also got promised a discount on an expanding armchair that would shrink or grow depending on the size of the occupier, which felt like something I should invest in for Pongo when I had a little more savings.

As much as I wanted to see Ines, I was still worried I was pushing her. It was clear she didn't want to be around people, and I fully understood that, but I also knew from experience that sometimes, the moments when you really, desperately feel like you should lock yourself away, are the same moments that you need people around you the most. So maybe a little pushing wasn't the worst thing in the world.

I did, however, decide that at least one person should know where I was headed, so mentioned the situation to Chloe before I left.

'Don't tell Diego,' I said. 'Or Bobby, for that matter. But I'm going to see Ines.'

Her eyes widened. 'Ines? Are you sure that's... I've heard

she's really not in a good place right now. And she's still a werewolf. Tomorrow night's a full moon.'

'She rang me last night. She just sounded so lonely. I figured, if I can do anything to help...'

'Well, you ring me if you need me? Okay?'

'I will. Promise.'

'And good luck for tonight, too.'

I froze. My brow creased.

I hadn't told her about tonight. Not *today*, anyway. Not about my mother.

'Whip's card,' she said quickly. 'It said, "Tonight will be difficult." I don't know what it is you're doing – and I get if you don't want to tell me – but I just wanted to say good luck, that's all.'

'Thanks. That... means a lot.'

'I just wanted you to know I'm here. If you want someone else to talk to. Other than Whip. Or Alex.'

'Alex?' I said.

'I just saw the way he was looking at you the other day. You know, when he came to the office.'

'He *was*?'

I had mocked her secretly and mercilessly for not noticing how Dylan felt about her. But Alex and I were different. We were just friends.

She smiled softly, grabbing her bag. 'Anyway, hope everything goes okay with Ines. I'll speak to you later, alright?'

FORTY-NINE

I arrived at Betty's twenty minutes before we were supposed to meet, assuming I'd get there first. As expected, there was no sign of Ines, and so I took a seat, only to hear a hiss from the table behind me.

'Elodie, psst. It's me.'

I turned around. A woman in oversized sunglasses and a strappy sundress tilted her glasses down, revealing her eyes. Even then, it took me a second.

These weren't the amber eyes I knew so well. These were a murky grey-brown, like a storm brewing over the sea

'Ines?' I whispered, still not entirely convinced I was seeing her right.

And it wasn't just the colour of her eyes. I had never seen her in a strappy dress. Jeans, jackets, and clothes you could get muddy in, that was what she wore. This? This was not Ines. No wonder the people I'd asked the day before said she hadn't been in. I'd been describing someone completely different. Who knew that putting *less* clothing on could be such an effective disguise?

I stood and moved over to her table. For a moment, I

wanted to wrap my arms around her and squeeze her tightly. But I was struck by the memory of the first time Chloe had hugged me, how my fangs had popped without warning. The memory still haunted me.

'Can I give you a hug?' I asked.

She nodded as a watery smile curled her lips. 'I'd like that.'

I wrapped my arms around her, feeling her warmth wick into my body as I squeezed her shoulders. The way she clung to me made me think she hadn't been held in a long, long time. Maybe even before everything had gone down.

When we broke apart, she wiped a tear from her cheek.

'He's got even bigger,' she said, glancing down at Pongo.

'Yup, he keeps doing that.'

Another cluster of tears broke free. Hastily, she wiped them away.

'I'm sorry,' she said. 'It's just... it's tough.'

'How are you holding up?'

'Not great,' she said honestly. 'It's just getting worse. I thought Dad would see my side. I don't know why I thought that. He gave me *one hour*, Elodie. One hour to pack up everything I owned and get out. All I could take was what fit in my truck.'

'I'm so sorry.'

'I should've known. All those years I did his job for him, all those years I was alpha in everything but name. It didn't mean a thing. He shouldn't have had the right to kick me out. *I* was the one who ran the pack. And it's just been one shit thing after another. Sophia and the others getting punished, but not stripped. I mean, I always knew she was his favourite. But that?' Her jaw tightened as a guttural growl rose in her throat, before she hurriedly shook it away. 'I tried taking myself away from things for a few days, head to the forest, and I even thought about getting off the island, but my car broke down. And to add insult to injury, I've just discovered my ex is engaged to a woman who's a shoo-in for the alpha in the peridot pack, and the beta they've elected is an arsehole white wolf who's basically undermined me at every chance he's had over the last two years. I'm pretty sure the only reason he didn't join Sophia's potion crew was because he knew he'd never get my role if he did. Oh, and they've given him my house. My house that I built with my own two hands.'

'It's hard to believe you're even still standing.' It sure as hell made my transformation, where my best friend was there to flavour my blood and guide me though the paranormal world, seem relatively tame.

'Do you have somewhere to sleep? I've only got a sofa, but if you need it—'

She shook her head. 'No. It's fine. Honestly. I've got a tent. It's amazing how much of the island you can see when you don't have any responsibilities. I've kind of been everywhere, and ended up right back in Ravens Hollow.'

'Sorry you got kicked out of the council meeting the other night. I wish I could have done something.'

'I wouldn't have expected you to,' she said. 'But the way it went down, I can't help thinking that maybe I should've let Sophia get away with it all. Hexed the whole damn town. Maybe she was right in the first place.'

'No. No, she wasn't. And you *know* that,' I said, taking her hand. 'You took the right route. I know it's hard to believe that now, but you have to. You have to trust that what you did will be better in the long run.'

'Maybe,' she said, though I could see she didn't feel it. 'So...' she forced a smile onto her lip. 'You said about something happening in your life too? Wanna share? Nothing like hearing someone else's crap to make you feel better about your own life.'

I let out a light laugh. It was true. Hearing how bad things were for her, really put things in perspective. It wasn't like I was living out of my truck and sleeping in a tent.

'I don't think that's wrong. I think that's perfectly human. Or Para. Or whatever we are. But I don't know if I'm ready to talk about it yet. The person it involves, I'm actually seeing them tonight. That's why I can't stay too long. I don't know how it'll go. I can't imagine it'll make me feel any *less* angry. But I need to hear them out. For *my* sake, as much as theirs.'

'Feeling angry is something I know about.' Her jaw twitched. 'Yeah. Angry, hurt, furious... I know those emotions. I know them all too well.'

A shadow passed across her features like a storm cloud rolling in.

'Ines,' I said gently. She looked up at me, shoulders sagging.

'Sorry. It's just... hard to let go sometimes.'

'I know. I know it is.'

Her hands were clenched in front of her. 'I don't know how long I can stay here before it all gets too much. Like I said, I thought about leaving, but why should I? Why should I have to do that?'

'You shouldn't,' I agreed. 'And I don't know much about para communities outside here. I wasn't in London that long before I moved. But I was staying with my best friend Donna, she's a witch. She might know of something. She knows the country pretty well.'

'You mean see if she knows any stray-friendly packs willing to take in a cast out wolf,' Ines said bitterly.

I hadn't meant the comment to upset her. 'I felt like a stray coming here,' I said. 'But the lot at *The Oracle* kind of accepted me. It's not worked out too badly. Fun job. Great dog. Boyfriend.' I didn't add the love bombing part. He was just caring. That was all.

'Boyfriend?' Ines eyes widened. 'You and the Chief Inspector? It's official?'

'It is.'

She sighed. 'Shame. I was always holding out hope for you and Alex.'

'Why does everyone think that about Alex and me? We're just friends.'

'Sure you are,' she said with a smirk.

'So... the Chief Inspector,' she mused. 'Never thought I'd see the day he'd actually settle down. You must be something really special. But what am I saying? I know exactly how special you are. And don't worry, I'll never tell.'

'I know. You're a friend,' I replied. 'And I only pick friends I can trust.'

For the first time, I felt like I might actually have made a difference, as the slightest hint of light returned to her eyes.

Over the next hour, I told her about Whip and about Pongo and even about Chloe and Mick, and more and more, I saw the change. the slow fading of her anger, the softening of her shoulders.

She needed that connection. That hope. That reminder that life *could* shift. That love was still possible. Even if it didn't come from the family she was born into.

'I'm really sorry to do this,' I said, glancing at my watch. 'But I need to go. I've got to meet this person.'

'The person you're angry at?'

'That's the one.'

A slight twitch tightened her jaw.

'It's alright,' she said. 'It's alright to be angry. You deserve to be angry. I don't know what they've done, but you're a good person. A great one. If you're feeling mad, you've got a good reason. So if you need to let it out, then let it out.'

She lifted her hand and rested it on my shoulder. A flicker of energy passed through us. Maybe it was her werewolf warmth. Maybe something else. Something to do with how I had healed her. But it was reassuring. Powerful.

'You're right,' I said. 'I *can* deal with her. I know I can.'

'Good girl. Go get her, Elodie.'

With that, I turned around, the weight of the conversation settling into something stronger. I was going to see my mother. The mother who had deserted me. And she was going to learn exactly how I felt about what she'd done.

FIFTY

As I walked toward the police station, my head throbbed with everything I was going to say to my mother. She wanted me to speak. Fine. I would speak. I would give her my words, all of them. I would tell her what it had been like as a child, being on my own. Waiting at school events, hoping that one day she'd turn up. That I'd look across the crowd and she'd be there, standing with the other parents. And for once, I wouldn't be the only one left behind.

I would tell her what it was like watching my father mourn her. What it was like rebuilding a life with someone new. And now that he was happy and free, I was supposed to ruin that? Shatter his world because she decided to come back? Because of her, I had to either lie or break the heart of the person who had done what she was meant to have done; loved me unconditionally and stayed even when it got tough.

And then there were The Guardians to think of. If I was right, if she was the starting point for their whole criminal enterprise, then how many lives had she helped ruin? How many other parents had skipped out on their life, leaving their families lost and mourning. How many young adults had abandoned their parents, leaving them with a lifetime of wondering? God, I had so many words waiting for her, they were practically boiling inside me.

It didn't just make me angry. It made me livid. Every cell in my body burned with the *fury*.

'Why are you pulling?' I said to Pongo as he tugged on his lead. 'Oh, you want to see her, do you? Well, you're the only one of us who does.'

I spotted her standing outside, shuffling her feet, like some upset toddler. Well, she wasn't the one who was allowed to be upset. That hair. That glamour. That *lie*. It wasn't just me she'd deceived. Every single person in Ravens Hollow had met a lie. Every good person, like Bobby and Chloe and all the faes. She had knowingly lied to them all.

As she turned and caught sight of me, her eyes lit with a smile. I did *not* smile back.

'Mother,' I said. The word had never left my mouth with so much venom.

'Elodie,' she said, stepping toward me. 'I'm so glad... I wasn't a hundred percent sure you'd come.'

'Really?' I snapped. 'You weren't sure *I* would show up? Hate to tell you this, Mother, but showing up is what I *do*. I'm punctual. I don't let people down. Unlike you.'

'I'm sorry, Elodie. You're right. I shouldn't have said that—'

'There are hundreds of things you shouldn't have done,' I cut in. 'One flippant remark is hardly the worst of it.

'Elodie, I, I...' She stuttered.

'Cat got your tongue, Mother? You've had twenty years to figure out what to say, and *now* you're struggling?'

'I just. Can we just talk inside? Please. I know you're hurt, but there's no reason to be cruel.'

'*Cruel?*' Laughter billowed from my lungs. 'You think I'm being cruel? If me finally being angry, finally speaking some truth, is cruel, then fine. But I'm *done*. I'm done with your lies. I'm done pretending. You didn't want to be in my life, and I don't want you in mine.'

'Please, Elodie—' She reached out and before I even realised what I was doing, I grabbed her wrist and threw her over my shoulder. Her back slammed onto the pavement, the impact reverberating through my feet. Pongo let out a sharp bark. I dropped his leash. I didn't care.

'You need to stop this, Elodie,' she said from the ground, her voice strained. Only it wasn't her voice. It was the voice of a frail elf, and I knew that wasn't who I had thrown at all. Not even close.

'Get up,' I said, as I circled around her, feeling the snarl curl on my lips. 'You know, I always wondered if older or younger vampires are stronger. Guess now's the time to find out.'

'You're going to fight me?' she said, rising slowly. The glamour still clung to her, but I saw it then, a flicker of fangs behind her lips. 'You don't want to do this.'

'Oh trust me, I do,' I growled.

'You think it will make you feel better, but you're wrong.'

'Oh, I don't think. I know.' That was when I swung. My fist caught her jaw hard as I recalled Whip's lesson and swept out my leg, knocking out her knees from behind, though she caught my shoulder stopping her from hitting the ground for a second time. And her grip was strong. She squeezed in around my collarbone as she pulled herself back upright quicker than a heartbeat. There were those vampire reflexes she'd tried to keep hidden from me.

'I'm not going to strike you, Elodie.'

'Well, I have no intention of stopping until you are out of my life for good.'

'Who are you? This isn't the child I raised.'

'You didn't raise me!' My voice was a scream, as I swivelled on the spot, and drove my elbow into her rips. 'You're not my mother! You stopped being my mother the moment you left me. I don't know what you are. But I don't want you in my life!'

Tears streamed down her cheeks.

'Elodie, please... I don't know what's wrong with you, but this isn't you—'

'You don't know me!' I screamed. 'You know nothing about me.'

'I know my daughter. I know the woman I've spoken to before now. This... this isn't you.'

Was she right?

Yes, I'd spoken to her before. The conversations hadn't exactly been warm, but they'd been calmer than this. Maybe that was because, before now, I hadn't felt strong enough. But now? Now I did. Now I was letting the anger take control, and it felt wonderful. Powerful.

'Elodie, there is something wrong with you,' she said again slowly.

'The only thing wrong with me is that I ever thought we could have a relationship,' I said. 'Believe me, that fantasy ends now.'

I struck again. But this time, she caught my wrist midswing, her grip locked tight around my bones. Too tight. Tight enough to snap something? I didn't know. But I didn't care. She could snap every bone in my body and I wasn't going to give up.

'You need to stop, Elodie,' she said, her voice shaking. 'Please. Focus on me. Whatever's happening, this isn't you.'

'This is exactly what you deserve,' I said, my voice trembling with fury.

'Maybe,' she whispered. 'Maybe it is. But when this passes, you'll have to live with that, and that's something I can't let you do.' Somewhere behind me, I heard Pongo barking. Sharp, frantic, desperate. And voices. Voices I knew. Whip? And Alex. They were both there. Whip with his love bombing. Gently caring Alex, even when I didn't want him to be. Well, I would get to them. But first, I had to deal with my mother. I didn't care what the punishment was for killing a vampire, now that I was one. I didn't care about laws or rules or council hearings.

I would take whatever sentence they gave me if it meant being rid of her. Because that was the only way this anger would be gone. If I truly eradicated the source of my hatred; this woman, this stranger who wanted to call herself my mother. What would happen if I bit her? I'd never bitten anyone before. Could vampires bite other vampires? I wasn't sure. But I was ready to find out.

I lunged again, but she caught me, threw me to the ground in almost exactly the same movement as I'd done on her. But I wasn't going to stop. I moved to stand, only for her foot to collide with my chest, pinning me to the ground.

'Fight me!' I shouted, as I struggled against her strength.

'You are not yourself, Elodie.'

'You don't know me! I cried again. 'You don't know me!' I wasn't going to stay down. If it took every last bit of anger I had in my body, I would keep going. In my peripherals, I could see shadows moving towards me. Whip, Alex. Raquel too. They were closing in. They were going to try to stop me from doing what had to be done. From hurting her the way she had hurt me. But I wasn't going to let them.

'Elodie, you are going to listen to me.' Raquel spoke, and I wanted to laugh. Whip couldn't do it. I was warded against him. But I was stronger than her powers, too. I could feel it. 'You're going to stop now. You're going to stop this. Stop fighting. Stop struggling.'

A growl rolled from my throat as I bared my fangs, showing her exactly what I thought of her suggestion. Amira still held me in place, boring all her power through her foot on my chest. But I didn't care. I pushed against her, hearing the crack of my ribs. I'd break every one of them, if I meant I got the justice I deserved.

'Elodie. Stop. Now.' Raquel was still speaking and Pongo was barking while Amira sobbed. Like she had any reason to sob.

'Alex, grab the cuffs,' Whip said, his voice calm but urgent.

'Got them,' Alex said. I turned to spit my venom at him. The man who was confusing my heart. Stopping me from having the love I deserved.

Yet before a sound left my lips, a feeling of cold washed over my wrists. A gasp shot out from my broken lips before the world tilted, just a little. Then everything went black.

FIFTY-ONE

I groaned. My head throbbed, like it had collided several times with a brick wall, yet as I went to move my hands – to press my fingers against my temples – a new pain shot up from my rib cage. What the hell happened? It took me second to realise that I was lying down on my side, but not on a mattress. On something much harder. And the pain in my chest wasn't the only reason I couldn't move my hands. It felt as if they were bound. Had I been kidnapped?! How? and Why? Had The Guardians found me?

I steeled myself against the pain as I pushed myself upright and open my eyes, only to find myself staring at metal bars. A cell. I was in a cell?

I winced, squeezing my eyes shut, trying to remember. What had I been doing? I'd been at work, right? I'd been at work, and looking at the migration pattern of Kelpies. There had been roses. And a centaur and then... *nothing*. Had the centaur kidnapped me? What about the rest of the people at the paper?

'Help! Help!' My throat cracked. Barely a sound escaping. Yet the door outside the cell door flung open.

'Alex?' I pushed myself up and lunged at the bars. 'What happened? What's going on?'

'Thank God,' he breathed, dropping his head into his hands. 'You're awake.'

'Alex, what's going on? Why am I here?' As I glanced at my hands, I saw the runed cuffs holding my wrists together. But they weren't the only surprise. My knuckles were black and blue with bruises.

'I'll get Whip. He can explain.'

'I don't remember... I don't remember anything.' My throat tightened. 'Why don't I remember what happened?' That was the moment it hit me. With a gasp, my hands flew up and covered my mouth. 'The demon? It was a demon, wasn't it? It got me too. Oh my God. Did I hurt someone? *Please* tell me. Please.'

'Whip just popped out to talk to some people,' Alex said quickly, his eyes darting towards the door. 'I wasn't meant to see you. He wanted to be the one who spoke to you about it.'

'Alex,' I said, tears stinging my eyes. 'Please. Tell me. As my friend. I need... I need...'

'It's okay. It's okay.' In one sweeping movement, he grabbed the keys from his belt, unlocked the cell door and pulled me into his chest. 'You're okay. You're safe now. Everyone's safe now.'

As I remained there, pressed against the warmth of his body, breathing in his honeysuckle scent, the realisation of his words struck.

'Did I hurt someone?' I asked, looking up into his amber eyes. 'Please Alex, tell me the truth. Did I hurt someone?'

His lips pressed tightly together before he dipped his chin slightly. 'You tried.'

'I did?' I didn't know whether the gasp that flew from me was because I would have tried to hurt someone – anyone – or that I didn't remember it. Not even a little bit. 'Who?'

'Your mother,' he said softly.

My mouth dropped open.

'Oh my God,' I gasped. 'Amira. Is she okay?'

'She's a vampire. She'll heal. But yeah...' He let out a shaky laugh. 'Remind me never to get on your bad side.'

I knew he wanted me to laugh. But I couldn't. 'Alex... I *don't remember* any of it.'

'I know. I know you don't. But we'll figure it out. Okay? You're not alone in this.' He planted his lips gently on the top of my head, only to suddenly back away. 'Whip's back,' he said.

A steady rhythm of footsteps made their way to the door, before Whip stepped through.

'Elodie,' he said, relief rushing over his face. 'You're back with us. Thank God.'

He moved past Alex, wrapped his arms around me, and kissed the top of my head. 'You scared the hell out of me.'

'My mother...' I whispered. 'She's okay?'

Whip glanced at Alex with a warning glare.

'She asked,' Alex said, defensively. 'And I wasn't going to lie to her.'

With a slight flare of his nostrils, Whip turned back to me and began unclipping the runed cuffs. 'Yes, she's fine,' she said. 'And believe it or not, you helped us solve the case. Find the demon.'

I blinked. 'What are you talking about? How did I help? I don't even remember anything.'

'No, you don't. But Chloe does.'

'Chloe?'

'You told her that you were going to meet Ines,' he said.

'I did?' I asked. 'Then why don't I remember?'

'Because Ines has been possessed by the demon. And from what we can tell, anyone who's had in-person contact with her loses the memory of it.'

I froze. 'Seriously?'

'Yeah. We don't have all the ins and outs, but Mick fixed her car the day he went crazy at Betty's. Prue had an interview lined up in her diary with her, the day she posted those videos of her crying.'

I was trying to take it all in, but there were still a lot of dots that weren't quite joining.

'But Prue wasn't angry, she was *upset*. And what about Flo?'

'We're not exactly sure when they had contact, but as for Prue, we're fairly sure we're dealing with a grief demon. One that amplifies negative emotions like anger, guilt, shame, self-loathing.'

'So Prue had all this self-hate building inside her...'

'Flo was bitter with her nephews for wanting to take the shop and wanted to make sure they got nothing.'

'That explains why she destroyed it.' I said finally seeing the full picture come into form. 'And Mick was jealous and hurt about Chloe. And me, I was angry with my mother.' I swallowed. 'Oh God. I'm such a fool. I should have seen it.'

'Why would you?' Alex said. 'There was nothing pointing to her until you. And you were trying to help Ines. Just being a good friend.'

The way his eyes locked on mine, I knew it wasn't just mine and Ines's friendship he was talking about.

'How is she now? Have you got her.'

'We have her contained,' he replied.

'Contained? What does that mean?'

'It means she can't hurt anyone else. We need to get someone from the mainland to exorcise the demon.'

I could hardly get my head around it. Poor Ines. Did she know that she was doing this? That she was hurting people? I couldn't believe that was the case. And now she was 'contained' but that didn't make me feel any better. A vision formed in my head, of somewhere cold and dark and even lonelier than she'd likely been since being cast out.

'And once you've got rid of the demon, then what'll happen? What'll happen to Ines?' I asked. Surely somewhere along the line, someone had to show some compassion. After all, I doubted the demon had picked Ines by accident.

Whip bit down on his lip, though his back stiffened slightly. Almost as if he was shifting from his role as my boyfriend and back into the Chief inspector.

'I've spoken with a couple of the others, and the paper's on board, so as long it's alright with the victims. We'll let Nyrah erase it from Ines's memory. She's got enough to deal with as it is.'

'You're going to wipe her memory without telling her?' Alex said sharply. 'You should give her a choice first.'

Whip's jaw tightened. 'She's a good person. She'll try to shoulder the blame. And she shouldn't have to.'

He turned to me.

'But it's not my decision. It's yours, Elodie. The victims need to agree. But I'll be honest, I think you have a lot of sway here. If *you* agree, I think the others will too.'

There was something in the way he said it, a softness. A

knowing. Maybe that was what he wished for; someone to erase all the bad things he'd done.

'I'm going to need a bit of time,' I said. 'Is that okay?'

'Of course it is.'

I tried to smile, but it was fleeting. 'Do I have to stay here any longer?' I asked. 'Because I really, really want to go home.'

'No,' Whip said gently. 'You can go. I'll walk you back.'

As I stepped out of the cell, I looked back at Alex.

'Thank you,' I said. 'Thank you for being there.'

He gave me a small smile. 'I'll always be here, Evergreen. You know that.'

I nodded and followed Whip out. When we reached the main area of the police station a ball of fur bounded up to me, only to stop a couple of feet away.

'It's okay, boy.' I said, crouching down and offering him my hand. 'I'm me now. I'm sorry if I scared you.'

Slowly, he took another step towards me, before sniffing deeply and bouldering into me. 'I'm sorry, if I scared you boy,' I said, feeling the tears tumble down my cheeks. 'I'm so sorry.'

I held Pongo in my arms as Whip drove me home, and it was only when I was sitting in my sofa, squeezed between the two males, that I spoke again.

'I can't believe I attacked her,' I said, imagining the way Mick had gone for Dylan, nonstop. 'I didn't know I was capable of that.'

'The emotions must've already been there,' Whip said quietly. 'The demon just turned up the volume. I'm sorry you had to go through that.'

'I should speak to her,' I said.

'When you're ready. Not before.'

I understood, but I was pretty sure that, for the first

time in a long time, I was now the one who owed my mother an apology. And sooner rather than later.

'I need to do it right away,' I said.

'I get it. But she's probably resting now. Why don't you come to my flat tomorrow night. And I'll keep the runed cuffs with me, just in case.'

I tried to smile, but I didn't have it in me. So instead, I let my head drop onto Whip's chest and stayed there until I fell asleep.

FIFTY-TWO

Bobby had insisted I take the day off work. I'd insisted I was fine. We compromised: I worked on the article from home.

It wasn't easy to write. How exactly did I say that there had been a flare-up of demon-induced grief on the island, without mentioning Ines, or the fact that the demon had possessed her?

I didn't want to lie to the public. So I didn't. I just didn't give them all the pieces. I left out names. Leaned on phrases like *a source close to the victim* and *the community is recovering*.

Not my favourite type of journalism. But when friendship and truth went head-to-head... sometimes you had to find a careful balance.

When I was done, I pinged it over to Bobby.

Sounds good to me, he replied.

Which left me with the other thing I had to do.

Speak to my mother.

I couldn't bring myself to message her directly. Cowardly, yes, but I asked Alex to deliver the message I wanted to meet. At Whip's flat, above the station. Just to talk. I felt like I was going against Jenna's instructions to keep Alex out of my private life, but he'd been involved in this from the start. He'd been the one who was there when I'd found out who she really was. She knew him, sort of, so it made more sense that he was the one to talk to her.

According to him, she agreed with no hesitation. Still, the nerves spiralled through me and I paced up and down Whip's short flat for a full hour before she was due to arrive. Maybe I'd had too much caffeine. Blood hastened healing and as I'd run out of Whip's red velvet brownies, that meant filling up on Weirdoughs. Still, I could feel the buzz in my veins. As much as I wanted Pongo by my side to comfort me, I also knew that Whip wasn't too keen on having him bounding about while he was cooking, so for now, at least, he was downstairs playing with Josephina. I'd go and fetch him at some point. Hopefully, when he was tired out a little.

'It's going to be fine,' Whip said, placing his hands on my shoulder. 'And if it's not, then I'll tell her, politely, to leave.'

'Do you mean tell her, or *tell* her?' I responded.

'Which ever one you need.'

I offered him a brief smile before slipping out of his grip and continuing my pacing. His flat was far smaller than his house in Pepper Bay, but far more lived in. The kind of place that felt like someone's home. The kitchen cupboard had mismatched mugs, the sofa had dents like someone had actually sat on it, and yes, even a couple of scatter cushions.

But there was one thing I wanted to see most.

I moved to the mantelpiece and picked up the photo frame. There was Whip, looking exactly the same as he did now, although judging by the clothes – eighties' shell suits – it had to be forty years ago at least.

Next to him was a woman, maybe in her early twenties. With jet black hair and perfectly symmetrical features. Her hand was around his waist as they laughed. Even though I knew they weren't technically related – step-siblings, at most – they looked like proper family.

'Your sister is beautiful,' I said. 'I don't think I've ever asked her name?'

'Katherine,' he told me. 'Her name is Katherine.'

'Katherine,' I nodded, picking up the frame, when the doorbell rang downstairs.

'That'll be your mum,' Whip said. 'Do you want me to let her in, or...?'

I hesitated. My throat tightened. 'Would you mind? I just... need one more minute.'

'Of course.'

Only as he headed downstairs did I realise how tightly I'd been holding the frame. My fingers had dented the metal. A frame that looked even older than the picture.

'Crap,' I muttered. I didn't think I'd damaged the photo, just the border, but still, Whip had told me he only had one of her. And the frame could well have been a present from her, too. A present from the sister he hardly ever got to see,

I twisted it gently, trying to smooth it out, when a throat cleared behind me.

'Elodie.'

I turned. Frame still in hand. My jaw dropped. My mother had removed the glamour. She no longer looked like the otherworldly creature who'd walked through Ravens Hollow with her peculiar angled ears. No. She looked like *her*; the mother from my memories. The one who left.

I couldn't speak. My heart lodged itself in my throat.

'I, I...' I started. 'Yesterday...I'm so sorry.'

She shook her head gently.

'You've got nothing to be sorry for. None of this was your fault,' she said. 'I know about the demon. I'm just sorry you had that much anger inside you. Enough for it to feed on.'

I tried to respond, but my throat was still blocked.

'Why don't you both sit down?' Whip said gently, appearing behind her. 'I'm just going to cook dinner. I'm doing ratatouille, if that's okay with you?'

'That sounds delicious. Thank you.' Whip offered a small, kind smile before disappearing into the kitchen.

Silence fell between us.

'I should... I should put this back,' I murmured, returning the photo before moving her to the sofa. 'We've got a lot to catch up on. A lot to work through, I guess.'

I expected her to jump on the opportunity to work on our relationship. After all, it was the first time I'd said I was actively willing to do so. But she didn't.

Instead, her gaze fixed on the photo frame. Unmoving. Unblinking.

She stood and walked over to it.

'Who's this?' she asked. She picked it up and turned it toward me.

'Who is this woman?' she repeated. 'This woman with Whip.'

'It's his stepsister.' I replied.

'Are you *sure*?' her voice quickened as though increased with panic.

'Yes. Yes, her name's Katherine. I mean, they're not technically stepsiblings, but he thinks of her that way.'

Her hand shook. 'No... no. You can't be right.'

'Why?' She turned to look at me, her voice barely a whisper. 'Because she's the one who changed me.'

I opened my mouth, unsure of what I was going to say. She had to be mistaken, didn't she? And yet her skin was ashen, her hands trembling. And she wasn't the only one. For a reason I couldn't explain, so was I.

'I think we need to get out of here, Elodie,' my mother whispered, taking my hand. 'I don't think we're safe.'

'No, no, we're fine,' I said. 'Whip's... Whip's...'

Why couldn't I finish the sentence? My boyfriend. The chief inspector of the police.

Instead, different thoughts filled my head. Thoughts about the fact that he was a magical, powerful siren of an undisclosed age, with a past I knew absolutely nothing about. One who had swept me off my feet and into a relationship before I'd even had time to catch my breath. Who had been responsible for placing wards on me since my first days on the island. And suddenly, it didn't feel half as romantic as it had done.

With my eyes locked on my mother's, I dipped my chin in a silent nod, gesturing towards the door.

Yet, as I took my first step, I found my path blocked. Whip was standing there, his eyes glinting, but not like they had the first time I met him, or any time since. No, this was something entirely different. And the gaze was locked solely on my mother.

'I'm sorry Amira,' he said. 'But I can't let you leave just yet. Turns out, I've got some questions of my own for you.'

I AM SO SORRY... I didn't set out with a plan for the book to finish at this point. It was as much a surprise to me as you.

However, don't worry... all will be revealed in Curses and Copy which you can pre-order now.

~

AND FOR THOSE of you in KU, I haven't forgotten you. I know the release is a way off, so I have created a special KU ALERT sign up so you will be notified the moment Curses and Copy is available for KU.

Sign up to KU ALERT

~

THERE IS a Bonus Chapter by way of apology for the wait. Get it here.

CURSES AND COPY
RAVENS HOLLOW INVESTIGATIONS BOOK 4

A failing ward, a missing witch, and revelations that'll shake Ravens Hollow to the core.

When Floyd, the bridge-guarding witch, disappears, it's more than your average missing person's case. Without him, the illusion spell that keeps our world hidden won't last long... exposing us and our secrets to the world.

I'm Elodie Evergreen, vampire journalist, and I just can't seem to catch a break. From glamoured elves to my relationship with our siren Police Chief, life has never been more complicated. I'm just hoping that finding Floyd is more straightforward than everything else on this island.

Unfortunately, suspects are everywhere, although my instincts keep pointing to Ophelia Willowwood, the enigmatic witch from across the pond.

And on top of that, Chloe and Dylan are braving a date, Pongo keeps sniffing out trouble, and new revelations are clawing at my past. I'm under more pressure than a werewolf at a full-moon party.

Find Floyd. Fix the ward. Don't fall apart. Easy... right?

Note from Ella

First off, thank you for taking the time to read **Demons and Deadlines**. If you enjoyed the book, I'd love for you to let your friends know so they can also experience this action-packed adventure.

If you leave a review **Demons and Deadlines** on <u>Amazon</u>, Goodreads, Bookbub, or even your own blog or social media, I would love to read it. You can email me the link at <u>ella@ellastoneauthor.com</u>

Don't forget, you can stay up-to-date on upcoming releases and sales by joining my newsletter, following my social media pages or visiting my website www.ellastoneauthor.com

ABOUT ELLA STONE

Lover of all things magical, mysterious, and mildly chaotic, Ella Stone writes fast-paced urban fantasy with a generous pinch of paranormal drama, a splash of slow-burn romance, and enough supernatural shenanigans to keep your heart pounding and your tea cold.

When not plotting vampire betrayals or helping were-wolves find some clothes (and occasionally their dignity), she's usually curled up with a book, surrounded by cats who believe they own the place—and, frankly, they do.

Her books include the *Dark Creatures* saga, the *Blood-sucker's Blog* trilogy, the *Witchlight Magical Mysteries* (co-written with the brilliant Heather G. Harris), and the brand new *Ravens Hollow Investigations*—a series full of magical crimes, dangerous alliances, and secrets that refuse to stay buried.

Expect charm, danger, and just enough mayhem to make things interesting. Welcome to her world. It's weird, it's wicked, and you're going to love it here.